THE KNIGHTS' TALES

The King of Jerusalem

"The White Knights" by Katherine Kurtz: A Veteran Crusader, Hugues de Payens, wants to use his newly formed band of "holy soldiers" to win him land and wealth—until a sacred messenger reveals the true purpose of Hugues's Knights Templar . . .

Richard the Lionhearted

"In the Presence of Mine Enemies" by Susan Schwartz: Once upon a time, valiant Ivanhoe saved beautiful Rebecca from the obsessed Templar Brian du Bois-Guilbert. Now discover what happens after the story ends . . .

Robert the Bruce

"The Last Voyage" by Patricia Kennealy-Morrison: Did the Templar fleet sink in a storm off the coast of Scotland—or are the Templars even now sailing between stars, bearing the heart of King Robert to the worlds of the Keltiad?

Lord Kitchener

"Sleeping Kings" by Debra Doyle & James D. Macdonald: Covert supernatural gumshoes Peter Crossman and Sister Mary Magdalene must find out why a fake True Cross, the Rudyard Kipling Society, and a First World War naval tragedy are clues in the quest for a lost Templar relic—the Spear of the Sleeping Kings . . .

Knights Templar Fantasy
Available from Warner Aspect

Edited by Katherine Kurtz

Tales of the Knights Templar
On Crusade: More Tales of the Knights Templar

By Katherine Kurtz and Deborah Turner Harris

The Temple and the Stone
The Temple and the Crown

CRUSADE OF FIRE

Mystical Tales of the Knights Templar

EDITED BY
KATHERINE KURTZ

WARNER BOOKS

An AOL Time Warner Company

WARNER BOOKS EDITION

Aspect® name and logo are registered trademarks of Warner Books, Inc.

Cover design by Don Puckey
Cover illustration by Greg Call
Handlettering by Carl Dellacroce

Warner Books, Inc.
1271 Avenue of the Americas
New York, NY 10020

Visit our Web site at
www.twbookmark.com.

An AOL Time Warner Company

Printed in the United States of America

First Printing: December 2002

10 9 8 7 6 5 4 3 2 1

ISBN: 978-0-446-61090-2
ISBN: 0-446-61090-9

In Memoriam
Francis Andrew Sherry of Achaea, GCTJ
1930–1997
Professed Knight of the Temple
Grand Prior of Scotland 1978–1993
Requiescat in Pacem

Contents

CRUSADE
OF FIRE

Introduction

ther than King Arthur's Knights of the Round Table, perhaps no other chivalric body in the world has inspired more intense or more long-lasting fascination than the Poor Fellow Soldiers of the Temple of Christ of Jerusalem, better known as the Knights Templar. Since this is the third anthology in this series about the Knights, any detailed account of their real-world history might rightly be regarded as unnecessary padding, but a brief summary is certainly in order for the benefit of readers as yet unacquainted with the Order.

They arose in the early twelfth century, in the immediate aftermath of the First Crusade and the formation of the Latin Kingdom of Jerusalem—warrior monks, melding the hitherto disparate concepts of chivalry and monasticism. Within less than twenty years, they would become the most formidable and feared fighting machine in all of Christendom. While their initial purpose was to protect the pilgrim roads of the Holy Land, now that travel was again possible in the land where Jesus once walked, they soon began to function as a crack military force for protection of the Holy Land itself—in effect, a private army answerable only to the pope—and a financial institution that would serve as banker for most of Europe and its crowned heads. In this latter function, they developed fiscal practices still in use today.

The success of the Templars rightly earned them a reputation for ferocity in battle and solidity in finance, but they also accrued an aura of mystery and even notoriety that has persisted to this day, underscored by the dramatic circumstances surrounding the Order's eventual demise. Even those who have never heard of the Knights Templar will be aware of the popular superstition that any Friday the Thirteenth is a probable occasion of bad luck—a combination long linked as ill-fated because of Christ's crucifixion on a Friday, after being betrayed for thirty pieces of silver by Judas Iscariot, the thirteenth disciple. The association was only reinforced when, on such a day in October of 1307, nearly all the Templars in France were simultaneously arrested and thrown into imprisonment.

Many were tortured horribly to extract confessions of an incredible variety of offenses including blasphemy, heresy, idolatry, and homosexuality. Apart from a few isolated instances of the latter, inevitable in any all-male organization, it is highly unlikely that any of the charges were true. Nonetheless, more than a hundred of the Knights perished at the stake before the Order was finally suppressed in 1312, and many had died as a result of their torture.

The manner of their ending, and persistent traditions of some kind of Templar survival, have fueled endless speculation about their actual influence, the true extent of their wealth and activities, their ultimate fate, and a thriving cottage industry that perpetuates even more speculation. Interested readers will find a bibliography of some of these titles at the back of this volume, along with those of more conventional histories.

The stories in this collection, while mostly set within the historical timeframe of the Order's existence, explore these persistent assertions that the Knights were far more than warriors and monks and bankers and counselors to royalty; that there was some mysterious and even mystical aspect to their existence and function that sometimes enabled them to operate outside and beyond the norm. And though their "official" status as a religious order spans less than two hundred years, put to an end by royal betrayal and lurid accusations, with the Order suspended by papal decree and its grand master burned at the stake, rumors of the Order's survival were rife even at the time. Though it seems likely that the Order's demise had more to do with jealousy and royal greed than from any real failing—other than naïveté, that the pope would protect them from their detractors—the fact remains that the Order kept its internal workings secret, and prospered with astonishing speed, and accrued enormous wealth and influence for which it was not answerable to anyone save the pope.

Just how this came to pass, we probably will never know for certain. Historical records of the Order are sketchy and often contradictory, but we can piece together many plausible speculations. Certain it is that in the first several decades following the First Crusade, just at the beginning of the twelfth century, the very notion of an order of warrior-monks was only just beginning to take shape in the mind of a French crusader knight called Hugues de Payens, a vassal of the Count of Champagne and kin to the counts of Troyes.

We don't know a great deal about Hugues. He would have been a young man in his early twenties when he took the Cross and left on crusade—probably a widower, certainly with a son left behind in France. He probably had come in the army of Geoffrey de Bouillon in 1096 and, like many of his crusading partners, stayed on in the Holy Land when Jerusalem was taken by the crusader army and Geoffrey was elected its king—though Geoffrey had declined to wear a crown in the Holy City, taking instead the more pious title of Advocate of the Holy Sepulchre: king in all but name, if for barely a year. It was a nicety quickly set aside by his successor, his brother Baldwin, who had no such scruples. Baldwin, in turn, was to reign in oriental splendor for nearly twenty years, during which he attempted to consolidate and stabilize the four crusader states making up the Latin Kingdom of Jerusalem.

To put this into perspective, we should consider the size of the Latin Kingdom, and the size of the Western population attempting to make it their own, and the fact that most crusaders, if they survived battle and the desert heat, went home to Europe upon finishing their campaigns. At its height, the area in question was roughly the size of the State of Maryland—perhaps 11,000 square miles, laid out roughly in a T-shape, with the stem stretched along the eastern end of the Mediterranean. Jerusalem and its environs lay at the bottom of the stem, with the Principality of Antioch immediately above it and the Counties of Tripoli and Edessa forming the cross-bar.

Muslim emirates surrounded each of these states on all landward sides, and the countryside was populated with bands of desert marauders who preyed upon travelers. Outside the Christian-occupied cities, Muslim troops might move freely—often within bowshot of the Western-held cities, whose inhabitants were able to do nothing about it. Had the emirates been able to unite under a single leader, as even the great Saladin could not accomplish, it is unlikely that a Latin Kingdom could have been formed at all, much less survived for as long as it did. At the height of the Latin Kingdom's power, the resident European population of the area probably never exceeded 20,000, with each state possessed of no more than

1,000 secular knights and barons, perhaps 5,000 serjeants, who were the fully armed infantry, and perhaps 1,000 clergymen. Over the next two centuries, Europe would continue to send periodic crusader armies to the defense of the Holy Land, until it became all too clear that the Latin Kingdom could not be held.

This, then, was the environment in which Hugues de Payens found himself, though history tells us nothing specific about his activities during this period. Some accounts suggest that he made several trips back and forth to France, but most agree in stating that, at the time he founded the Order, he had been in the Levant for twenty-two years. Knowing that he had left behind a son in France, we can speculate that at least a part of his original motivation in taking the Cross may have been the seductive possibility of winning lands and even a title in the Holy Land, if the crusade was successful. If so, however, that was an ambition that would come to have no meaning, once his son grew to manhood and took holy orders, thereby binding himself to the Church rather than carrying on the de Payens name and lineage. By 1128, when Hugues achieved papal recognition for the Order, the heir of his body had become Abbot of Saint Columb's at Sens, and was beyond the need of any secular inheritance.

Meanwhile, during those years between arriving in the Holy Land and conceiving of the institution that would leave an indelible mark on history, Hugues' life probably would have been little different from any other knight who had chosen to stay on after the end of the First Crusade. Despite the hardships of desert warfare, there would have been a certain satisfaction and even a heady excitement to being part of a victorious army, especially as a member of the knightly class. As the colonization of the new Latin Kingdom got underway, the very nature of the land to be governed would have required constant military activity to retain the precarious toe-hold the Westerners had established in the midst of their Muslim enemies.

It is more than likely that this would have been the principal occupation of Hugues and his crusading partners, some of whom undoubtedly became co-founders of the Order with him. In the beginning, as their function shifted from active warfare to peacekeeping, perhaps they even enjoyed the opportunity to be a law unto themselves—young men searching for adventure—despite the hardships of life in the desert.

Only vaguely and as a matter of passing note would Hugues and his companions have become aware of the Hospital of St. John of Jerusalem, established in the previous century and perhaps officially founded in 1113, when the Hospital received a charter as a religious order dedicated to nursing sick and injured pilgrims. As yet, however, the Order of St. John had not taken on any military function to reduce the numbers of pilgrims who needed such assistance. That was still to come, following the example to be set by a military order still to be born.

The hard fact was that outside the cities that marked the hearts of the four crusader states—Jerusalem, Antioch, Edessa, and Tripoli—the Holy Land still was not safe for pilgrims, though that had been the ostensible reason for the First Crusade. The two-day journey between the port of Joppa and the Holy City was particularly dangerous, for bandits and brigands made their camps in the caves along the way, whence they sallied forth to prey on pilgrims bound for the holy places.

The danger had been underscored just before Easter of 1119, when travelers on a Lenten pilgrimage to the River Jordan were set upon by Muslim raiders from Ascalon and Tyre. Unarmed and weakened from fasting, three hundred had been slain outright, and another sixty taken prisoner. This incident or one like it may be have been what finally focused the energies of Hugues de Payens and the companions who founded the Order of the Temple. Perhaps it happened something like this.

White Knights

Katherine Kurtz

The shadows were lengthening on that late spring afternoon, not long after Easter, when a French knight called Hugues de Payens and a handful of brother knights en route to Jaffa paused to water their horses at one of the springs near Lydda, a frequent destination for pilgrims wishing to visit the tomb of Saint George. Their journey from Jerusalem had already led them past the bones of many an unlucky victim of Muslim raiders, in varying states of decay. Hence, when another pilgrim band came limping into sight, just at dusk, Payen de Montdidier was quick to spot the furtive riders shadowing them to the south, where robber caves overshadowed the road from Ramleh.

"How many?" Hugues asked, when Godfrey de Saint-Omer had pointed out the danger.

"Perhaps a dozen," said Archambaud de Saint-Aignan. Like the others, he was well aware of the slaughter of pilgrims near the Jordan a few weeks before. "But they've come from the opposite direction. They won't have spotted us already here. If we can retain the element of surprise, we can take them."

"Rossal, you and Gondemere move the horses away from the water," Hugues said decisively, beckoning for two more knights to join them. "The rest of you—hide yourselves among the rocks, and make ready."

Quickly dispersing to follow his instructions, the others found vantage points as he had directed. Hugues waited with young André de Montbard behind the shelter of a clump of date palms until the first of the pilgrims came abreast of his location, then snaked out a hand to grab the lead-man by the sleeve and yank him aside, at the same time clapping a hand over his mouth while André stepped into sight and counselled urgent silence by means of a finger laid vertically across his lips.

"Don't cry out," André whispered. "We mean you no harm, but you are being followed—stalked, in fact. There are bandits in this area. Proceed to the oasis, but be ready for trouble."

Fortunately, the pilgrim had his wits about him, and made no sign of alarm as Hugues released him to continue on his way. The others stumbled past without apparent notice, either not seeing them or too weary and thirst-driven to pay them mind.

The surprise of the pursuing Muslims was complete, as was the victory of the defending knights. When it was over, and all the attackers were slain or fled, Hugues and his men carefully cleaned their weapons as the pilgrims began the gingerly task of clearing away the enemy slain and making camp.

"Will they come again?" one frightened pilgrim asked, glancing back nervously toward the rocky heights where the remaining attackers had disappeared.

"Not tonight," Hugues replied. "But we'll post guards, to be certain they don't."

Later that night, having stood his watch, he lay dozing beneath the desert stars, head propped against his saddle, vaguely aware of the small, uneasy night sounds of their camp. Earlier, he and the others had shared meager rations with the pilgrim band: succulent dates, pungent goat cheese, the flat, unleavened bread of the Levant, and sour red wine from vineyards outside the walls of Jericho. Out at the edge of the firelight, three of Hugues' comrades-in-arms kept quiet watch, far more aware than the pilgrims of the dangers presented by the desert.

He never quite slept that night, but he did dip in and out of a drifting, dreamlike state in which he seemed to sense someone standing at his feet, silently gazing down at him. He was not exactly frightened—he sensed no menace there—but nonetheless he found himself trembling as he opened his eyes to the stars overhead, beginning to dim in the haze of predawn. The image that solidified in memory, as he swept his anxious gaze over the sleeping men around him, was of a tall, handsome figure clad all in white: he was overcome by a shiver of incredible awe, and beauty so profound that he felt tears well in his eyes.

Then the moment was past, put to flight by someone coughing nearby and someone else loudly breaking wind. The sound jarred him to full consciousness, and he elbowed himself upright amid the folds of his cloak, a little light-headed with emotion.

Around him he could hear the soft shuffle of the horses stirring along their picket line, the whisper of booted feet crunching in the sand—the sentries stretching their legs in the pre-dawn greyness—and, closer, the varied snores of the sleeping pilgrims and the men not on watch. Beside him, André shifted and moaned softly on his bedroll, one arm flinging across his eyes, then settled.

After a few more seconds, as Hugues' racing heart calmed, he made himself exhale softly and lie down again, wondering what the vision might have meant, finally dozing. Not until several days later, as he and the others sat nursing their wine in a shabby tavern in Jaffa, did he really think about it again— and then, only when André de Montbard broached a very startling notion.

"That skirmish we had at Lydda," André said, not looking up as he ran a callused fingertip along the rim of his wooden cup. "I can't get it out of my mind."

Hugues glanced at him sharply, the white-robed image momentarily flashing before his inner sight.

"Why not?" Payen said lightly. "We trounced them. It's past."

"Aye, and it was well done," Bissor agreed. "A bit of a payback for what they did at the Jordan. It was time *someone* did it."

"True enough," André replied. "And not only for the Jordan. It has occurred to me that maybe we're to be that 'someone.' All of us," he added, looking up at the bearded faces turned to him in query and consternation.

Payen looked astonished, Archambaud quite taken aback. Robert de Craon was gazing at him very intently, Gondemere and Rossal nodding in agreement. Hugues found himself glancing to Godfrey for some sign that his second-in-command was as appalled at the notion as he was; but the Fleming was staring at André with a look of rapt attention.

"André, that's crazy," Archambaud said. "We can't take on the entire Levant."

"We don't have to take on the entire Levant. Only the enemies of Christ."

"Only the enemies of Christ?" Payen echoed, with an ironic laugh that was almost a bark.

"With nine men . . ." Robert added, also bemused by the thought.

"It's a start," André replied. "My nephew started with less than thirty."

Several of the others stirred uneasily, for André's nephew was the remarkable Bernard of Clairvaux, abbot of the now flourishing Cistercian Order. What gave the statement particular significance was that, when the twenty-one-year-old Bernard had determined to take monastic vows at Citeaux, he had persuaded nearly thirty others to join him, including four of his five brothers, his father, and another uncle.

So infectious had Bernard's enthusiasm been that the previously moribund community at Citeaux had grown sufficiently in the next three years to hive off three daughter houses. The one at Clairvaux, established on lands given by the Count of Champagne, had elected Father Bernard as their abbot, at the age of twenty-five. Now, still not yet thirty, the charismatic little priest was regarded increasingly as the conscience of Christendom, counsellor and sometimes chastiser of kings, bishops, and even popes.

"André, your nephew and his companions all became monks," Bissor pointed out.

"Maybe knights could be monks as well," André replied.

Bissor snorted. "Even if we wanted to, the Church would never allow it. You know that clergy are forbidden to shed blood—and that's what we do best."

"Well, we do practically live like monks already," Robert noted. "And didn't we come here to do God's work?"

"Well, *some* of us also hoped we might win lands and titles," Rossal said lightly.

"And have any of us done that? No," André retorted. "On the other hand, we took a vow to recover the Christian holy places—which, to a certain extent, we have done. Except that pilgrims still die trying to reach those places. We could do something about that. We *did* do something about that at Lydda—and we shed Saracen blood to do it. Maybe that's what we're meant to be doing now. Isn't that the reason we all came?"

* * *

The more immediate reason they had come, at least to Jaffa, was to deliver letters from the king to his factor at the port and to provide escort for the supplies going back to Jerusalem. This they did, though their departure was delayed for a day while drovers organized the caravan to carry the goods.

On the long ride back, while his eyes restlessly scanned the rocky escarpments and caves above the road, Hugues thought about what André had proposed that night in the tavern. So far, no one had brought it up again, but as they went about their business in the next few days, Hugues had found himself unable to forget for long. He wondered whether it was on the minds of the others, as well.

To his surprise, he found himself actually considering how knights might somehow be monks as well, devoting part of their time to prayer and penance as well as fighting, perhaps reciting the daily Office as monks did, all in the service of God. Though a part of him argued that they had fought the crusade in the name of God, another part was well aware that the idea of warrior-monks was absurd.

Perhaps it came of living too long in the Levant. The heat preyed on a man's mind, and the constant proximity to the Christian holy places—and the Jewish ones, and those of the Muslims—insinuated pious pretense into unguarded moments of contemplation that, otherwise, might be focused on the interests that usually occupied a man of knightly station.

Or would have occupied him, had he stayed in France, in the milieu into which he had been born. There, Hugues had always assumed that his religious observances owed as much to social convention as any reflection of true religious fervor—though he had been as vulnerable as any other man to the siren-call of Peter the Hermit, preaching the First Crusade.

But even then, when he had taken the Cross and ridden out on Holy Crusade with Geoffrey de Bouillon—had it really been more than twenty years ago?—Hugues had told himself that he did it as much for the very practical possibility of earthly gain as for any thought of heavenly merit to be won. In this, he was little different from most who answered the call to crusade: faithful enough to their holy mission, especially in the beginning, but also well focused on the realities of their way of life. Of a certainty, Hugues had never regarded himself as particularly pious—other than just before battle when, like those around him, he found himself whispering fervent prayers to Our Lady and St. Michael for protection. At heart he was a soldier—and had been, for most of his life.

Why, then, could he not put the notion of warrior monks out of his mind?

That night, as those not on watch huddled around the campfire, Hugues glanced into the darkness around them, then leaned closer to Payen, Archambaud, and Gondemere, motioning them closer. Young André, the uncle of Bernard of Clairvaux, was on watch with Godfrey and Rossal. Bissor and Robert were checking on the horses. Farther beyond their immediate campsite, the men and beasts of the caravan slept obliviously.

"I've been thinking about what André said about knights being monks," he murmured.

Archambaud gave a dubious snort. "You don't think he was serious, do you?"

"He sounded serious to me," Gondemere said. "And his nephew *is* Bernard of Clairvaux. Maybe missionary zeal runs in the family. For a moment, he half had *me* ready to take vows. What about you, Payen?"

Payen de Montdidier scratched distractedly at his beard and considered. Though beards were out of fashion back in France, the more savvy among the Crusader forces had soon discovered that facial hair elicited at least a modicum of grudging respect among their Muslim foes, who regarded a beard as a sign of manliness, esteemed by their Prophet. Conversely, the long hair affected by many Europeans was seen as effeminate—which was not the primary reason that many crusaders soon hacked their hair off short, but it was certainly more comfortable and practical in the desert heat, under arming cap, mail coif, and steel helmet. All of them in their little band now wore their hair cropped short, and beards even the Prophet would approve.

"The idea does have a certain appeal," Payen said. "A band of warrior monks, vowed to serve God by protecting His holy places."

Archambaud nodded gravely. "It is why we came: to serve God."

Gondemere drank deep of the sour local wine, unconvinced.

"How would we survive? It is one thing to fight for a western prince, who would give us our maintenance. Who will maintain us if we fight for God?"

"God Himself?" Archambaud said, with a raised eyebrow.

"Perhaps," Hugues replied.

Somehow, as he said it in the firelight rather than the harsher light of day, it sounded almost possible.

That night, after he had stood his watch, he dreamed again—the first time since the skirmish by Lydda. This time, he managed to drag himself to consciousness far enough for his dream-self to sit up, still dreaming, to confront his white-robed visitant.

Would you be His knight, Hugues de Payens? the apparition seemed to say to him, celestial-blue eyes seeming to pierce his very soul. *Would you be His servant?*

The questions so startled him that he woke up in a cold sweat, heart hammering, and never did manage to fall asleep again that night. He did not want to think about what the dream might mean. Even more, he did not want to think about who or what the shining figure might have been.

But he spoke about it privately with André the following day, after they had seen the supply caravan safely into Jerusalem, for unloading in the king's granaries and store-rooms. And later that night, when the knights had retired to rather ruder lodgings on the south of the city, that served as their occasional quarters, he shared his growing idea with the others.

"I'll certainly agree that armed patrols on some of the worst roads would be no bad thing," Godfrey allowed, when Hugues had explained what he proposed.

"No bad thing at all," Rossal said cheerfully. "God knows, we've done precious little else of any real import here since securing the city. And the need is clear."

Young Robert de Craon snorted into his cup of wine and grinned. "Those Saracens we trounced at Lydda will certainly remember the lesson—the ones who survived, at any rate. I can't deny that it gave me great satisfaction to be able to give back some of what they've been meting out to pilgrims. Policing the roads is something that's been needed for a long time."

"But Hugues isn't proposing mere policing, are you, Hugues?" Godfrey said thoughtfully. "Clearly, you see it as a military band—but you're also suggesting that we take monastic vows. I thought we'd agreed that the Church would never allow it—clergy shedding blood."

At Hugues' quick glance, André shook his head.

"Monks aren't clergy in the same sense that priests are," he said. "As monks, we would bind ourselves to a godly code of conduct, part of which would be to use our swords in God's service." He shrugged. "I know it has never been done before, but why not? It comes to my mind that this was foretold more than twenty years ago—long before I joined this fray. A few of you were at Antioch in '97. Surely you must have heard the stories—how white-clad angels came to the aid of our armies, mounted on white horses and led by Saint George."

"That will have been an English version of the story," Bissor said with a snort. "George is *their* saint. Our lads were claiming it was Saint Michael."

"Does it really matter?" André countered. "If the saints and angels were leading our armies into battle with swords in hands, perhaps we could take that image as our ideal."

"I remember how the troubadours at the court of the Count of Champagne used to sing of such visions," Payen said, his eyes shining. "They were guardians of the Holy Grail as well as warriors of the Light. It is a goodly ideal."

"Soldier-monks, sworn to protect pilgrims," Godfrey said. "The image is powerful."

"Aye, it is," Archambaud agreed.

"Indeed," André said, nodding. "It is what we were born and bred to do, after all: to fight. And we came here prepared to offer up our lives in God's service, for the rescue of the Holy Land and the salvation of our souls. Why not give ourselves to Him entire? Some of us came for other reasons as well, in the beginning, but by now I think it's clear that we aren't fated for the sort of success some of us hoped for— lands, and wealth, and families to leave them to when we're gone. We've been living more or less like monks, as it is; why not *be* monks?"

That suggestion devolved into a further discussion of just how this might be accomplished, with André setting down their ideas—for he was one among only a few of them who could read and write.

Payen was another, and reviewed his notes with Hugues after the others had retired to sleep, jotting down a few amendments in the margins.

"I think it might just be possible," Hugues said, when the two of them had read over the document again.

"So do I," Payen replied.

"What persuaded you?"

Payen smiled in his shaggy beard. "I saw those white-clad angels at Antioch, Hugues—or at least, I think I did."

"Then, perhaps this is the reason," Hugues replied. "That we should *become* that vision, fighting in God's holy Name." He paused thoughtfully. "I thought to approach the patriarch about it. It may be that he would sponsor us."

"Warmund?" Payen grinned. "I think he would welcome anything that helped keep order. So would the king."

Hugues nodded. "Yes, but it's Warmund we must win over first. This notion of soldier-monks may take some convincing."

"Then, we must be certain to take André with us," said Payen. "And make certain that the patriarch knows André is the uncle of Bernard of Clairvaux."

The next morning, the three of them rode to the patriarch's quarters, adjacent to the Temple Mount—a part of the Holy City sacred to those of all three of the great faiths contending there: Jews, Christians, and Muslims. King David had chosen the spot for the great temple built by Solomon. There the boy Jesus had preached to the Elders, and there He had later entered as the Prince of Peace, before His Passion.

With the advent of Islam, followers of the Prophet had built the great al-Aqsa mosque atop the Temple Mount. Beside it rose the great structure known as the Dome of the Rock, which sheltered beneath its foundations the black stone known as the *Ka'aba,* said to be the very stone on which Abraham had been willing to sacrifice his own son in obedience to the command of Yahweh, and where, later, the

Prophet Mohammed was believed to have sprung heavenward on the back of a white horse.

Now turned to Christian worship, following the recapture of Jerusalem two decades before, both buildings were part of the great complex known as the Haram al-Sharif or Temple platform, at the south end of which Baldwin II had his headquarters. Across the city to the west, near the Church of the Holy Sepulchre, was the palace of the patriarch, Warmund of Piquigny, who presided over his see of Jerusalem with an oriental splendor similar to that of the king.

"The patriarch will see you now," said a deferential, softly spoken little man in the white robes of the Canons of the Lord, bowing them into a smaller chamber beyond the public one usually used for audiences.

Gathering his courage firmly in hand, Hugues led his two companions into the patriarchal presence, there to be enfolded in the prelate's fragile embrace before he could kiss the episcopal ring.

"Hugues, my son, the sight of you brings delight to these old eyes!" the patriarch said, after bestowing a kiss of peace on the younger man. Still smiling as they drew apart, he murmured vague greeting to the other two as well, though he made no move to extend his hand for the more formal salute they would have owed him in more public circumstances, only waving them to seats on an array of stools set before a larger chair.

"Please, gentlemen, be seated and take your pleasure of this excellent wine that has lately arrived from Sephoria—further proof that the Apostle Nathanael was in error when he claimed that nothing good can come out of Nazareth."

Smiling at the Biblical reference, the three settled as directed, as the patriarch's gesture also summoned the monk to fill silver cups before quietly retiring.

"Dear Hugues, I do wish you would not be so much a

stranger," the patriarch went on, settling into the cushions of his chair. "Your visits reinforce my hope that we may yet bring our European culture to this savage land. I am convinced of the good work we do here, in Christ's name, albeit very slowly, but I find myself becoming more Eastern with every day that passes." He indicated his beard and the wide priest's stole of Oriental embroidery he wore over his black robes—more like desert robes than the habits affected in the West. "Papa Paschal would not recognize such vestments in Rome."

Hugues fingered his own beard and smiled faintly, glancing at Payens and André before returning his attention to the patriarch.

"In truth, my lord, we come to you on a matter that likewise would find little recognition in Rome. At least you draw upon a millennium of evolving tradition."

At the prelate's look of question, Hugues launched into a somewhat tentative description of what the three of them proposed, Payen and André adding their comments—though no one essayed any mention of dreams and angels. When all of them seemed to have run out of words, Warmund looked among them in wonder and growing approval, gnarled fingers twining in his luxurious beard.

"Knights who are also monks," he said slowly. "You are right, it has never been done before." He paused a beat. "You truly wish to do this thing—to give yourselves to God, as servants of prayer, and also to fight His foes?"

When the three of them only nodded silently, Warmund started to speak several times, then said, "An unusual idea—*most* unusual—but this *is* an unusual place. . . ."

As he reached for his wine, forgotten until then, he realized that none of his guests had touched theirs, and gestured for them to take up their cups.

"Please, drink, my sons," he urged. "Your throats must be dry, after so much speaking."

As they nervously did so, he gazed into his own cup, clearly considering what they had said, then returned his attention to them.

"Yes, it is an intriguing proposition," he murmured. "And in a sense, there *is* precedent. For at confirmation, does not the bishop strike us on the cheek and swear us all as Christ's legions, to aid Him in the battle against evil? Why could you *not* be monks as well as warriors? Certainly, there is need for a policing force such as you describe, to protect travellers on the pilgrim roads to the holy places."

"Will you allow us to try this vocation, my lord?" André said boldly.

Warmund drew a deep breath and let it out slowly, then nodded.

"Yes, I believe I shall. . . ."

They went next—all nine of them, this time—to the king, who received them in his audience hall within the palace he had built next to the citadel of Jerusalem, the "Tower of David," overlooking the Jaffa Gate. Only a year upon his throne, Baldwin II was yet a young man, full of fire and high ambitions. Still outraged over the Jordan massacre, he listened to Hugues' proposition with interest.

"You propose to patrol the roads?" he said when Hugues had finished. "And to live as monks?" He tried unsuccessfully to control a faint smile. "That hardly sounds either fitting or even possible for knights, good sirs."

Gondemere flushed bright red and lifted his chin. "It is true, Sire, that little of a knight's life recommends it to that of a cleric. And some of us have little to be proud of in our past lives. That is what brought many of us on crusade: to fight against the enemies of Christ and thus make some recompense for our past, to save our immortal souls. With God's help, we can do this thing—and help save the bodies of other sinners so that they may save their souls as well."

Baldwin slowly nodded. "God knows, *something* must be done. But, warrior monks—have you spoken to the patriarch about this?"

"We have, Sire," Hugues spoke up. "He is prepared to receive our vows, that we shall live as holy monks and also dedicate our swords to Christ's service. We—*will* need assistance, however: quartering for ourselves and our horses, provisioning for ourselves and our beasts and a handful of servants."

"In other words, what I have been supplying while you have been in my service," Baldwin interjected with a wry smile. "But I find no fault with your previous service, or its terms," he added, holding up a hand to allay any objection. "And if you desire to extend that service to God's service as well . . ." He glanced at the chamberlain attending him. "Make inquiries regarding a suitable lodging for these good knights," he commanded. "We shall try this bold experiment, and see if it produces good fruit."

"Thank you, Sire," Hugues said.

Inclining his head in answer to their bows, Baldwin watched the nine turn and retreat up the hall.

"A *very* bold experiment," he said musingly to his chamberlain, when the men were out of earshot. "I know not whether it can succeed, but knights under the discipline of a religious rule could be a very useful—and controllable—tool. We shall see."

Within a month, the nine of them were kneeling before the patriarch in his more formal hall of audience, swearing him the traditional monastic vows of poverty, chastity, and obedience and offering up their swords in Christ's service. Ranged to either side of the patriarch, several dozen Canons of the Lord looked on, spectral as ghosts in their white robes.

"Because you have sworn poverty for our Lord's sake," Warmund declared, "I give you no habit or other outward sign of your service, but only the duty to wear my patriarchal cross in place of the crusader cross you have worn hitherto." He handed each of them a strip of crimson cloth, the width of two fingers and as long as a man's hand, demonstrating on Hugues the manner in which it was to be positioned over the lower arm of the crusader crosses they already wore on their shoulders, thus forming the patriarchal cross with its double cross-bars.

"By these, you shall be known as my knights as well as Christ's," he went on, when he had given out all nine strips. "I charge you to do honor to both of us."

Bowing deeply, his forehead touching the floor, Hugues murmured, "Not to us, but to God's Name give the glory, my lord. We shall serve Him as best we can, under His mercy and His blessing."

"And thus do I give you His blessing," Warmund said in reply, standing to raise his hands above the kneeling nine, "and I ask that He grant you His infinite mercy and guidance. *In nomine Patris, et Filii, et Spiritus Sancti, Amen.*"

Later that afternoon, Warmund accompanied the nine to King Baldwin and presented them and their cause, explaining what had been done and commending their services to the king as keepers of his peace and defenders of pilgrim travellers. Baldwin, in turn, welcomed this augmentation of his peace-keeping forces and granted them space for lodgings adjacent to his own palace, near to the site said to have housed King Solomon's stables. He gave them, in addition, the modest income of several pieces of property near the city.

"You have chosen to live as Christ's poor knights," he said, "but you cannot serve Him if you starve. In time, if your cause be just and your purpose be God's purpose as well, the means will come, to see your order grow."

Having heard the words both of patriarch and king, the Canons of the Lord gave the new-formed order a square beside the Dome of the Rock, to be used as a place to recite their monastic offices.

"It will not be easy for knights to live like monks," their prior said to the nine. "You will require a rule of life, and chaplains to minister to you. For now, you may use our rule and our priests. And may God prosper your holy work."

That night, after they had recited the office of evening prayer for the first time as a fledgling monastic community, and most of the others had bedded down for the night in what was to become their new home, Hugues and Godfrey lingered over the remains of the fire on which they had cooked a very meager evening meal. Thus far, other than the prayers, it had been little different from making camp in the field.

"Has the desert sun addled our minds?" Hugues said in a low voice to Godfrey. "We could have gone on indefinitely, the way we were. We didn't have to become monks to fight Saracens and protect pilgrims."

Godfrey simply shrugged, staring into the fire as he poked at it with a stick of kindling.

"No, we didn't. But somehow, it feels right."

Hugues slowly nodded. "It does. God help us, but it does."

The next day, after morning prayers and another sparse meal, they rode over to inspect the site given them by the king for their new lodgings.

"Surely we cannot live *here*," Rossal murmured, as they picked their way on foot through the rubble outside one of the buildings.

"This will be a trial of our vow of poverty," André de

Montbard said cheerfully, as he ducked his head to peer through the doorway of an obviously derelict building. "Surely you didn't think that God would give us only easy challenges?"

"True enough," Payen agreed. "And think what we may find, within these walls." He slapped one gauntleted hand against the side of another open doorway. " 'Tis said that King Solomon's stables lie beneath the Temple Mount. What better quarters could we ask, as Christ's knights?"

Gondemere snorted, though he looked more intrigued than seriously concerned.

"I can see the potential," he said. "There will be a great deal of rubble to clear, but we can manage that. It will be easier than mining under a wall to broach a castle's defenses."

"Then, let us begin," Hugues said. "We have much to do, in the Lord's name."

It was a far different labor than any of them had anticipated, but they entered into it with a glad will. They had retained the dozen or so serjeants and servants necessary to maintain nine fighting men and care for their mounts, but even with this assistance, they spent several weeks making their new quarters habitable: first clearing away rubble, then laying out areas for sleeping and cooking, a place for storage and maintenance of their armor, an area for stabling the horses and keeping their harness, an area for the serjeants and servants. While the men performed most of the heavy manual labor, the knights pitched in as needed. It was decidedly unknightly behavior—but so was being a monk. And the sooner their poverty became tempered by sufficiency, however basic, the sooner they might take up their true vocation.

Except that their vow of obedience was next to be tested—and not their obedience to any earthly authority. Having inspected the work of the past few days in what was about to become their armory, Hugues was contemplating their shift back to a military functioning when his ears began to ring and the air grew suddenly heavy and still around him. He could vaguely hear the distant voices and tool-sounds of others working in adjacent areas, out of sight, but everything seemed muffled and distant, as if his ears were full of water.

With a grimace, he gave his head a shake to clear it, but the ringing persisted. And then, brighter than the torchlight, a golden radiance began to wash over the rough-hewn wall, as if sunlight spilled across a threshold—except that the rays of the sun had never penetrated this deep into the earth.

Blinking, Hugues rubbed at his eyes and shook his head again, for the ringing in his ears was growing more intense, and he felt himself becoming light-headed. It was not until he put out a hand to steady himself against the wall that he saw the man standing a few strides away, simply gazing back at him.

Or—not a man, though he had the appearance of one. For no man had ever worn such shining raiment, or stood thus with his feet a hand-span above the level of the floor. As Hugues' jaw dropped and one hand lifted in automatic gesture to shade his eyes from the brightness, the being inclined its head, as if acknowledging his regard. The words the other spoke came not from any earthly lips, but resounded in the depths of Hugues' soul, clear as a resounding bell and beautiful as the morning.

It is well begun, the other seemed to say, *but the Lord's work lies not yet upon the pilgrim roads outside.*

Stunned, not comprehending, Hugues merely gaped at the apparition. Was it not to protect God's pilgrims that they had pledged Him the service of their swords, as knights?

Not alone by the sword shall ye serve Him, came the being's next words, as if reading his very thoughts. *Neither is it yet ordained that ye should venture forth from this place. Labor faithfully in God's vineyard, and He shall prosper the work of your hands, whether or not ye wield a sword.*

Without any warning, Hugues found his knees buckling beneath him, and he was sitting in a heap on the dusty floor.

"I—don't understand," he murmured.

All shall become clear, in God's time, said the voice within his soul. *Beyond this wall—far beyond this wall—ye shall find what is needful. . . .*

The other's hand lifted to slap the stone wall beside him with a solid, meaty sound that made Hugues start backward in surprise, for he had not supposed that this heavenly apparition—for such it surely must be—had physical presence to render such a sound. Yet even as he gaped in dismay, the light was fading, along with that shining presence, and he could hear properly again. His heart was pounding, his hands shaking, but he had no doubt of what he had seen and heard.

Slowly he got to his feet and put out a gingerly hand to touch the wall, confirming its solidity, then brought a torch to look at the stone more closely. To his surprise, he discovered that the wall was formed of blocks of cut stone, not merely cut away from the surrounding rock like the chamber itself.

A constructed wall, then. And what lay behind it?

Dig here, a voice within him seemed to say.

He dug: first, using his dagger to scrape out the fine crack around one of the stones and prise it loose; then, as more blocks gave way and he could see that another course of stones lay behind the first, he used his bare hands to widen the opening in the first course. After an hour or so, André came in, saw him digging, and wordlessly joined in. By time for evening prayers, they had cleared most of the first layer and broached the second—to find that a third lay beyond that.

After prayers, they talked about it with the others as they took their evening meal, though they drew apart from the serjeants and kept their voices low. It was becoming clear that the knights would need a chamber where only they would meet—a chapter room, as it was called in monastic parlance.

The serjeants and servants had made promises to their individual masters, and had agreed to live the same monastic discipline as lay brothers, but Hugues sensed that this was not for the rank and file of the fledgling order.

The next day, he and André took the others to see what they had done, and only there, with André to keep watch against intrusion, did he fully tell the others about his vision, and ask their opinions. All were intrigued with the possibilities, and all agreed that the matter should be pursued.

"Who knows what we might find?" Archambaud said, gazing off into the distance. "This has been a holy place for thousands of years."

"Might it be Solomon's gold, then?" Payen asked.

Godfrey gave a shrug. "Gold? Ancient artifacts? Who knows? Maybe the Ark of the Covenant, sacred manuscripts, the secrets of the Magi—who can say? But Brother Hugues has been vouchsafed this vision for a reason, so it behooves us to do our part."

Trusting to the guidance of Hugues' vision, they decided that the manual labor necessary to penetrate the Temple's secrets was likely to be of an extended nature. Furthermore, if they were to keep up the pretext of patrolling the pilgrim roads, they would need to enlist the efforts of the serjeants and even the servants to assist with the digging.

"So long as we make certain to be there when and if any breakthrough occurs, it should be safe enough," Rossal declared. "I sense that there will be some secrets that are not meant for all—and we must make at least a token show of doing the thing we set out to do, which is to patrol the roads and protect pilgrims."

In fact, they ended up doing precious little patrolling of roads, though they sent out skirmish groups often enough, and in enough different directions, that though no pattern was set, they were seen to be going somewhere, doing something—if, indeed, any remarked at all, to see these tiny bands of knights in cast-off clothing and worn armor and harness, riding on unknown business along the roads outside Jerusalem and Jaffa and Jericho.

Occasionally, the knights did actually encounter pilgrim bands needing their protection, and word did trickle back to patriarch and king—enough that both patrons remained indulgent about the limited success of this odd band of warrior monks whose mission had always seemed unlikely anyway. Though Hugues lived in daily dread that this patronage might be withdrawn for lack of results, neither king nor patriarch wavered in their support. He could only attribute this good fortune to divine grace.

Further grace came in the guise of unexpected support from France, though Hugues was never to decide just how much was providence, how much coincidence, and how much through the good offices of André. Though the order made no active effort to recruit new members, being focused on their excavation work, André wrote periodic letters to his nephew, Bernard of Clairvaux, asking his guidance in the spiritual life of their tiny brotherhood. Hugues guessed that it might have been by this means that word of the order's existence found its way, in turn, to the attention of men such as Fulk Count of Anjou, who came in 1120 to spend time with the brethren as an associate member; and perhaps it had been Fulk who mentioned them to Hugh Count of Champagne, who had been the overlord of most of the members of the order. Later, Hugues was to conclude that the praise of such men perhaps had helped to guarantee the forbearance of their official patrons, the patriarch and the king.

Meanwhile, as the weeks and months of digging gave way to years, they began to find the odd artifact, the occasional coin or fragment of carved stone. And gradually, as they penetrated ever deeper beneath King Solomon's ancient Temple, they began to break through into systems of vaulted tunnels with keystone arches—usually blocked by rock falls before they had gone more than a few yards, but sometimes admitting further into the warren of passageways that honeycombed the ancient site. On one particularly memorable day, the work party broke into what they later learned to be the very stables of Solomon, where Rossal and Gondemere found a battered bronze boss still attached to remnants of a leather headstall such as might have graced one of Solomon's own steeds.

"Well, maybe not the king's own horse," Rossal acknowledged, as Gondemere proudly showed their find to the others. "But even if it only pulled one of the chariots in some minor battle, at least King Solomon might have *seen* it."

Later that night, after evening prayers, they took Hugues and the rest of the nine down into the site, where Gondemere showed them how he had found the item.

"We think this may have been part of the old stables," he said, as he held a torch high and gestured toward shadows beyond. "We hadn't time to explore farther before prayers—and we didn't want to let the serjeants go farther in until we'd seen it ourselves."

Hugues nodded, taking up a torch and venturing farther into the corridor, Godfrey and André at his back as he ran a hand along stones whose hard edges still appeared as fresh as the day they were cut.

"I wonder why they closed this up," André murmured, sticking his head through the opening of a large, cut-stone loose-box.

"The annals say that when Jerusalem was under siege to the Romans, the city's inhabitants knew it was likely to fall," said Gondemere, who had learned to read Arabic and even Aramaic and Hebrew. "I have heard it said that they took some of the treasure out of the city, but there have always been rumors that some was left behind, in trust for survivors who never came back."

The other six had come after them, crowding to see the wonders of this new section just opened that day, when suddenly a bright light began to glow from behind them, as if someone else approached with a torch.

But it was no torch; rather, a growing brilliance that caused all of them to draw back with hands lifted to eyes, even recoiling from a sudden blast of furnace heat and an impression of flames.

Squinting against the brightness, Hugues could hardly believe what he was seeing—a vision akin to the one he had seen before, here in the bowels of the earth. But this time, three armored men seemed to stand within the flames, gazing at him intently, fire glinting from golden breastplates and helms, and pinions of flame sweeping from each set of powerful shoulders.

Speechless, Hugues stretched one arm toward them, a part of him wondering how much the others could see. But another part knew that this vision was for him alone, and he bowed his head in acknowledgment of their coming, arm still raised in reverent salute.

Hugues de Payens, a whispering voice seemed to say inside his head.

Trembling, Hugues dared to raise his head again, unbidden tears now streaming down his cheeks from the glare.

"Speak, holy messenger," he managed to murmur, conscious of the eyes of his fellows turning toward him in question.

Go forward in His holy Name, and ye shall find what is needful, the voice replied. *Like us, let your motto be thus: "Not to us, O Lord, not to us, but to Thy Name give the glory." If ye live by these words, ye shall prosper in His grace. . . .*

With those words, the light faded and the beings dissolved

into naught but the flickering torchlight, leaving Hugues silent and awestruck.

"Hugues, what is it?" Godfrey murmured, seizing his arm to stare into his face.

"Let him be," André said, for he sensed what Hugues had seen. "Let us press forward, for I think we draw near to that which is ordained."

Indeed, what they found was beyond what any of them could have imagined: not only gold—though there was enough of that—but more subtle treasures that would only slowly yield up their secrets. Curious relics with mystical powers yet to be unlocked . . . a cache of parchments carefully rolled in earthen jars—it would take years to translate them all! . . . and, wrapped in silk within a box made of olive-wood, a set of thin miniature tablets carved from some transparent green stone, etched with what proved to be a series of codes and ciphers, readily adaptable for use with Latin lettering—perhaps a legacy of Roman times.

Those of them equipped to probe the treasures' mysteries spent the next several years doing so, while the others, along with the serjeants and servants, maintained the outward show necessary to avoid unwelcome questions. Though the order continued to attract little official note, word of their existence and its purpose had begun to attract the notice of other pious knights, some of whom became associates of the Order, not under full vows, but availing themselves of membership for a set period of time before returning to secular life. Fulk of Anjou had been the first, but he was not the last. And by 1125, when Hugh of Champagne resigned his estates to his heir and journeyed to Jerusalem to become a full member, King Baldwin had become sufficiently impressed with the Templars' performance to designate Hugues as Master of the Temple.

"For you are its master, old friend," Baldwin said, handing him the document of conferral. "The patriarch agrees. But with this title will come added responsibility, and added demands. It is time you sought recognition of your Order from the Holy Father."

Hugues bowed his head, troubled. "What notice would he wish to take of *us,* Sire?" he replied. "We are but an odd sort of monks."

"Odd enough, perhaps, but would I had hundreds more as odd." Baldwin managed a wan smile. "I am preparing a campaign against Damascus. If the Holy Father recognizes your Order, and sets his seal on your holy mission, others may also take up the Cross and come to the aid of our cause."

"Ah."

"You have within your power a means to achieve this," Baldwin said.

Hugues looked up in question, wondering whether the king could have any inkling just what kind of power he and his brothers were in the process of achieving.

"Indeed, Sire. And what power might that be, that a pope would bow to it?"

"Why, the power of persuasion, of course," Baldwin replied, with a dismissive sweep of his hand. "I know that your Brother André de Montbard is uncle to Bernard of Clairvaux. I am told that no man in Europe can resist Father Bernard's entreaties."

Smiling faintly, Hugues relaxed. "I have also heard that, Sire."

"If Father Bernard were behind you, the Holy Father would be hard-pressed not to give the Order his recognition. That, in turn, would attract the notice of other fighting men—and donations of land and gold to support them in their holy work. To support *me.*"

Hugues inclined his head. "Then, you wish me to send Brother André to Father Bernard?"

"I do."

When Baldwin said nothing more, Hugues glanced off into the distance.

"I could ask him to give us a Rule of our own, I suppose, now that we are figuring out how this odd combination of knight and monk works. We would need that before the Holy Father would even consider giving us his recognition."

"Why do you make so little of yourself?" Baldwin replied. "You have been the driving force behind the Order. Without you, it never would have come into being. Nor would it have achieved the success it has to this point."

Hugues snorted. "We lose as often as we win."

"But *we* win far more often than we did before you joined us, Brother Hugues," Baldwin replied. "Will you send Brother André? I will write a letter for him to carry."

It was late in 1126 by the time André de Montbard headed out from Jerusalem, with Hugues' blessing, Gondemere as companion, and the king's letter to Bernard of Clairvaux. The journey back to France took many months, but the welcome André received at Clairvaux was genuine. Though Bernard was his nephew, the two of them were of an age, and the reunion re-established the friendship they had enjoyed as boys. When Bernard had heard his uncle's plea, and read Baldwin's letter, he took pen in hand and composed his own letter, asking the pope's permission to compose a Rule for the Order of the Temple and requesting that a church council be convened to hear the petition of the new order and grant it recognition.

Permission came almost at once, for Bernard's stature in the Church was growing almost daily. A church council was set for the turn of the new year in Troyes, and letters were sent back to Jerusalem to summon Hugues and his brethren. Meanwhile, Bernard began work on the Rule for the new Order, based on that of his Cistercians, and André and Gondemere settled into a welcome few months of true monastic life, unencumbered by military duties and free of all obligations save to pray daily.

Meanwhile, back in Jerusalem, Hugues received the papal summons in some wonderment, but immediately set plans in motion to allow for the departure of himself and several more of the founders for Troyes. He had already dreamed of the summons, the very night before, so could entertain no doubts but that heaven favored this enterprise. He left Robert de Craon and Hugh of Champagne to look after the affairs of the Order while the rest were absent, along with the serjeants and lay servants.

"It may be several years before we return," Hugues told them, the last night before he left, after turning over the Order's seal to Robert, "but the king desires this, so he will assist you if needs must be. God be with you, my brothers."

"And with you, brother," Robert replied, as he and Hugh of Champagne dropped to one knee for Hugues' blessing.

They arrived in Italy late in 1127, where Hugues was granted an audience with the pope. A papal chamberlain bade Godfrey and the others to wait outside, but when Hugues emerged from his papal interview, a tiny smile lifted the corners of his mouth within his beard, and a new spring animated his step. From there the warrior band returned to France, recruiting as they went. The thirteenth of January found them kneeling before the bishops and abbots of the Council of Troyes as Hugues made formal request to be granted the recognition of the Church and a Rule from Abbot Bernard's hands. In the days that followed, André spent several hours sequestered in private with his famous nephew, though he declined to tell the others what they had discussed.

To the joy of all of them, recognition was soon forthcoming, along with the requested Rule from Bernard. And with the Rule came a further gift that brought a surge of joy to the heart of Hugues de Payens, who had labored so long to bring his dream to reality.

"It is fitting," said Abbot Bernard, "that this new Order of

Knighthood be marked by a sign worthy of its holy calling. Therefore, I give you the kindred habit of the Cistercian Order: purest white, in token of your vows to live in chastity for Christ's sake."

From beside him, one of his monks shook out the folds of a knee-length white mantle, which Bernard laid around Hugues' shoulders and fastened at his throat. At the same time, more of Bernard's monks removed the white mantles from their own shoulders and moved to similarly garb Hugues' seven companions. Hugues, in that instant, saw the vesting as God's confirmation that they should take the Antioch visions as their ideal. He wondered whether Bernard had learned of the visions from his uncle, or whether it had been God Himself.

"By this garb, you shall be known as Christ's knights," Bernard went on. "And as a further mark of your common purpose, I give you a battle standard to bear before you on the field, to serve as a rallying point in the heat of battle."

From behind him, another monk brought forward a banner pole, cased at one end in heavy canvas which, when removed, allowed him to shake out the folds of a noble standard, black on the upper half and white below. This he placed in the little abbot's hands, to be lifted aloft in salute to the One Whom they all served, before being passed to the kneeling Hugues.

"Bear this standard to the glory of God's holy Name," Bernard said, "symbolic of the rising tide of Light against the darkness. May you be steadfast defenders to God's friends and enemies to His foes. *In nomine Patris, et Filii, et Spiritus Sancti. Amen.*"

Thus it was that these Knights of the Temple, mantled in the purity of their vocation and steadfast before the banner of battles to be won, strode out of the hall at Troyes and into history and legend.

INTERLUDE ONE

Whatever the circumstances of the Order's beginnings, and whatever its founders discovered beneath the Temple Mount, be it gold or ancient documents or mystical relics or even nothing, the subsequent success of the Order led later historians to *believe* that more might lie behind it than a mere religious establishment. By the time Hugues de Payens returned to the Holy Land from Troyes, having spent a year recruiting in France and even England, more than three hundred new knights had joined him, now clad in the pure white robes of the Cistercians.

For those who recalled the tales of mysterious white-clad knights assisting the crusader army at Antioch—or who had seen them!—the appearance of these Knights of the Temple must have conjured powerful imagery that worked both to their favor and to their disadvantage. In an age of faith, such mystical antecedents might provide a helpful psychological advantage on the field of battle, especially since the Templars' Rule forbade them to retreat unless the odds were more than three-to-one against them—and then, only at their commander's order; nor could they hope for ransom, if captured. But the secrecy that soon surrounded the Order's internal workings, while both customary in a religious order and necessary for intelligence operations and financial confidentiality, would become a powerful weapon against them later, in the hands of other enemies besides the Muslims.

Meanwhile, the Rule given them by Bernard of Clairvaux—himself of the knightly class, and later a saint—drew on some of the same ideals of chivalry then taking shape in the courts of Europe, especially in Provence, in what was to become the literature of the Grail legends and the concept of courtly love. The romance and mystical element fostered by this development were reinforced by the air of mystery surrounding the internal workings of even the most benign religious orders; and the added need for secrecy regarding the gathering of intelligence for the war effort, and confidentiality in dealing with finance, were heightened by the pride and even arrogance that soon crept into the Order's general demeanor, building on its success as a military force.

Popular legend sometimes identified the Grail Knights as Templars. As a real-world reflection of this Arthurian ideal, the Templars came to symbolize not only the heroic virtues of chivalry, knightly puissance, and honor but the more perilous aspects of mystery and religious fervor, eventually inspiring the accusations that brought the Order down. Whether or not any part of the charges was true, a king and many others came to believe that they were—and with the same result, in the end.

In the years immediately following the Order's founding, however, both glory and disaster were still in the future. The very nature of their chosen work must have appeared daunting, for not only must they convince the world that this new combination of warrior and monk was viable, but they must begin to live that role. In the wake of papal recognition, the

Knights presumably began patrolling the pilgrim roads in earnest, perhaps actually reducing the danger to civilian visitors to the Holy Land, but their evolution into a standing army did not occur overnight. They lost their first full-fledged battle after returning to Jerusalem, when Baldwin II led them against the Saracens at Damascus; and later defeats would also make their mark on history.

But something in the very concept embraced by the Templars was sparking the public imagination. Though their popularity grew in spurts, with donations of land and gold augmented by fresh recruits, they soon found that some of their energy had to be diverted to administering the lands and wealth that were coming their way. Their example must have been well taken, because during this period the Order of St. John expanded its hospitaller function to include a military arm. By the end of the twelfth century, the combined forces of the two orders had established themselves as an indispensable part of the defense of the Holy Land—and needed to be, because in 1187, the Muslims took back Acre and soon, Jerusalem itself.

This is what we might regard as the height of any "romance" regarding the Crusades, when Richard Coeur-de-Lyon, perhaps the first historical role-model for the chivalrous image that became Europe's parfait knight, rode off on crusade and into those legendary realms beyond history. As the son of Henry II and Eleanor of Aquitaine, he was bound to be caught up in some of their mystique, but it is for his reputation as a peerless warrior that we mainly remember him—and for his honorable interaction with his Saracen adversary, the legendary Saladin.

We also know Richard for his association with the Knights Templar, best etched in the general memory by their presence at his back when, in the Robin Hood stories, he returns to Sherwood Forest disguised as one of them, to finally make his presence known and confront his brother John—who later, when obliged to sign the Magna Carta, had at least one Templar as his witness. In years to come, this Richard/Robin Hood/Templar connection showed up in Sir Walter Scott's *Ivanhoe*—of which, more later.

Our next story, meanwhile, concerns an infamous incident in King Richard's crusading history that has long puzzled historians. It was sufficiently out of character for the noble Richard that Deborah Turner Harris decided to explore this incident in the context of later speculations about Richard's Templar allies.

Harvest of Souls

Deborah Turner Harris

In August of 1187, the Crusader port of Acre was taken by the Muslims, first conquest in a whirlwind *jihad,* which climaxed in the seizure of Jerusalem.

After two years of Islamic occupation, Acre was again besieged, this time by Christians seeking to reclaim the Latin Kingdom. Pinned down in their turn by the armies of Saladin, the Franks tried repeatedly to force their way into the city, only to be beaten back by the defending garrison.

Then came the summer of 1191, when England's warrior-king, Richard Coeur-de-Lion, arrived to take command of the Crusader offensive. His coming signaled decisive changes in strategy and tactics. Encamped at Tel Kharruba, six miles to the east, Saladin summoned his emirs to a council of war.

"Four years ago, I swore a sacred oath to drive the *Ifranj* from these shores—a task which has yet to be completed," he told them. "Too long have we dallied here like fat farmers too lazy to gather in the harvest. The time has come to muster our forces for a full-scale attack."

"Why now, great lord?" asked one emir.

"The coming of England's Lion-king has put fresh heart into our foes," answered Saladin. "His galleys have strengthened the blockade on Acre's harbor so that no vessel of ours can break through. The garrison is at the point of starvation. Unless we march to their relief, Acre assuredly will fall—perhaps within a matter of days."

"How can you be sure?" asked another commander.

Saladin beckoned forward a ragged, emaciated figure. "This is Mas'ud al-Hassim," he explained. "Last night he dared to swim the harbor under cover of darkness, diving under the hulls of our enemies to bring us word from the city's defenders."

All eyes turned to the swimmer.

"Repeat the words of the garrison as you delivered them to me," Saladin instructed.

"*We are at the end of our tether and no longer have any choice but to capitulate,*" Mas'ud recited. "*If nothing is done for us by tomorrow, we will request that our lives be spared and we will hand over the city.*"

Saladin rounded on his emirs. "Hearing this plea, will you not marshal your armies for battle?"

"The infidel forces are as numerous as the sands, and their positions are well-fortified," came the response. "They will not be overcome without great loss of life. Is this one city truly worth the sacrifice of so many for the sake of so few?"

"Acre is the gateway to Syria," said Saladin. "If you allow the Christians to reclaim it, they will be a thorn in the side of the Prophet for another hundred years to come."

A lengthy debate ensued, but left the emirs unmoved.

"I cannot lead where you refuse to follow," Saladin conceded bleakly. "Very well. Return to the security of your encampments—and hope that this obstinacy of yours does not bear bitter fruit."

Once the emirs had departed, a harsh voice spoke from the shadows.

"If my lord will deign to pay a visit to my tent, perhaps there, by the grace of Allah, he may find better counsel than that offered by his officers."

The speaker was a gaunt, gray-bearded *mullah* whose black eyes burned like twin embers in his stern face. Wordlessly Saladin accompanied him to a pavilion set apart among a cluster of boulders. Silk screens inscribed with verses from the Koran had been erected inside to create an inner sanctum. On the floor at the heart of this enclosure, wreathed in sacred symbols of warding, stood a jeweled casket, taller than it was wide, with a steeply domed lid.

"There is no need to let Acre slip through your fingers uncontested," the *mullah* observed softly. "When the swimmer Mas'ud returns to the city, he must take this chest with him. Send orders to the garrison commander instructing him to deposit it in the royal apartments of the palace. Whoever amongst our enemies first finds it and breaks the seals will become the scourge of his own people."

Saladin stared at the chest. The gems surmounting the lid seemed to glitter with a malignant life of their own. Abruptly he made a gesture of warding.

"This is not an honorable way to wage war," he muttered, "even upon unbelievers."

"Was it not an *Ifranj* warrior—an accursed Templar—who burdened us with this abomination in the first place?" countered the *mullah*. "The time is ripe to return it to him and his kind. Let the infidels' own greed for plunder be their undoing. And let the guilt be upon their heads for whatever evil may follow."

On the eleventh of July, a fleet of Genoan galleys arrived at Acre, bringing a fresh consignment of munitions. That evening, the Frankish army once again put their siege engines to work in an effort to breach the city walls. All through the night, the skies over Acre rained down a ruinous storm of fire and stone. Not until first light did the attackers pause to regroup.

The Knights Templar had deployed their great catapult opposite one of the city's main bastions. Throughout the predawn hours, the bombardment had been conducted under the direction of seasoned desert campaigner Sir Jocelin de Courbet and his junior counterpart, Sir Alain de Briare.

By appearance, both men were vastly different. Jocelin was tall and broad-shouldered, with hazel eyes and tawny-gold hair, projecting an air of leonine vigor. Lean and dark, Alain looked almost boyish by comparison, but he carried himself with veteran assurance. Their white mantles, emblazoned in scarlet with the cross pattée, proclaimed their knightly profession for all to see. Only others similarly gifted would have perceived them to be members of *Le Cercle,* a secret brotherhood within the Order whose special vocation it was to safeguard the Templars' mystical treasures.

Now both of them scanned the damage done by their machine during the night. By daylight, the city ramparts looked as if they had been savaged by a behemoth.

"How much more of this punishment can the garrison withstand?" Alain wondered.

"They are men under authority, as we are," said Jocelin. "And their courage, like ours, is rooted in their faith." He added, "How much would you be prepared to endure, if our positions were reversed?"

"I would stand as long as my captain bade me," Alain conceded.

Jocelin nodded. "War often places heavy demands upon our loyalties. But that does not exempt us from doing our duty."

He spoke from painful experience. Four years earlier, at the springs of Cresson, the Order's acting Grand Master, Gerard de Ridefort, had rashly led his knights into battle against a vastly superior Saracen force. Scarcely had they engaged the enemy when they were driven back with heavy losses. Fighting to cover his superior's withdrawal, Jocelin had been grievously wounded in hand-to-hand combat with three enemy janissaries, only narrowly escaping with his life.

Temporarily invalided, he had been spared the even greater disaster which befell the Templars shortly thereafter at the Horns of Hattin. Among those slain on the field were several key members of *Le Cercle*. Alain de Briare was one of several junior initiates sent from Europe to rebuild the ranks. Since then, the younger knight had amply proven his worth, and Jocelin had come to value him not only as a colleague, but also as a friend.

A strident trumpet blast rang out. It was the signal to recommence the bombardment. Under the direction of their officers, the Templar engineers winched back the catapult's great throwing arm and wrestled a massive stone ball into its cradle. Planting his feet, Alain braced himself to yank the firing cord.

"Wait!" exclaimed Jocelin. "Something's happening!"

All eyes turned toward the city ramparts. Atop the roof of the castellum, invisible hands unfurled a makeshift white banner. Shortly thereafter, the barbican gate swung open, disgorging a party of Saracen warriors on foot. Advancing to the middle of the field, they cast down their weapons in a gesture of capitulation.

A great shout went up from the front lines. The cheering swelled to a deafening roar as news of the garrison's surrender spread throughout the ranks. The negotiations, which followed, were a mere formality. After two years of bitter conflict, the moment of triumph was at hand.

Shortly thereafter, all Templar officers were summoned to a meeting with the Grand Master. Leaving their men to secure the catapult, Jocelin and Alain set off for the Order's field headquarters. Here de Ridefort's successor, Robert de Sable, acquainted them with the terms of the surrender.

"In exchange for their lives and the lives of their families, our adversaries have agreed to hand over the city and all its contents, even the ships in the harbor. A ransom of two hundred thousand pieces of gold is to be paid, and fifteen hundred Christian prisoners are to be freed. As a final obligation, the True Cross is to be restored to us."

"Those are sweeping concessions," said Jocelin. "Will Saladin actually honor them?"

"If he does not," Robert de Sable said baldly, "the lives of twenty-seven hundred men, women, and children stand forfeit."

"What's to become of the hostages in the meantime?" asked Alain.

"We have allowed them one hour to make provisions for their dead," answered the Grand Master. "Then they are to commence vacating the city. Some of the horse pens are being dismantled to make room for a temporary stockade. The prisoners will be held there under guard until Saladin purchases their release.

"Once Frankish control of the city is assured," he went on, "our royal patrons will make their entrance. King Richard will take up residence in the palace, while King Philip has graciously accepted the hospitality of our Order. The triumphal procession will commence at the Port of Our Lady. Let all knights and sergeants apply to the Marshal for suitable mounts and report to me there."

Once inside the ramparts, the Frankish forces dispersed. The Crusader vanguard under Conrad of Monferrat took possession of the castellum. The Hospitallers diverted toward their headquarters near the north wall. The Templars struck out for their stronghold at the tip of the peninsula overlooking the bay.

They entered warily, the clatter of their horses' hooves echoing hollowly off the walls of the gate passage. Leaving the horses under guard in the forecourt, the Templar advance guard set off on an inspection tour of the commandery.

During the occupation, the fortress had been manned by a Saracen naval contingent. Kitchens, cellars, and residence halls had been left in a state of disarray, but evidence of wanton vandalism was slight.

"I wasn't sure what to expect," Alain confessed. "I thought we might find the place in shambles, with every room stripped bare."

"This castle is almost as rich a prize as Acre itself," Jocelin reminded him. "Saladin would not have allowed it to be looted at his expense. No, the fortress and its contents would have been entrusted to a captain of proven loyalty, someone who could be relied upon not to exploit his opportunity. For that we can be thankful."

The moveable assets of the Templar treasury had been depleted, but no one was mourning these losses. Even those outside the ranks of *Le Cercle* knew that the Order's greatest treasures had been transported abroad for safekeeping. There they would remain for the time being, pending the resurgence of the Latin Kingdom.

While lay servants set to work refurbishing the apartments appointed for King Philip, orders were dispatched to the captains of the Templar supply fleet, calling for food and other necessities to be relayed ashore. The swells below the castle water gate were soon dotted with laden barges. Jocelin and Alain went down to the quay to help direct the landing operations. They were deep in the midst of these labors when a sergeant arrived, bearing written instructions from the Grand Master.

"King Richard has occupied the palace, and finds it adequate to his needs," the message read. "His chamberlain informs me, however, that they have an insufficiency of wine. The *Marguerita Preciosa* is carrying a consignment of Bordeaux in her hold. See that it is brought ashore and presented to His Majesty as a gift in honor of the occasion."

Alain pulled a face. "Only this morning we were warriors of God. Now we are reduced to mere purveyors."

"Consider it a valuable lesson in humility," Jocelin recommended with a laugh. "Now help me get these flitches of bacon unloaded."

An hour later they were on their way to the palace with a wagonload of wine casks. They arrived to find the main entrance clogged with carts and sumpter mules. A knowledgeable porter directed them around the side of the building to the kitchen entrance, where they were greeted by a grateful royal butler and a swarm of servants only too willing to help with the wagon's unloading.

"Thank God that's over with!" said Alain.

"Not quite, I'm afraid," said Jocelin. "Protocol demands that we present the Grand Master's compliments to His Majesty."

Alain rolled his eyes. "If you insist."

A paved courtyard separated the kitchen precinct from the residential wing of the palace. The guards on duty at the door, seeing their Templar livery, admitted them without demur.

The instant Jocelin set foot across the threshold, a sudden blinding pain pierced him between the eyes. The blow staggered him in his tracks. He caught his breath, choking on the stench of brimstone—no earthly reek, but a noisome emanation of spiritual evil.

Alain's sinewy hands came to his support. "What's wrong?"

"A *foetor diabolis,*" Jocelin muttered harshly. "Somewhere within these four walls there lurks an unclean spirit!"

Alain made a gesture of warding. "In God's name, how did it gain entry?"

"How else but through human agency?" Jocelin countered.

"A member of Saladin's garrison?" Alain was incredulous. "But the Muslim faith, like our own, strictly forbids trafficking in the black arts!"

"The prospect of defeat can make men desperate," said Jocelin, "and desperate men will sometimes make unholy alliances."

Shielding himself with a prayer of invocation, he directed his perceptions toward the spirit realm. At once he became aware of a raging dissonance in the air, assaulting his soul like the howling of a captive beast.

No free-ranging predator, then, but a malignant entity thus far confined; bound for the present, but poised to wreak havoc, if some unwary soul should unwittingly release it.

This last impression shed a sinister new light upon the summoner's purpose, and gave Jocelin insight into the outward guise of what contained the danger. The container would be rich and tempting, inviting the finder to open it and release its diabolical inhabitant.

Intensifying his efforts, Jocelin tried to discern the location of the receptacle. A tugging at his senses intimated that it lay on an upper level. Dizzying images flashed through his mind: a vaulted bedchamber strewn with chests and boxes . . . an ornately wrought casket with a steeply domed lid.

The casket gave off a powerful emanation of evil. Jocelin harbored no doubts that this was the demon's prison. The gems that encrusted the casket lid scintillated with sparkling allure. Such bait was rich enough to tempt even a king. . . .

He roused with a jerk. "We must go to the king's chambers!" he ordered sharply. "Pray God we're not too late."

The entry hall gave access to a flight of stairs. With Jocelin leading, the two knights mounted the steps two at a time. The stair passage opened into a long gallery on the first floor.

The anteroom to the royal apartments lay beyond, bustling with servants and petitioners. The Templars shouldered their way brusquely through the ranks. Two household guards sprang forward to bar their way.

"We have an urgent message for His Majesty," Jocelin stated curtly. "Stand aside and let us pass."

His tone commanded unquestioning obedience. Mere moments later, the two knights found themselves in the presence of Richard Plantagenet, where they made the briefest of obeisances.

"Your Majesty, we have cause to believe that your enemies have laid a trap for you," said Jocelin. "As you value your immortal soul, you must allow us to search your apartments."

King Richard eyed them with frank astonishment. "Brothers, I trust your good will as I trust my own right arm. But what exactly are you looking for?"

Before Jocelin could respond, a sudden rending shriek rang out, coming from the adjoining bedchamber. A wild-eyed manservant appeared on the threshold. Gibbering incoherently, he bolted for the outer door.

The Templars sprang to investigate. At a glance Jocelin recognized the vaulted chamber of his earlier vision. The king's personal baggage, half-unpacked, lay scattered across the floor, but Jocelin's gaze was drawn at once toward a table to the left of the door.

On the tabletop stood a richly embellished casket, its domed lid gaping wide. Broken fragments of lead sealing littered the casket's base.

Inside lay a hideous severed head, its skin wrinkled and

discolored. The features were inhumanly crude and distorted. The sense of immanent evil filled the air like a miasma.

"God and Saint Michael preserve and protect us!" Alain gasped.

King Richard appeared behind them.

"Blessed *Jesu*," he exclaimed, "what monstrosity is this?"

At the sound of his voice, the Head's withered eyelids peeled back. Bloodshot yellow eyes raked the room. The fanged mouth gaped, displaying teeth like daggers.

With a blood-curdling laugh, the Head lifted into the air. A tentacle descended from the root of its neck. With terrifying speed, the tentacle thickened to a trunk, sprouting arms, legs, and a tail.

"Run, Sire!" Jocelin cried, rounding on the king.

Instead, Richard held his ground. With an oath he reached for his sword.

"Your Majesty, keep back!" shouted Alain.

Even as the words left his mouth, the abomination lunged. Sinuous arms enveloped the king in a throttling embrace as the slavering mouth pressed itself to his in a rank, possessive kiss.

With a choked cry of revulsion, Richard struggled to break free, but not even his battle-tried strength could suffice. Like water infusing a sponge, the demon's form merged with his.

A fit of convulsions seized the king's tall frame. Jocelin leapt to catch him as he collapsed.

"Secure the door and windows!" he yelled to Alain. "Ward every latch and bolt!"

While Alain sprang to seal the room by Word and Sign, Jocelin eased the king to the floor. Richard lay twitching, a white froth bubbling between his clenched teeth. As Jocelin gathered his own inner resources for an assault, the demon took control of its victim and attacked, investing Richard's body with its own inhuman strength.

Steely fingers clutched at Jocelin's throat. He could feel the entity trying to subdue and possess him as it had overcome the king, but he gritted his teeth and fought off the demon's assault with a counter-assertion of power.

> *"Servant of the Temple am I,*
> *Heir to the wisdom of Solomon.*
> *By his sign and by his seal*
> *I abjure and deny you!"*

With a bestial screech the demon recoiled. Wrenching himself free, Jocelin gasped, "Alain, to me!"

The younger knight flung both arms around Richard's powerful shoulders, Jocelin adding his weight, and together they forced the king flat to the floor. As they struggled to restrain the demon, Jocelin continued his exorcism.

> *"Servant of the Cross am I,*
> *Follower of Christ Jesus Emmanuel.*
> *By the blood of atonement*
> *And the water of salvation,*
> *I charge you to come forth!"*

Richard went limp. The next instant, a black shadow erupted out of his body into the air. Screeching, it spread itself across the ceiling in a pulsating mass. Tentacles of shadow thrust violently at every crack and crevice, seeking an avenue of escape.

"It's trying the wards!" cried Alain. "They may not hold much longer!"

Jocelin's head was pounding and his mouth tasted of ashes. Outside the room, heavy fists were beating an importunate tattoo at the door. One final verse remained to seal the interdict.

With dwindling strength, eyes fixed on the darting shadow that was the demon, he focused his will.

> *"Servant of the living God am I,*
> *Consecrated in the fellowship of the Word.*
> *By every article of sacred Law,*
> *By the one Name that is above all names—"*

Before he could complete his pronouncement, a rending crash rocked the door in its frame. There was no mistaking the ruinous impact of a battle-ax. As a second stroke followed hard upon the first, the hinges abruptly gave way and the door burst wide.

The demon uttered a gleeful howl. Coalescing like dirty smoke, it rushed from the room in a roiling cloud, the two Templars springing after. The guards fell back with cries of alarm as the cloud swept past them. Jocelin and Alain could only watch aghast as the creature escaped through an open window into the open air.

The captain of the guard rounded on the Templars with a scowl. "I want to know what happened here," he growled. "If any harm has come to His Majesty, your heads will—"

"Silence, fool!" snapped a voice. "It is entirely due to these reverend brothers that I am not only uninjured, but once again in command of my senses."

Richard Plantagenet emerged from the inner room, looking deathly pale but otherwise composed. His appearance would have deceived anyone less discerning than the two Templars. "Return to your posts," he ordered his men curtly. "Sir Jocelin and Sir Alain will attend me."

Chastened and relieved, the royal guards made reverence and withdrew. Once they had gone, the king groped his way toward the nearest chair, slumped down in it with a shuddering sigh, and closed his eyes. For a long moment he remained very still, breathing in an oddly measured way, like a man nursing an internal injury. After a moment, Jocelin fetched a goblet of wine from one of the side tables.

"Here, Your Majesty, drink this," he said.

Richard's eyelids flickered open. He took the proffered cup and drained it thirstily. Watching his face, Jocelin asked, "How much do you remember, Sire?"

The king's features twisted. "Enough."

His blue eyes lost their focus. "The creature was Hunger itself," he muttered distractedly. "There can be no appeasing it. My own spiritual imperfections conspired against me and made me weak in its presence. It had me in its grasp, and I could not break free—"

A shiver gave him pause. Mastering himself, he leveled his gaze at the two Templars.

"So this was the entrapment that you feared. Never would I have believed it possible that our adversaries would stoop to such treachery—nor did I guess that knights of the Temple were adept at casting out demons."

"That is a special vocation," Jocelin admitted. "Relatively few are called upon to embrace it."

"Then I give thanks to Providence that you were here to dispel the creature," said Richard.

"We only partially succeeded," said Alain with a crestfallen sigh. "Your men broke in on us before we could send the entity back to the Pit where it belongs."

"Your guards were only doing their duty," said Jocelin, "but I fear for the consequences, now that the *diabolus* is at liberty. Such creatures prey on humankind, and their strength grows with feeding."

"Then it must be apprehended at all cost," declared the king. "You appear to know the ways of demonkind. Will you hunt it down?"

"Whatever gifts we possess are yours to command, Sire,"

said Jocelin. "But the task won't be easy—and it may take time."

Outside, the sun was three hours past its zenith. Abroad in the streets of Acre, the afternoon shadows were lengthening.

The narrower lanes were cooler, and shadier, reduced almost to twilight by the close proximity of the buildings. In the cellar of an abandoned house, a deeper, more sinister darkness lurked like a predator in ambush.

A troop of soldiers came marching along the narrow street, noisily bragging of improbable exploits. Spectral as fog, the *diabolus* slipped out of the house and followed them, fluid and silent as it dogged their footsteps along the lane.

An intersection loomed ahead. A straggler to the rear stooped to tighten the lacing of his boot. The *diabolus* surged forward to pounce, then abruptly sheered off, repelled by a blaze of holy Light.

Its source was the sign of the Cross inscribed on the man's forehead. Never before had this mark of Christian baptism been so excruciatingly visible. The Accursed Brothers' interdict had lifted the veil from the demon's eyes.

Hitherto blind, now it could not help but see. And the sight of the Cross was too painful to endure. All the soldier's companions likewise bore the mark of baptism. Frustrated and sullen, the *diabolus* drew back and slipped away.

The neighboring by-ways swarmed with human activity. Loud voices filled the air with boasting and bravado. The demon ranged closer, drawn by the clamor of rival passions. It slipped around a corner into one of the main thoroughfares, then checked abruptly at the sound of chanting.

A liturgical procession emerged from a courtyard. Wreathed in incense smoke, the party advanced along the avenue, singing hymns and aspersing the cobbles with holy water as they came.

To the *diabolus,* the fragrant smoke had a new and terrible savor: that of the Temple incense of old, as potent as the water that sealed Christian baptism. The Accursed Brothers had invoked the protection of both, and the *diabolus* could not defy either. Cursing them, it turned tail and fled, flitting through the streets till it reached one of the city gates.

A disconsolate huddle of prisoners stood at the gateway, waiting to file out. The *diabolus* homed in on them eagerly, for no taint of Temple incense clung to them; no mark of the Cross shone forth from them in intolerable radiance. These were adherents of the Prophet, unshielded by the terms of the Accursed Brothers' rite of exorcism.

Mingling with the shadows on the ground, the *diabolus* approached the captive band, singling out a victim. Its assault was swift and deadly. Weakened by hunger, the man succumbed with a shudder and a groan.

A companion came to his support. Touch enabled the demon to extend its mastery to a second victim. Within minutes, it had gained control over the whole party. Infected one and all, the Muslim prisoners set off toward the hostage compound, carrying the *diabolus* in their midst like a secret plague.

It was after dark by the time Jocelin and Alain returned to the Templar preceptory. The report they rendered to Robert de Sable dealt only with the commonplace dispatchment of his orders. Their encounter with the demon was a matter reserved for their fellow-initiates.

Most senior of these was a grizzled veteran, Brother Terricus. For two troubled years following the battle of Hattin, he had served as Grand Commander of the Order until the election of Robert de Sable had released him to return to his esoteric studies. Other members of *Le Cercle* included Johan de Vries, a knight from the Low Countries, and two Spanish brothers, scions of a noble family of Castille. Each of these had received a covert message, apprising him of the demon's appearance and the need to take counsel together.

After Compline, the six men repaired to a sparsely furnished chamber deep in the heart of the castle treasury. Arriving singly by candlelight, they assembled round a table in the center of the room. Once the door had been secured, Terricus called the meeting to order.

"Mere hours ago, the Frankish reclamation of Acre seemed assured," he observed heavily. "Since then, as you know, that victory has been undermined by the manifestation of a *diabolus* in our midst. But for the intervention of Brother Jocelin and Brother Alain, this demon might have gained dominion over our most royal champion, Richard Coeur-de-Lion. The entity is still at large, and as long as it remains so, our hopes of restoring the Latin Kingdom will be in jeopardy.

"Such entities sow discord wherever they appear," he continued. "Only a few hours ago, a band of English soldiers had the effrontery to tear down the standard of Duke Leopold of Austria and cast it into the city fosse. The ill will engendered by this insult has opened a serious breach in the Crusader ranks. And there will be worse to follow unless we act quickly to eliminate this demonic influence."

"The *diabolus* has already escaped from us once," said Jocelin. "To ensure it doesn't happen again, we must cast a circle of interdict around the city and the encampment. That will both limit our search area and prevent the entity from fleeing into the desert beyond our reach."

This proposal met with unanimous approval.

"But all of us are too weary to do anything more tonight," said Terricus. "We'll set to work tomorrow, the stronger for a good night's rest."

Early the next morning, the members of *Le Cercle* obtained de Sable's permission to go on reconnoiter. Accompanied by a trusted following of sergeants, they set out for the fringes of the Crusader encampment, where they spent the next several hours toiling under the desert sun, sowing the ground with consecrated salt and chrism oil. By late afternoon, the circle of containment was complete.

That night, following evening devotions, Jocelin and his counterparts reconvened in the treasury chamber. They warded the room on all sides and sealed the door with lozenges of beeswax inscribed with holy symbols of protection.

A heavy pall of undyed silk transformed the table into an altar. Upon this Alain laid a square of parchment bearing the figure of a circle thrice quartered into twelve equal segments, this overlying a rudimentary plan of the city and surrounds. Candlesticks of burnished bronze were set in place on either hand. Lighted, the candles gave off a sacramental fragrance of frankincense and myrrh.

From a pouch of chamois strapped to his belt Jocelin took out a bowl-like vessel of clear blown glass. It was the size and shape of half a small orange, with a flattened base and a wide, collared neck. This he set carefully on top of the parchment sheet, then likewise laid out a steel pin, a small piece of cork, and a misshapen nodule of gray rock.

The younger members of *Le Cercle* looked on with frank perplexity.

"Have faith in Brother Jocelin," Terricus exhorted wryly. "These objects have a place in our search."

Jocelin went on to explain. "*Diaboli* are storm-bringers. When such an entity is present, it infuses the air with an invisible emanation akin to lightning. By determining the source of the emanation, I believe it may be possible to determine the demon's whereabouts. The key is vested in this lodestone."

Picking up the nodule, he displayed it for closer inspection.

"Celestial in its origins, a lodestone possesses a unique affinity for elemental influences. This affinity can by passed on by contact to its kindred ores, iron and steel. By rubbing this pin against the stone—thus—we render it sensible to emanations of the kind we are seeking."

He paused to survey his companions. "Given freedom of movement, the pin will normally incline toward the Pole Star, as befits its heavenly yearnings. But in this instance, the more imminent attraction should be that of the *diabolus*. Pray with me, brothers, that this experiment will succeed."

All bowed their heads.

"Almighty God, Lord of all things Seen and Unseen," Terricus intoned solemnly, "bless and sanctify unto us this creature of earth that it may reveal the enemy in our midst."

The others responded, "Amen."

Alain was standing by with a stoppered bottle of holy water. At a nod from his mentor, he used this to fill the glass bowl. Jocelin thrust the pin through the morsel of cork and deftly set it afloat.

"Father, Son, and Holy Spirit, we beseech you," he prayed fervently, "hallow our intentions and show us the way."

A tense silence ensued. For a long moment nothing happened. Then with agonizing slowness, the pin shifted a few degrees from right to left, counter to the direction of the sun.

The witnesses waited with bated breath. With dragging reluctance the pin continued to turn. Ponderously it wavered round to the east. Here it halted, its sharp tip trembling.

Snatching up a stick of charcoal, Alain drew a corresponding line on the parchment diagram beneath the bowl. The pin's quivering intensified, sending tiny ripples washing to and fro. Suddenly the water erupted, ejecting the pin from the bowl in a miniature fountain of spray.

A brief flurry of activity ensued as the witnesses hastened

to retrieve the pin and mop up the water. Then everyone gathered round to survey the mark on the diagram.

"The orientation is east by northeast," said Terricus, "toward Montmusard."

The others nodded thoughtfully. Prior to the Saracen occupation, Montmusard had been a thriving suburb. Warfare had since reduced it to a no-man's land of ruined houses and ravaged gardens—ample concealment for any fugitive.

"That at least gives us a starting point," Jocelin observed. "Tomorrow we'll apply the same test at closer quarters."

The next day, he and Alain once again prepared their apparatus. This time they corked the bowl and inverted it, keeping the water contained whilst still allowing the pin to spin freely.

"I hope this works," said Alain. "King Richard is anxious to press on with his campaign—and he is not a man renowned for his patience."

Accompanied by their usual escort, they set out for the east quarter of the city. Dismounting at the Hospitallers' Gate, they left their horses in the keeping of their sergeants and ascended onto the ramparts above.

This eminence afforded them a panoramic view of Montmusard and the outlying Crusader encampment. Thanks to King Richard's tireless leadership, work was already afoot repairing and strengthening the city walls. Some of the hardier Muslim prisoners had been enlisted to help with the labor. All up and down the walls, small parties could be seen mixing mortar and clearing up rubble under the supervision of their guards.

Jocelin led the way to a sheltered embrasure below one of the turrets. Satisfied that they were safe from observation, he directed Alain to ward their immediate area. Encompassed by this narrow circle of protection, he took out the glass vessel. Cupping it between his hands, he murmured a prayer for guidance and waited expectantly to see the results.

The pin began to move widdershins. Pivoting slowly, it swung around in a circle. Continuing on without stopping, it made a second revolution, then a third. Gathering speed, it launched into a spin.

The spin became a blur. Like a runaway wheel, it seemed to be racing out of control.

"This is impossible!" Alain exclaimed blankly. "It's as if the demon were everywhere!"

"Everywhere—and nowhere," Jocelin muttered.

The spin was affecting his vision. He experienced a pang of vertigo. The bowl in his hands was heating up. Just as it was becoming too hot to handle, there came a sudden sharp crack and the vessel shattered.

Both men recoiled as splinters flew in all directions, showering the pavement like a sparkling rain. As Alain watched the last fragments settle, he said flatly, "I don't think we'll be trying *that* again in a hurry."

Jocelin blinked, trying to clear his vision. "Do you see the pin?"

Alain bent to retrieve a misshapen twist of metal. It was uncomfortably warm to the touch. "I think this might be it," he said.

Jocelin took a moment to put his thoughts in order. His conclusions were paradoxical.

"The demon is certainly close at hand," he said. "The diabolic emanations in this vicinity are almost overwhelming. With indications as strong as these, we should have been able to pinpoint their source. Instead, it seems the closer we get to the demon, the less certain we are of its location."

"Maybe it's a question of amplitude," Alain hazarded. "Maybe such strong emanations register only as chaos."

"Maybe," Jocelin agreed, without conviction. He frowned. "I have the feeling we're missing something. But I can't work out what that might be."

He heaved a frustrated sigh. "Let's return to the fortress. Maybe Brother Terricus will be able to shed some light on the problem."

The two knights rejoined their escort at the foot of the rampart. They were poised to mount up when a gruff voice hailed them from the adjoining gateway. The voice belonged to a burly man-at-arms in the livery of the Commune of Acre. Jocelin recognized him as one of the sergeants of the guard assigned to keep watch over the Muslim prisoners. The guardsman approached them somewhat diffidently.

"I'm sorry to trouble you, reverend brothers, but one of the prisoners in my charge begs a word with you. He claims it's urgent. Would you mind giving him a moment of your time?"

"Not in the least," said Jocelin. "Take us to him."

The prisoners were assembled in a group outside the gate, where the sergeant singled out an intelligent-looking man of middle years, with an active manner and compassionate dark eyes. Twin prayer-locks of lustrous black hair framed his lean face on either side. This distinguishing feature, together with the manner of his dress, proclaimed him to be not a Muslim, but a Jew.

Jocelin greeted him courteously. "I am Brother Jocelin and this is Brother Alain," he informed the man. "What business did you wish to address to us?"

"I am Joachim ben Abraham, physician to the garrison of Acre," the other explained. "Since passing into captivity three days ago, a number of my fellow-prisoners have fallen ill. The malady is characterized by fever, fits of trembling, and bouts of delusion. Medicinal prescriptions exist for easing such complaints, but I have none of the ingredients at my disposal—unless you, of your charity, might be disposed to supply them?"

Disease was a common—and dreaded—feature of desert

warfare. In the closely packed confines of a siege camp, even minor illnesses could spread like wildfire.

"Make up a list of the compounds you require," Jocelin told the physician, "and I will see that they are delivered to you."

As they rode away, Alain remarked, "At least we've accomplished something worthwhile this morning."

"Aye," Jocelin agreed with a grimace. "We have more than enough trouble on our hands already without an epidemic."

That night brought no new counsel. The next day, the fifteenth of July, Leopold of Austria set sail for home an embittered man. Many German crusaders departed with him, as many as the ships could accommodate. They left behind them an atmosphere darkened by resentment at what some regarded as a cowardly defection, though others recalled the affront to Leopold occasioned by the tossing of his standard into the city ditch.

When Jocelin and Alain came to report to King Richard, they found him in a mood to make light of the Germans' withdrawal.

"They have shown their true colors," he growled. "Let them go, and good riddance. A crusade is no place for half-hearted laggards. When we enter the Holy City in triumph, theirs will be the regrets."

His brow darkened, however, when he heard that the demon thus far had eluded the Templars' search efforts.

"We must be rid of this burden, and speedily!" he declared. "Jerusalem beckons like the morning star. With our greatest prize still before us, I begrudge every day we are forced to linger here."

Tensions between rival factions continued to plague the Crusader army. Many of the resident merchants and nobles of Acre, previously driven out by the Muslims, had returned to claim their property, only to find themselves supplanted by newcomers from abroad. Aware that King Richard's interests lay elsewhere, they appealed to King Philip for justice. When he upheld their claims, the newcomers were obliged to withdraw, adding more fuel to the embers of contention that were smoldering throughout the Crusader camp.

Relations between Philip and Richard, never more than lukewarm, were further tested over the question of who should be awarded the crown of the Crusader Kingdom. Richard favored the previous incumbent, Guy of Luisignan, while Philip supported his own kinsman, Conrad of Monferrat. Clashes in the streets between opposing parties became so intense that the Templars were obliged to bear a hand in keeping the peace.

Eventually it was agreed that Guy would assume the crown for life, whereupon the succession would pass to Conrad and his wife Isabella. No sooner had this compromise been reached than a new storm appeared on the horizon: King Philip blandly announced his intention to abandon the Crusade and return home to France.

Neither argument nor blandishment prevailed to make him alter his plans. On the thirty-first of July, he set sail for Tyre on the first leg of his homeward journey, leaving behind the greater part of the French army under the command of the Duke of Burgundy. But no one could gloss over the fact that the Crusader forces were being steadily eroded by attrition.

"Had we set out on the march a fortnight ago, our strength would have been the greater by a thousand men!" King Richard complained angrily to his Templar advisors. "What makes you so sure that we are still harboring a demon in our midst?"

"The signs are, if anything, stronger than ever, Sire," said Jocelin. "If the army leaves Acre, it will be traveling under a curse that will undermine our every action." He added gravely, "Only recall how it felt to be under the demon's dominion, and you will be reminded what we have to fear."

Richard uttered a frustrated growl deep in his throat, but some of the fire died out of his eyes. "What would you have me do?" he asked. "Remain here forever? We are as much prisoners as our Muslim hostages!"

"Have patience, Your Majesty," urged Jocelin. "We are not yet at the end of our resources."

Mollified, at least for the moment, Richard gave them leave to depart. Just outside the palace gates, the knights were hailed by an agitated young guardsman.

"Brother Jocelin? Brother Alain?" he queried anxiously. Receiving nods of confirmation, he continued in a rush. "Sergeant Etienne of the city militia bade me find you. One of the prisoners in the stockade has been killed. He thought you should know. It's the physician—the Jew."

Jocelin experienced a sudden sinking in the pit of his stomach, and asked, "Do you know how it happened?"

"He was stoned to death," the young guard answered. "That's how it looks, anyway. By his fellow-prisoners, our sergeant guesses."

Jocelin flashed a sidelong glance at Alain. "We'll ride back with you to the stockade," he informed the young guard. "If this is a question of murder, it warrants a full investigation."

They went directly to the stockade. Several other members of the city militia were hovering about the gate, looking tight-lipped and uneasy. Sergeant Etienne caught sight of the Templars and came to greet them.

"I'm glad you've come, reverend brothers," he said grimly. "Maybe you'll be able to make sense of what happened here."

Signaling three of his men to accompany them, he led the way into the stockade. An area at the northeast corner of the compound had been roped off. Two more members of the city militia were standing watch with loaded crossbows. Sergeant Etienne pointed toward a shrouded bundle on the ground inside the enclosure.

"The body's just there," he told Jocelin. "We only discovered it an hour ago. I thought you might want to take a look, so we left it lying where we found it."

"That was well-considered," said Jocelin. "Let's see what clues remain to be found."

Stepping easily over the ropes, he and Alain made their way over to the corpse, where Jocelin knelt and lifted the shroud. The body exposed to view had been savagely battered, but rags of clothing that clung to the shattered bones belonged to Joachim ben Abraham.

"This was the work of many hands," Jocelin observed soberly. "And the weapons are all around us."

The adjoining ground was littered with bloodstained stones. Set-faced, Alain reached down and gingerly picked one up.

The stone seemed to cleave to his fingers. A sickening jolt rocked his vision. A fiery veil descended over everything in sight, and for an instant he seemed to be seeing through other eyes.

An image flared before him, of Joachim retreating in terror. A molten flame seemed to belch up from Alain's belly, filling his mouth with the taste of sulfur. A murderous bloodlust seized hold of him. With a supreme effort of denial, he hurled the stone at the ground between his feet.

Instantly his vision cleared, though he found he was breathing hard. A steadying hand gripped his shoulder.

"You saw something just now," said Jocelin. "What was it?"

Alain swallowed hard. "I was looking through the eyes of a murderer. Whoever cast this stone was demon-possessed."

Jocelin nodded grimly. "The marks are on the body, too."

The full horde of Muslim prisoners was crowded together at the far end of the stockade. Their faces made a blur. Jocelin was suddenly reminded of the spinning compass needle. He heaved himself to his feet and confronted the legion of faces with all the fortitude at his command.

The horde stared back at him. Every eye was a window into infernal darkness. An icy chill clawed at Jocelin's spine as a terrible truth began to dawn.

He felt the blood leave his face. With a shudder he wrenched his gaze away. When he looked again, the prisoners had turned their attention elsewhere. But he did not doubt the truth of his discovery.

He pulled Alain aside. "I know where the demon has been lurking," he confided hoarsely. "It's made a haven for itself among these prisoners. *All* of them."

"All of them?" echoed Alain. "But—"

"Look for yourself," Jocelin urged fiercely. "It's there to see—in their eyes."

Alain glanced toward the prisoners, then flinched away. "I believe you," he muttered. "Now what are we to do?"

"Tell the rest of *Le Cercle*," said Jocelin, "and hope they can suggest a way forward."

They left Sergeant Etienne and his men with instructions to dispose of the body decently. "The motive for this killing remains a mystery," Jocelin informed them noncommittally. "We'll know more when we've had time to unravel the evidence."

With manifold other responsibilities to uphold, it was several more hours before the members of *Le Cercle* were free to assemble as a group. The news Jocelin had to impart, illuminating as it was, added further weight to their existing burden of anxieties.

"I accept the evidence that the victim was killed by his fellow prisoners," Johan de Vries conceded bleakly. "And I am prepared to believe that they were acting under the spur of demonic possession. The question remains: What was it that set this unfortunate physician apart from his companions?"

Jocelin had been pondering this same question, and considered thoughtfully before speaking.

"As a Jew, Joachim ben Abraham was a servant of the Temple," he said. "The other prisoners in the compound, without exception, are servants of the Prophet. This distinction, I believe, is a vital one." He paused.

"Proceed," Terricus instructed.

Jocelin chose his next words carefully. "In our attempt to exorcise the *diabolus,* Alain and I invoked the power of the Temple and the Cross. But the traditions of the Prophet lie outside our realm of experience—and for this reason, we made no reference to them in our canticle of interdict.

"The result of this omission," he continued, "is that the Muslim prisoners alone, in the whole of Acre, have been left vulnerable to the demon's influence. The demon has claimed them for its own, and we, in our comparative blindness, have no authority to cast it out."

"Meanwhile," mused Terricus, "Joachim ben Abraham was killed because he was an outsider."

Jocelin nodded. "The *diabolus* could not tolerate his presence. More deaths will follow if even one of the demon's hosts is allowed to go free. But I believe there is a remedy—if we offer ourselves with an open mind."

"What remedy is that?" asked Brother Tomaso, the younger of the two Spanish brothers.

"The Muslim faith has its own saints and mystics, its own esoteric traditions," said Jocelin. "There is a sect known as the Sufi who are widely revered for their spiritual gifts. If we are to broaden our knowledge of the ways of the Prophet, our best recourse, I believe, is to seek out a Sufi master and solicit his aid and teaching."

"The Assassins have stood apart from our conflict with Saladin," Alain ventured. "I have heard it said that some of their holy men follow the Sufi way."

Jocelin resumed. "I know a Byzantine merchant in Beirut who occasionally employs members of the Assassin tribe to guard his caravans. Perhaps through him we may find someone willing to assist us."

"What are we to tell King Richard in the meanwhile?" asked Johan.

"Tell him what we have learned," said Jocelin. "Tell him we need more time."

Beirut was enemy territory. Terricus secured the Grand Master's permission for a scouting party to penetrate the city and assess its defenses. In keeping with the plan, Jocelin and Alain put aside their Templar livery in favor of humble laborers' garb. With Jocelin's golden coloring masked by walnut dye on skin and hair, they embarked aboard a lowly fishing boat on the first stage of their quest.

The voyage took two days. Disembarking a few miles south of the city, the Templars fell in among the local peasants making for the main gate with livestock and produce to sell. Jocelin's fluency in Arabic satisfied the city guards. Once past the sentry post, he and Alain made their way to the house of Patroclus the Isaurian.

Portly and aging, Patroclus no longer traversed the caravan routes in person. He greeted his guests with expansive good humor.

"Were your disguise any less impeccable, friend Jocelin, I would be obliged to inform the authorities," he boomed amiably. "As it is, I long to know what brings you back to this city."

"I am looking for spiritual counsel," said Jocelin. "Perhaps you can direct me."

The account he rendered to their host was as straightforward as he could devise. Patroclus pondered the problem over a dish of stewed lamb.

"I will ask around," he promised. "If any of my associates can direct you toward someone with Sufi affiliations, you shall have the report immediately. In the meantime, please avail yourselves of the hospitality of my house."

Three days passed in barren silence. On the fourth, Patroclus at last brought hopeful news.

"A caravan leader of my acquaintance tells me that he recently escorted three Muslim holy men from Antioch as far as Berothai," he told Jocelin. "Perhaps these will be the men you seek."

Berothai had been an Aramaic stronghold during the rule of King David. Jocelin and Alain set out at dawn the following morning. Traveling on muleback, it took them three days to thread their way through the foothills of the Lebanese Mountains. On the fourth day, they reached the fertile vale known as the *Beqa'a*—the Valley of the Lebanon.

Berothai itself was little more than a village perched among ancient ruins. Finding no trace of the Muslim holy men there, Jocelin and Alain set out to explore the surrounding terrain. The shadows were growing long when they heard a voice hailing them from the height of a neighboring hill. Looking up, Jocelin discerned three figures etched against the sunset sky.

"Come," he told Alain. "Providence has led us aright."

Dismounting, the Templars led their tired mules up the steep incline. Simply attired in the earth-colored robes of wandering dervishes, the three Sufis each carried a staff and a begging bowl betokening their mendicant vocation. The eldest of the three greeted the Templars with a bow.

"Peace be with you, brothers," he intoned solemnly. "I am called Nadim, and these are Jubael and Amadh. Thanks be to God that the waiting time is over!"

Jocelin registered a blink. "You were expecting us?"

"An angel of prophecy told us that *someone* was coming," said Nadim. "It remains for you to tell us why you are here."

Jocelin sensed that nothing less than the truth would suffice. Following his instincts, he delivered an unvarnished account of the facts.

"Twenty-seven hundred lives are at risk on account of our ignorance," he concluded simply. "Will you or will you not share with us the wisdom which will save them?"

Nadim and his counterparts put their heads together. A whispered conclave ensued. At last the Sufi elder spoke.

"A mile from here lies a dry watercourse," he told Jocelin. "Tomorrow you and your counterpart will go there and bring us back a stone of your choosing. That will tell us things we still need to know."

The two Templars exchanged guarded looks, but both knew of the sort of wisdom being invoked by their Sufi counterparts, and knew not to question it.

The following morning dawned pitilessly bright. Tethering their mules in a grassy hollow, the Templars set off on foot for the wadi. They spent the day scrambling over rocks under the baking sun, choosing and discarding. The shadows were stealing across the valley when Jocelin spotted a smoothly-rounded fragment of bluish-gold among the baked white pebbles of the dry riverbed.

He ventured closer. The stone in question was a silky oval the size of his palm. Wind and water had hollowed out a window in the middle of the stone. Suddenly sure of himself, Jocelin plucked it from its matrix and stuck it in his scrip.

It was after dark when he and Alain rejoined the Sufi brethren. There the one called Nadim took Jocelin's trophy and turned it over in his fingers, examining from all sides.

"What made you choose this stone above all others?" he inquired.

The question caught Jocelin off guard. "I don't know,

khalifa," he confessed truthfully. "This stone's color attracted my eye and its smoothness felt pleasing to my hand. More than that I cannot say."

He was ashamed of his answer. It seemed wholly inadequate. But Nadim smiled.

"The true Seeker is also a true Finder," he observed sagely. "The man who takes satisfaction in humble things will be slow to condemn and swift to understand. It remains to be seen if we can dream the same dreams."

He poured a measure of pale gold liquor into his begging bowl. It looked like honey, but had the scent of many spices. Nadim took a sip, then offered the bowl to Jocelin.

The liquor was headily sweet on Jocelin's tongue. Almost at once he felt his senses swim.

"The roads to Heaven are many," said Nadim. "Let us seek a common way."

Jocelin's eyes were already closing. He had no choice but to surrender—not to sleep, but to trance.

At first he seemed to be floating in pearly mist. Presently the mist cleared, and he saw below him a vast landscape of peaks and valleys. On the highest pinnacle of all stood a shining city, its bastions crowned with stars. Flights of bright birds swooped and soared among its towers in a joyous, ever-rippling stream.

The birds were every color of the rainbow. As Jocelin marveled at their grace, there came a voice.

"All souls ascend to God on wings of longing. And all are pleasing in His sight."

With these words, the vision faded. When Jocelin next opened his eyes, the sky was suffused with daylight. Nadim was sitting on a rock nearby, his face to the rising sun. Without looking round, he remarked, "The birds were beautiful, were they not?"

Jocelin sat up. "You saw them too?"

"The gift of vision can be shared," answered Nadim, "where two are of one mind."

He rose to his feet and came closer. "On that account, I give you my *beraka*—my blessing—in a form you can carry with you. It will empower you to reclaim a harvest of souls."

He presented Jocelin with the smooth stone from the riverbed. When Jocelin received it, he experienced a subtle tingling in his fingertips. Even without the aid of vision, he could tell that the stone had been invested with a potent mystical energy.

"Thank you!" he exclaimed with profound gratitude.

"*Baraka bashad!*" Nadim responded. "May this be the first of many sharings!"

After they had eaten, Jocelin and Alain set out southwest toward the coast. The day passed without incident, but that night a cold hand of fear seized Jocelin in his dreams, for he heard, as if at a distance, wailing cries of anguish and bereavement. He awoke with a start and found himself bedewed with icy sweat.

Dawn was still an hour away. He reached over and shook Alain awake.

"We must get back to Acre as fast as we can!" he told the younger knight. "A disaster is imminent, and only we have the power to prevent it."

They made the best speed that their mules could manage. Even so, hunger, heat, and rough terrain reduced their progress to a snail's pace. Tightening their belts, they pressed grimly on, aware that every passing moment was precious. Late in the afternoon of the twentieth of August, the sight of familiar landmarks told them they were approaching their journey's end.

Their weary mules could muster no more than a slow trot. The sun was sinking toward the western horizon when Alain spotted an ominous circling of carrion fowl in the sky to the east. As they pressed on, their ears were assailed by distant ul-ulations of mourning. When at last they reached the Crusader picket lines, crushing news awaited them.

"The Muslim hostages have all been executed—man, woman, and child," the sentry reported bleakly. "The killing started shortly before noon. I expect it's finished by now."

Sick at heart, Jocelin understood the promptings of his dream. He asked, "Who gave the order?"

"His Majesty the King of England," the sentry replied.

Appalled, the two knights hastened on to the Templar com-mandery. Here Brother Terricus supplied them with a fuller account of the events.

"After you left, King Richard became increasingly restive," he informed them. "The day before yesterday, a ship put into port, carrying aboard her a body of black-clad knights calling themselves the Brothers of the Signet. Claiming esoteric au-thority from an unnamed source, they gave the king a new proposal for ridding the army of the demon in its midst: Sim-ply kill all the prisoners in the creature's possession."

Alain bridled. "Why didn't you take steps to prevent this?"

"We weren't given the chance," said Terricus. "These Brothers of the Signet volunteered to spearhead the execu-tions. Without pausing to consult us, Richard accepted their offer."

"And so it was done," said Jocelin, his voice as bleak as winter. "Have you any idea who these knights were?"

"I suspect they may have been renegade members of our own Order," Terricus responded grimly. "There is evidence to suggest that some of those who went missing after Hattin were enemies in disguise. In days to come, we shall have to be on our guard against malicious dissemblers. God grant us the wisdom to unmask them before they can undermine our mission.

"As for these Knights of the Signet," he continued, "once

they had had their fill of slaughter, they departed as swiftly as they came. The demon likewise has vanished—we don't know where. In the final reckoning, twenty-seven hundred people are dead. And the whole Crusader army is now tainted with their blood."

Jocelin slowly shook his head. "It bodes more ill than you think," he said heavily. "In consenting to the slaughter of these prisoners, King Richard has abandoned his own nobility of purpose. Whether he realizes it or not, it's doubtful that he will achieve the conquest of the Holy City."

"And if he fails," said Alain darkly, "all our labors will have been wasted."

"No!" Jocelin protested, surprised by his own vehemence. "Nadim expressed the wish that this would be the first of many sharings. I believe he spoke with a prophet's tongue. If we abandon all hope of reconciliation with our enemies, is this not a triumph for the forces of darkness? Very well, let us struggle on, crippled though we may be, in the blind trust that God will one day heal our divisions and bring a happy issue out of all our shared afflictions!"

"Those are the sentiments of integrity," said Terricus. "Whether the Templars' Crusade leads ultimately to Jerusalem, or to some unknown land—whether it takes years, or decades, or even centuries—may these words of yours bear fruit in times to come!"

INTERLUDE TWO

A mysterious head, of course, eventually figures in the accusations that brought the Order down, when Philip of France was plotting their downfall a century later. Though no evidence of a head or its veneration was ever found, nonetheless the charge of idolatry was one of the principal features of the list of accusations against them.

The very vehemence of the assertions has led to much speculation as to what such a head might actually have been, ranging from an actual head (perhaps that of John the Baptist) to the imprint of Christ's face on the Holy Shroud (or painted copies thereof) to some demonic relic contained in a head-shaped physical receptacle. (While one head-shaped reliquary made of silver was actually found among the few Templar items seized at the Order's suppression, it housed head bones of one of the 1,001 virgin martyrs; and given that the Templars were never accused of giving the item anything more than the proper respect due to the relics of a saint, nothing was made of this find.)

We will never know whether the massacre of King

Richard's hostages owed anything to the influence of a mysterious head. Likewise, we will never know whether Richard's legendary meeting with Robin of Locksley ever took place, backed by Templars.

But the latter made for an excellent sub-plot when, a good six hundred years later, Sir Walter Scott got hold of the legend in *Ivanhoe*. Unfortunately, he decided to make a Templar the villain: Sir Brian de Bois-Guilbert, who conceives a forbidden passion for Rebecca, daughter of Isaac the Jew, and seizes her with the intention of making her his mistress.

Rebecca, in turn, has fallen in love with the eponymous Sir Wilfrid of Ivanhoe, while tending wounds he sustained fighting in a tournament at which the Saxon heiress Rowena, already the object of Ivanhoe's love, was to award the prizes. (Unbeknownst to any of them, a disguised King Richard had also fought in the tourney, and Robin of Locksley had won the archery prize, thereby setting up for a mostly happy ending—though not for Rebecca.) By the end of the book, Sir Brian is dead, Ivanhoe receives King Richard's blessing to wed the fair Rowena, and Rebecca sadly returns with her father to York, having selflessly set aside her undeclared love for Ivanhoe.

But did you ever wonder what happens *after* the end of the book? Susan Shwartz did. Go with us now as we return to the Templar Preceptory of Templestowe, picking up Rebecca's story some fifty years later.

In the Presence of Mine Enemies

Susan Shwartz

The last time Rebecca, daughter of Isaac, approached Templestowe, she'd feared only for her life. With her soul at risk, she forced herself to rise, then staggered off the road toward the fortress the Templars had abandoned fifty years ago. Thick undergrowth hid her, and the wind that tracked her seemed to have died down. She knew better, though, than to chide herself that this was only Yorkshire weather, that she'd gotten soft after fifty years in Granada. The hunt was up, and she was the quarry.

She stilled her shaking hands and murmured a prayer for guidance. She had come back to York seeking a champion for her people, and she had failed in her quest. More than that, she had been discovered and forced to flee.

At least for now, she found sanctuary in the forest. The greenwood, Englishmen called this wilderness of trees and thickets? Here, in the moon's eclipse, the wood was black, shadowy, full of fears—but less dreadful than what she'd fled.

She'd heard shouts and rhythmic, angry hoof beats on the road, but she was no stranger to anger and fast pursuit. She even knew something of tourneys and battles, usually from treating the wounded. She was also no stranger to fear. She'd been terrified enough when Brian de Bois-Guilbert abducted her, fighting, screaming, and scratching as the Templar carried her into precincts forbidden to women, and doubly so to Jews. And she'd been tried for sorcery. But those had only been fears for her life, not her soul.

She raised herself to aching, aged knees, and looked back toward the road. Earlier that night, hunters had sought her, spurred on by bloodlust, inspired by greedy clerics and that thrice-damned apostate Theobald. Bad enough they'd threatened Norwich; now they wanted to bathe York in the blood of innocent Jews again.

But even the threat of a massacre such as York had suffered in the early days of King Richard's reign wasn't what made Rebecca murmur prayers and wonder if, tonight, she'd be fortunate enough to die with the *Sh'ma* on her lips, affirming God's unique, ineffable, and holy name.

Ghostly horns rang out, hollow and more horrible than the awesome notes sounded on the Day of Atonement, more terrible than Gabriel's horn would sound at the end of days. Shadowy banners whipped in the night wind. Some were white and black, some depicted two knights on one horse, some showed symbols she knew Christians considered holy, but turned upside down. They were not her symbols of faith; nevertheless, she shuddered at what put them to use.

The Wild Hunt frightened her more than Templars or an angry mob. Still, it was of this land, and she could deal with menaces native to this land. The true menace to her soul wasn't so much the Wild Hunt, but the Hunt's master for the night, half male, half female, its vile brow crowned with horns. Baphomet: not Baal, not Mohammed, not even some other ancient idol out of dark history, but an evil for these times that fed on souls as well as lives.

The Hunt was up, and the Mort was blown on deathly horns, not just for her but for her people. The killing had started last century in York, then raced through the years. Now, it had raised fire and sword in Norwich. If she failed, it would move on London, until not a Jew remained, first in England, then in the entire world.

For so many years she had tried to calm her father. They were safe in Granada, she assured him. They had no more need to fear. But Isaac had been right. Even after they'd left York, she could hear him late at night, muttering with his trading partners—he no longer allowed himself the luxury of friends—long after he thought she'd banked the household fires and gone safely to bed.

In York, she had been her father's surviving child, his heir, his princess. Isaac shielded her from the stories that made him wake in the night and strike his breast, weeping and praying until dawn. He hated his memories: looters erupting from burning houses in York's Jewish quarter, hunched and more terrifying for their long shadows cast by the flames; men whose arms and sigils should have denoted noble blood standing by and watching innocent blood shed; and the Jews of York—his brothers and sisters in the faith—lined up and slaughtered.

"May their bones be ground on millstones of iron!" Rebecca had heard Isaac cry out almost all the nights of her life. Curses by night; fear and cringing by day. She had spent her girlhood pitying her father—and her adulthood loving him and forgiving herself.

At bay here in the woods near Templestowe, Rebecca squeezed her eyes shut, searching for the source of hope, the white light that meant guidance. She felt herself waver, faint, and fall half-in, half-out of a tiny pool.

She lifted her face out of the chill water and wiped it almost clean of mud. Revived by the shock, once again she squeezed her eyes shut until lights exploded in the darkness: *white light . . . gold . . . the color of her young champion's hair.*

Her love for young Wilfred of Ivanhoe had been as forbidden a thing as the Templar Brian de Bois-Guilbert's passion for her. But where her love had been silent and unselfish, she had been spared all but the long, long loneliness of her life: no husband, household, or child ever to call her own.

Brian de Bois-Guilbert, though, had died, destroyed by his own lawless passions. They had buried him on the field where he fell. And then Lucas de Beaumanoir led the Templars away from Templestowe rather than submit to King Richard.

Rebecca had been relieved to flee with her father to Granada, to the heat and the sunlight and the illusion of safety granted in Sefarad to *dhimmis,* to People of the Book. In the blessed distance from the young Saxon lord and his new wife, she had even gained a measure of peace. But she had never forgotten. Her people never did.

Isaac, though—her father had never fully recovered from the last assault, not just upon himself, but upon his daughter's life and honor. Eventually he had died as he had lived, a fearful, broken man. He would have died a second death if he'd returned to York.

You did not let fear conquer you when you sprang to a window and threatened to hurl yourself to the courtyard below if Brian de Bois-Guilbert approached you, she told herself. *So you will not submit now!*

She drew her hands over her cheeks to cool them—fine hands, despite the spots and prominent veins of age, healer's hands— then glanced down at the water. The ripples stirred by her fall were subsiding, turning the water into a mirror blackened by leaf muck and reflections of the tossing branches overhead. . . .

As above, so below . . . the trees . . . the tree . . . the Tree of Life . . .

*   *   *

Once again, a canker gnawed at the Tree of Life. Rebecca bat Yitzhak, once of Evoric, as they called York here in Sefarad, did not have to be a *gaon*, a scholar-prince, or even one of the old men who huddled about the latest shipment of manuscripts from Burgos, Cordoba, or Cairo itself to know it. She looked down at her hands, idle, for a wonder. In her youth, Rebecca had wished to sit (most meticulously veiled) at the feet of Moses ben Maimon in Cairo. But the Caliph's own physician had pronounced it a crime to teach women the Law, so she had learned her medicine instead from the celebrated women's physician Miriam in Constantinople.

Decrees such as ben Maimon's—in the form of treatises and *responsa* from the scholar princes—were cheap. To Rebecca's way of thinking, they weren't nearly as useful as righteous action. What could wise men do when the Children of Israel were slaughtered at York? Where were they when Rebecca's life hung in the balance between a Templar who vowed to turn apostate for her love and a Christian whose life she'd saved? Even almost half a century later, she still had to school her heart not to ache at the thought of Wilfred of Ivanhoe, and how he'd smiled at her.

Light played on the fountains of the innermost courtyard of Rebecca's home, sparkling off the patterned turquoise tiles of the basins and the gold stone doorposts with their Hebrew signs. Those dancing lights were the only jewels she had permitted herself since leaving England—those and her good name. Besides, the high taxes paid by People of the Book won them welcome, for at least this little while, but it was still well not to appear too prosperous.

Rebecca liked to think the hospital she had built over the years had won her and her people some security here in Exile. The good works she and her father had done since leaving England had even eased his guilt at surviving the massacre in York. At least, that had been her hope. In the fifty years since she turned her back on England, she had aided hundreds, of all faiths and races. She had become virgin matriarch to women, their children, and grandchildren who had no other home. Her "family," they called themselves, but flesh of her flesh? Never that.

During long, sleepless nights, she numbered her failures. She had not had a household and children. She had not made pilgrimage, *aliyah,* to Jerusalem either, torn as it was between the knights of Europe and the *dar al-Islam.* Still, if she'd never heard a husband and children rise up to praise her with Sabbath proverbs that she was far above rubies at a table of her own, yet she could not complain her life had been empty. Or loveless.

Now, at more than three-score and ten, she had reached an age when she had earned the right to sit in her courtyard, reading the poetry of ibn Gabirol while adopted grandchildren played the mournful, wandering tunes that her people and Islam shared.

But *Ets Chayim,* the Tree of Life, rustled, bringing half a century's refuge to an end.

When messengers brought word that the community in England went once more in peril of its life, Rebecca laid aside her poems. It was time to set to work again.

In the days that followed, she had turned over governance of her hospital to Abigail: steady enough, now she'd married off her last son to a real manager. She gathered her gold and kept her own counsel. She wished, she explained—and the Holy One, Blessed be He, forgive her for the lie—finally to reach Israel, perhaps to study in Safed in the years before she made her way to Jerusalem and, at long, long last, slept in the shadow of the ruins of the Second Temple.

Because she had never lied to them before, they believed her. Because she owed no obedience to father, brother, husband, or son, they had no choice but to let her go. She had made them her heirs; even though they loved her well, that ought to dry their tears.

Cleverly, she made her plans. Not for her now the fast, clean trading vessels of the merchant fleet in which she'd inherited her father's share. They were too likely to be seized by pirates bearing noble names and the protection of kings, some even bearing the cross of the knightly orders.

For Rebecca, safety lay in discomfort. She joined a caravan across the Pyrenees into France. Once safely across the mountains, she journeyed quiet as a blowing leaf from town to walled town with traders, always taking care to choose those who were not so poor as to be easy pickings or so rich as to be fat targets. Even so, she had to dodge troops of knights, even the occasional Templar (who merited an even wider berth) before she boarded a leaky, rolling vessel any decent trader would not have bothered to repair. The sky was cold and gray, the water even more so, and only her hidden store of medicines kept her from being sick.

As a girl, Rebecca had been her father's jewel. When she traveled with him, she had been carried in a guarded litter or had ridden her spirited horse. Her courage had not been all a virtue. It had exposed her to . . . even now, memories of Brian de Bois-Guilbert's intrusive gaze made her flush, just as—no, she would not think of how helpless Ivanhoe had been in her care, how his fair hair had fallen over his flushed brow when she had smoothed it back to bathe it, or how he had thanked her as he would a lady of his own race, long after he knew her heritage.

Let the dead be dead. As the rabbis said, the only whole heart ever was a broken one.

She had learned from her mistakes as a young girl, the golden apple of her father's eye. Even with knights on the road—perhaps because of them—any woman, unguarded, was a target now, while a rich, aged Jewish woman might as well denounce herself for sorcery and have done with it.

So Rebecca avoided the quickest, easiest crossings that would have let her land at Plymouth or Southampton and head forthwith to London. Instead, she made the grueling voyage to the northern coast. From there, meanly dressed, she could travel by cart to the Jewish community in Norwich. Once she was there, she could hire or buy another cart that would carry her inconspicuously to York.

Tracks of pain scored Rebecca's heart as she jounced over the Roman roads toward Norwich. She remembered this silver sky, these green fields, these hedges arching over the narrow roads like the entryways of her house back in Granada. She remembered the forest scents.

She also remembered odors considerably less than fresh: best not to think on that. Her first night back in England, she let her carter convince her to stop at a wayside inn, barely more than a hut, that offered her only fetid air, unclean food, dirty ale, and noise. It was rich with noise.

"Look at this!" shouted a man whose tunic boasted no patches and fewer stains than some of the others in the tavern. He hurled a crudely lettered parchment down on the rough table, scarred by a thousand drunken guests, their belt knives, and their rough boots.

"Am I a monk, to be a lettered man? What's it say?"

"And how'll we know it's the truth?" shouted a third man, whom the stench of pigs, of all unclean beasts, accompanied like a filthy cloak.

Rebecca swallowed quickly, wishing she could reach for a phial she knew she had. It contained drops that would end the sickness that made her want to flee, calling notice to herself, but they'd probably think it was poison. She swallowed and grasped the stool she sat on until splinters pricked her fingers.

"Poor saintly little Will," the first man said. "That blessed innocent." He drank deep, wiped his mouth on his sleeve, then blew his nose on the already-filthy rushes. "He'd been kind to that accursed race, and what did he get for his pains? Dead in a ditch, with Hebrew letters—probably some curse to steal his soul—carved into his skin."

"And how do you know it's true?" the swineherd demanded again. Keep pigs he might; but he'd also kept his wits about him.

"Master Theobald told the Bishop of York. He used to be a Jew himself—"

"The Bishop?"

"Quiet!" snarled the lettered man. "No, Theobald. That's his new name. He got it when he was baptized. He'd put up all those years with the annual sacrifice—you know, they kill an innocent right before Easter—but this one was just too much, and he confessed, seeking justice. . . ."

"Have they hanged him yet?"

"He's got remission for his sins." The man with the parchment waved it, trying to gather people's attention. "I think it's a damned shame we let this go on. . . ."

Three men yelled assent. When the swineherd seemed inclined to protest further, they grabbed him, one each to an arm, a third, to push his face down into a bucket of swill, then hurl him out the door.

Clean Tunic—the literate, prejudiced one—swaggered to the head of the table, demanding ale for everyone. In a moment, he might notice Rebecca. She didn't like that idea at all. Even less, though, did she like the quick-eyed, silent men who watched the man's performance, but glanced too carefully into every corner.

Who glanced at *her.*

There was no time to fear a mob; simply to escape it before it sought a convenient victim. Drawing her hood over her face, Rebecca slipped outside. Her bones creaked in the unfamiliar dampness of the air, but she made it to the stables. If the truth were to be told, they were slightly cleaner than the inn.

She found her carter sleeping by the horses. If he hadn't been willing to move at her command, if he had dismissed her warning as the fears of an old woman, she would have hitched up the cart herself and driven through the night. Instead, he humored her as the elder kinswoman she was—some third cousin on her mother's father's side. What a fool, to think because he sat and ate with them, because his family had lived here for a hundred years, these English wouldn't turn on him! They had turned on her father in York, and on others in Norwich. And if she judged from the rage that filled the stories she had heard, the tinder to set that fire ablaze was close at hand.

Thereafter, Rebecca refused to stop at wayside inns. Beneath her cart's straw, carefully kept foul, and its splintery planks, were parcels of clean food. If she and her driver ate moderately, they would have enough to last. She had a store of old cloaks she would claim to be selling: they would keep her warm when, at nights, she withdrew some distance from the roadside to sleep, guarded by her apparent poverty and the wards she cast after she heard her driver's snores.

Staring up into the darkness of the forest canopy, Rebecca found it easy to believe she heard the rustling of the Tree of Life itself, urging her to hurry. As day followed day, she rose earlier and earlier, complaining until her carter lashed the reluctant horses to greater speed. He—as well as the horses— would be glad to see the last of her.

As the cart creaked behind the exhausted horses toward the city's gates, Rebecca saw that Henry, third of his name, and son of John, had lived up to his reputation as the builder-king. Workers passed her on the road, heading for jobs on the great cathedrals that made the king a debtor-king, too, no better than his father or his uncle before him. The workers had high hopes and heavy tools: reason enough for Rebecca to avoid them.

Armed men also thronged the road. Humbly, Rebecca's cart gave them place: she huddled amid her bundles and her driver bobbed his head. It was possible, she suspected, that some of those haughty knights owed her money. After all, everyone with a reputation to maintain, immense cathedrals to build, or an army to pay borrowed gold.

Unlike his father John, King Henry had his choice of bankers: not just the Jews but the Flemings and the Templars, and on better terms. And if Henry did not need the Jews as lenders. . . . Rebecca pretended to watch the road, her eyes dark with concern. At any moment, any laborer in the field, any rider spurring down the road, any drover plodding homeward with his beasts could decide to rid the world of one more Jew.

She reached Norwich before sundown on the Sabbath. She gave her carter the horses, cart, and the last of her supplies; in the years since she had been in England, it had become harder and harder for Jews to buy food from strangers, let alone food fit for them to eat.

Hastening as much as she dared, she made her way to King Street. Once the sun set, she could not seek entrance into the Jewish quarter, and she did not want to be seen trying.

The house fronts had been freshly cleaned, the street swept. But no cleaning could conceal the scars from rocks hurled at walls. Even though it was not yet dark, the householders had shuttered their windows.

The quarter was smaller than when she had last been here— perhaps two hundred souls in all. The night wind was growing chill. She hastened to a house, larger than the others, which she remembered. Jurnet, who lived there when she was last in England, had been her father's partner on a venture or two—as well as a notable musician. Word had come in Granada years ago that he had died. When she reached York, she learned that his son, named Isaac, after her father, had also died.

When she rapped on the door, a woman, younger than Rebecca but far, far older in appearance, emerged and took her by the hand.

"Rebecca bat Isaac?" she asked. Rebecca could see her attempting to reconcile the old, impoverished woman on her doorstep, tired and covered with the dust of the road, with what she'd heard of Isaac's princess—and then giving up. After all, people did grow old in fifty years, assuming the Holy One, blessed be He, let them live that long.

"I am Avegaye," the woman said. "You must be starving. Come and wash. It will be sundown soon."

As the sky darkened above the cramped street, Avegaye led Rebecca to a narrow room whose wood panels shone with cleanliness. Light gleamed in a brass lamp Rebecca identified as coming from Damascus. The linen smoothed over the feather bed was scented with lavender. Water fragrant with the roses of England steamed in a copper pot over the fire, bringing tears to her eyes. The tire-woman sent by Avegaye with clean linen helped her wash and change, chattering of the family as she did.

Yes, Isaac ben Jurnet had been imprisoned. Yes, he'd been fined 10,000 marks, but he'd paid and thus survived to be released and live in such peace as Jews could know, until 1235 of the Christians' reckoning.

Theobald? When Rebecca mentioned him, the maid looked as if she wanted to spit.

"Pardon me, I beg," she said quickly, "but may they grind his bones for an apostate and a murderer!" Her face worked as if she fought not to weep. In it, Rebecca saw the scars of terrible fear.

Then, the girl took a deep breath and scrubbed one hand over her eyes, visibly seeking to calm herself.

"Would it please the lady to join the family for the Sabbath meal?" she asked. Her voice was so carefully expressionless that Rebecca despaired of getting more information out of her.

Rebecca followed her down the stairs to the main hall, where Avegaye kindled the Sabbath lights.

Like the woman of the house, Rebecca hid her face with her hands, unworthy to look upon the bright Presence, but heart-glad of its manifestation again in this weekly blessing. She sighed in a contentment she wished could last, not just for the Sabbath, but for all time. Lights, blessings, the wholesome aroma of hot bread, and the scent of spices rose about her like a circle of protection, guarding not just her but every Jew in Norwich.

Within this circle of peace and sanctity, she felt encompassed by stout walls. But she had spent time in fortresses, and knew how quickly they could fall. Judging from the way that the Sabbath peace slipped like an ill-fitting hood from people's faces when they did not think she watched them, the others knew too that the peace of the Sabbath was fleeting.

It was the old story, she told herself that night as she retired. The kings, knights, and monks sought the Holy Land. But it wasn't enough to kill on sacred ground. They had to get an early start in dealing death at home. The Rhinelands, York, Norwich—where would they strike next?

All too soon, the Sabbath passed in a fragrance of spices and a glow of silver, an intimate circle of cleanliness and warmth. After sundown, when fires could be lit and food again cooked, the maidservants withdrew, leaving Rebecca among the men. She was Isaac's only heir; though the older men—some almost her age—frowned at her, her wealth gave her a right to that place. Avegaye sat in a corner to bear her company. As was proper, her hands were busy with mending, but the way they trembled and jerked showed how uncomfortable she was.

David, son of Isaac, son of Jurnet, spoke first. Though he was far from the eldest man present, he was clearly the most influential; and this house was his. Kindly—it was obvious he looked upon Avegaye if not as a foster mother then as a beloved aunt—he praised the dinner she had cooked, a pottage of lentils, chicken rich with saffron, a deep red wine almost good enough for *Kiddush.*

"Yes," said an older man, who had been introduced to Rebecca as a physician. "We're getting food delivered regularly. At least, they're not trying to starve us out the way they did in Stephen Langton's day, when the king had to order merchants to sell us food."

"We paid in gold," muttered Mosse Mokke, son of the family's agent. In the tavern where Rebecca had first heard of the apostate Theobald, they'd have spat.

"He's right, David. This isn't your father's day. The constable who protected him—"

"Mordecai, my family is ten thousand marks the poorer for that protection!" David laughed.

"You're alive!" the physician retorted.

"And if you don't mind, I'd like to stay that way," David replied.

"No one's asking you to throw your life away." Mordecai continued what was, clearly, an old argument. "But someone is going to have to speak for us."

"Anyone who does will draw such attention to himself, he'll be a marked man." Avegaye looked appalled at her own interruption. "And his life won't be worth a mark."

David looked down at the polished wood at his place, the head of the table. He was *parnas,* community leader, here; if anyone was to speak to the Christians, it should be he.

Avegaye's tears fell upon her sewing. She pricked herself with the needle, blotted the tiny wound with the linen she held, then wrung her hands.

Rebecca looked up and down the table. No man would meet her eyes. She remembered that expression—half anger, half shame—from her days in England. After all, if a man knew he had only to kill a Jew to escape his debts, why not? It wasn't as if the Jew's son—or daughter—could strike back; forgiveness of debts to Jews had even been written into the Great Charter of England. She remembered how her father had humbled himself, praised men he should not have lowered himself to speak to, in the hopes of staving off the nightmares: men dying, children wailing, women trying to keep their skirts decently about their feet as they were herded off to the slaughter.

Rebecca cleared her throat.

"Would *you* speak to the constables?" Jurnet's grandson demanded, looking at her.

How shocked the young man was! But then, he had never seen her, clad in silks, following her father and Prince John into the tournament at Ashby-de-la-Zouche. He had not watched as Christian ladies were forced to give place to her. He had never seen them eyeing her garments, hating her for the splendor of her glittering diamonds.

God forgive her, she had even taken some pride in their envy. And she had repented it every Day of Atonement since then. If they only knew. She had already been punished by the Lady Rowena, who knew only that Rebecca was unhappy and would not forsake her faith. Rebecca had given the lady her jewels as a wedding gift—why not? The Saxon woman held in her white hand the only treasure Rebecca had ever truly wanted and could not have.

David ben Isaac cleared his throat. He saw only an old woman, almost a hag, not the passionate girl Rebecca had once been, or the physician she still was. Like old men, old women often wandered in their thoughts and were to be taken lightly.

Much to everyone's surprise, Rebecca laughed.

"Why would any Christian heed me when even you, my kinsmen, regard my presence as intrusion?" she asked. "I am old, it is true, but I am not yet in my second childhood; very likely, I will not live to see it. I was merely remembering—your pardon, old people do such things—my youth which, yes, I spent—

much to my regret—in the presence of great lords of England. But I am old now, as you are all too courteous to say. Those lords' sons have no reason to listen to me. And it is all too easy for them to wrest wealth from old hands, especially the hands of an old Jewish woman. So, I am not the one to intervene. What we need is not a constable, but a champion.

"I was headed back to York," she added. "To see to my father's businesses there, which have been mine for almost thirty years now." It didn't hurt to remind them that the old woman who dared to sit among them was easily as rich as any of them. "In York, once, I needed a defender, and one came to my aid."

"He'd be an old man now! Will these English respect anyone who cannot bear a sword?"

Rebecca drew a deep breath. Even now, the words hurt, though not as much as when a messenger had first brought word from England.

"Wilfred of Ivanhoe is dead," she said, "but his son lives. And these Saxon lords are bred to war."

She turned and laid her hand over Avegaye's. "You have ruined that linen," she said.

"Look at her," she told the assembled men, whose dark eyes fell before her own. "I am old. I have no place here. I will run your risks long enough to place them in the hands of someone who *can* speak for us."

It was not a plan they liked. It was the best plan they had. And, in the end, they agreed with her.

Rebecca had thought she succeeded in slipping out of the city unobserved, save for the guards. She had paid them well for her early-morning departure, but men-at-arms had a way of not staying bought—especially when it was a Jew who bribed them.

She had made all haste to York and seen to her affairs in such heart as a Jew's business could be in these times. The Jews of the city were frightened. By night, their quarter was locked from the rest of the town. They themselves paid for Christian guards upon the wells, lest anyone accuse them of poisoning the water. And Theobald's name was much in the air.

It was time, and past time, to seek the champion she had promised the Jews of Norwich she would find. So, disdaining the useful seclusion of a litter, which might cushion old bones but would call attention to the presence of a wealthy woman, she set off on foot toward Ivanhoe's ancestral lands.

Rebecca had been so certain that the son and heir of Wilfred of Ivanhoe and Rowena would rise to defend her. Ivanhoe and she owed each other their lives; Rowena owed her her life's happiness. When had she realized that she might have gained years and learning, but not wisdom?

Perhaps when she first saw that Wilfred son of Wilfred had replaced the wooden palisade Cedric the Saxon had built with walls of stone. The hall in which her father had been so humble a guest had not been torn down, but was used for storage: young Ivanhoe received his guests in a fine Norman-style keep.

Cedric had been proud to offer hospitality to all who came to his door, be they Templar, palmer, knight, or Jew. As a beggar woman, humbly clad but clean, Rebecca was duly granted entrance and placed far below the salt. Did she decline to eat meat or sip ale? Bread and water were brought her, but no effort was made to persuade her to eat more.

Her father had told her that, in Cedric's day, the hall was as filled with drafts as with hounds. Clearly, improvements had been made here. This hall did not reek with smoke. Tapestries and carpets Rebecca could have priced to the last quarter-mark hung from the walls. The rushes scattered on the stone floor were clean—fragrant, even—with herbs.

Cedric had worn a short tunic in the manner of his Saxon forebears. His grandson's garments swept the floor: lavish brocades from Persia, heavily trimmed with sables of

Moscovy. Yet he was drab in comparison with his wife Denise, who wore all the jewels Rebecca had given Rowena. A Saxon lady—a loaf-sharer, as the old term was—would have risen to serve her guests, carrying the great cup herself from one guest to another until all had drunk; Lady Denise shared a cup only with her husband. Her eyes, if they rested at all on her humblest guests, flashed as if she calculated to the farthing how much their food cost her. She whispered to her husband each time before he spoke; and when he rose to speak, what he offered his guests was not the hearty *Waes Hael* of Cedric's time, but a Norman French greeting that contained at least two grammatical errors.

Rebecca bent over her bread and water, trying to make herself small. She was painfully aware that one of the guests at the high table was an abbot, while three more were knights—and that the men seated nearest her were peering at her too closely for her comfort, never mind their courtesy. She knew she might bring less suspicion on herself if she could bring herself at least to nibble at the meat, a rare treat for the poor in England. But people who sat this far down the board would not have the choice of venison, beef, or mutton. They would be served only pork. And the mere thought of touching swine's flesh made her gorge rise—and that would certainly betray her.

When a man leaned over the board and pressed her to take a slice, she shook her head, thanked him in a whisper, then lowered her head as whispers swirled about her. She heard the name "Theobald" and bent her head over her wooden cup. Vows to eat no flesh were common, but so was rumor; and it was rumor she feared.

The talk grew profane—something about a horse that had thrown its rider, then run off into the woods. Raucous laughter followed, enraging the man whose beast had disgraced him. Conversation grew ribald, then bloody. Rebecca had never understood the connection between lust and murder, but it was one she feared.

She glanced up at the high table. She had loved Wilfred and respected the little she had seen of his father. Neither would have permitted such uproar in their hall, even this far below the salt, when the only guest made uncomfortable was a beggar woman.

But the current lord nodded to his wife, then turned to smile at my lord abbot.

She had to admit she would find no champion in Ivanhoe. She blinked back the easy tears of age. Her disappointment was cruel: he had seemed like such a fortunate choice! With parents like his, he could not be a coward. He carried himself well, and the arms hanging over his high seat looked well used. But, judging from his clothing, his French, his wife, and his conduct, he, unlike his father, was a son of the times and went with the times. He would value his reputation as a reasonable man, in favor with the king, too much to risk it—or anything else—for an ancient obligation.

Rebecca laid aside her bread and fled the hall.

Old as she was, she could run like a girl at need—she'd learned years ago that babies ready to be born did not wait on a physician's lagging steps. Still, a man in fighting trim could outrun her. The men who followed her, however, did not even try.

She had heard tales of hunters in the forest who stalked the quarry, a slow pad-pad-pad of steady footsteps until the poor beast exhausted itself, flung itself off a rock, or turned at bay.

She was no brute beast, and more lives than hers were at stake.

But speaking of brute beasts—she could hear hoofbeats now. She almost laughed, remembering the story she had heard at table of the horse that had thrown its master and run off. The wretched creature would be loitering nearby, doubtless hoping to be taken to a stable and fed.

Rebecca placed two fingers in her mouth. As a girl, she had had one trait more unladylike than all the others for which she had been rebuked: She could whistle like a boy. Perhaps they would think a boy had come to catch the horse, and perhaps they would not. But if the horse came at her call, it would not matter: she could escape.

But where would she go?

For now, that didn't matter. First, she had to get away.

The Lord God of Hosts was with her. At her whistle, shrill as any hostler's, the horse ran up to her. She twined her fingers in its mane and forced herself to leap until her foot touched a stirrup. She had mounted horses more gracefully in her youth, but she had had grooms to aid her then, and she hadn't been running for her life.

She lacked spurs, but the beast was well-trained. When she touched its flanks, even with her soft leather shoes, it moved. And at the shouts of outrage that rose behind it, it began to run, then broke into a gallop that left her only the power to cling to the saddle. The wind whipped away her veil and made her hair stream in the night wind.

Hast thou given the horse strength? Hast thou clothed his neck with thunder? As the horse raced away from her enemies, Rebecca laughed with exultation. Ahead of her, the track was straight and shining.

Her laughter was short-lived as she recalled there was no moonlight. Overhead, the sky was even reddish: the moon was in eclipse. And yet the track shone, not white, but red.

Pursuit came swifter than she hoped. They slew swiftly for stealing horses—but it was a cleaner death than some she could think of.

Then, behind her, she heard screams as if her pursuers had been ambushed. Men shouted and horses screamed in terror, then fell silent. On each side she heard rustling as if the forest teemed with hidden sentries.

The thunder of hoofbeats rose again behind her. Over them rang a horn call and a baying of hounds that made her cower in the saddle.

No blood underlay those sounds. This night of the moon's eclipse, it wasn't just Christians Rebecca had to fear. The bloodlust in England had released a force more malefic than Theobald and his masters, older than Christendom, and one that hated Christians every bit as much as it hated Jews.

Had it let her pass?

She had been *bait* for the men it had already slaughtered.

And she had no champion.

At the very least, she could lead the ghastly hunt away from York and from Ivanhoe's son. Rebecca knew this road; she had ridden it, every sense keen with rage and fear, as Brian de Bois-Guilbert's prisoner.

If she decoyed the Hunt away to the Commandery at Templestowe, that could be her final gift to her people. She'd even be aiding Ivanhoe by preserving his son. Templestowe, once so rich, had been abandoned fifty years ago.

Panicked at the scent of the ghostly Hunt, her horse fled down the road. Froth streamed from its mouth; sweat matted its sides. It could not last much longer. Behind her came the deadly call of the Wild Hunt, even closer now.

She dared a glance behind her. Ghostly banners waved, bearing sigils evil to Christian, Jew, and Muslim alike. And leading the pack, mounted on a horse taller than all the rest, was a naked figure with a man's shoulders, a woman's breasts, and a horned brow.

Her horse gave one last gasp and collapsed in the roadside. Rebecca kicked loose from the stirrups and fell as she had been taught so long ago. For a moment, she lay in the road, wondering if her life were worth the trouble of rising.

Get up, *fool,* she told herself, and staggered into the temporary shelter of the woods. Even through the trees, she could see the heavy polygonal architecture of the Templar stronghold looming.

Again came the horn call. The fortress' gates gaped wide. True, it had been long abandoned—so it, too, might be filled with things that could not bear the clean light of day.

Rebecca stifled a groan. Bad enough she had to protect her people and her old love's unworthy son. Did she have to defend the Templars too? That would be too much to bear. *Why me, Lord*? she wanted to moan, but restrained herself.

For a moment, Rebecca longed simply to stand up and call "Here I am!" She would have time to praise God, and then she could die. She even had a dagger with her, whose little Damascus blade could give her a swift and painless death.

Coward, she called herself.

Kiddush ha-Shem, the sanctification of God's name by a martyr's death, was one thing. Suicide was another. King Saul had been a suicide: dark, moody, subject to rages that approached madness.

Absurd as the thought was, King Saul might well have resembled the Templar Knight Brian de Bois-Guilbert, who had tried to ravish her and had offered her a devil's bargain: Run off with him to the Holy Land or die.

He had attacked her life and honor. And yet, he had come to her before her trial and exchanged forgiveness with her.

Abandoning concealment, she plunged through the undergrowth. Her breath cut like daggers, and her heart pounded. Much more of this, and she would die where she fell.

But the ground leveled under her feet and widened into the field she remembered. She could almost see it as it had been fifty years ago. There the Templars had assembled, row on row. There, Sir Brian de Bois-Guilbert waited on horseback. There she stood, dressed in white. There, between her and freedom, stood the gibbet and the pyre. There, Ivanhoe had come riding. And there, Brian de Bois-Guilbert had fallen. When they had lifted his visor, his face had been dark with blood. They had buried him where he fell, in ground unsanctified by the uses to which it had been put.

He would not wish to see this place—and his grave, even in unsanctified ground—dishonored.

Even spent as Rebecca was, it was but a second's work to race to where he had been buried. The Templar had offered once to be her champion. Now, she had no choice but to accept his offer. Her faith forbade trafficking with the dead. But what rode toward her was worse than any spirit she might summon.

Stooping, she picked up a sharp stone. Swiftly she inscribed a circle in the earth, then forced herself back to her feet.

The horns rang out and the Hunt drew nearer. Wind whipped about her, threatening to drive her to her knees. She steadied herself, drew a breath so deep it seemed to fill her to her toes, and intoned the ancient invocation: *Ateh Malkuth . . . ve geburah . . . ve gedulah . . . le olahm . . . amen.* For Thou art the kingdom, the power, and the glory, forever.

Within the circle she had drawn, the wind subsided.

Outside it, the Hunt reined to a stop. Immense white hounds with ruddy ears and glowing eyes loped to the edge of her circle of protection and waited. Behind them walked, or crawled, creatures she had no wish to see.

She raised her hands and invoked the Archangels: Raphael in a rush of clean air; Gabriel, whose horn call seemed to lend her strength; Michael, brave in armor, his cloak whipping about them both; and Uriel, as strong as the earth the Wild Hunt outraged.

Does Babylon do better deeds than Zion?

The challenge came from Uriel. Protection she might have for the asking, but Uriel would challenge her reasons and her means.

She drew another breath. So titanic were the balanced energies she had summoned that they robbed her of breath. Then, the winds that heralded Raphael inspired her, and she could speak.

"I seek a champion for my people and the world," she said.

This one? He was defeated by his own weakness. Thus, Archangel Michael, dismissing a warrior he deemed unworthy.

"I owe him an ancient debt. And he owes me."

And you wish not just to save your life, but to redeem him?

A blessed coolness washed over Rebecca's face: Gabriel blew his trumpet. Outside the circle, the horns fell silent. The Hunt was waiting, but it would not wait forever.

"I do," she said.

Then be it as you wish. The challenge and its consequences lie on your head, Uriel said. Permission, yes, but also a warning.

About the circle she had drawn, the air thickened, coalescing into a pillar. She saw the eyes first, and remembered them, dark with passion, flaring into new life and awareness.

Then the figure of a man took shape: Brian de Bois-Guilbert as he had been in life. He wore Templar's white, the breast of his long tunic inscribed with a crimson cross. Under the cloak and tunic of his order was full mail, a hauberk covering his legs and body down to the solerets that protected legs and feet. In one hand he carried his helm; in the other, a lance. His sword was girded at his side.

Slowly, mockingly, he bowed and greeted her, adapting words from Esdras: "You most foolish of all women, can you not see my sorrow and what has happened to me?"

Her reply came swiftly. "Zion, the mother of us all, is afflicted with grief, and in deep humiliation."

He shook his head almost imperceptibly. "Even greater wit than beauty. How could I have looked away?"

"God struck you down rather than allow Ivanhoe to die and me to burn," she said.

"And this is my reward," the Templar's spirit observed. "I am trapped on the other side, unable to free myself. Are you satisfied with your victory?"

"I did not summon you from death to trade riddles with you," Rebecca snapped. "Purgatory is part of your faith, not of mine."

To her astonishment, the Templar's spirit laughed. "Ah, lady, I always said we were two of a kind. Even now, separated by the veils, we belong together. That pale young Saxon Wilfred never deserved you. He was a dream. But you—you are a ruling passion. And I died for it."

Rebecca managed not to shake her head in amazement at de Bois-Guilbert's audacity, even now. It was, she thought, a thing that their two peoples had in common.

"Lady, why have you called me?"

Silently, Rebecca pointed to Archangel Michael.

Brian de Bois-Guilbert stood erect. He set his lance in the earth, drew his sword, and saluted the warrior archangel. The warrior he had been before his death had been confident, even rash. As a spirit, he faced Michael like a soldier, submitting to punishment he had earned.

The Archangel turned his face away.

You failed.

Even as a spirit, the Templar flushed in shame and anger. Then, visibly, he collected himself and knelt on both knees.

"The lady has forgiven me; for what binds me has been slain, and what surrounds me has been overcome. My desire has been ended, ignorance has died, and now I am released from the fetter of oblivion. My lord of warriors, will *you* not release me?"

The knight bent, lowering his proud head until it rested on the stone that covered his grave. Rebecca had seen such prostrations in the East. "I beg you to forgive me and let me redeem myself."

Michael drew his sword and touched the spirit on the shoulder. *Even death shalt die. And the grave give up its dead, as a woman in her ninth month.*

Archangel and knight turned to Rebecca. Their regard was more than mortal flesh could withstand.

She fought not to swoon, then bent and scratched out an opening in the circle. As the air about that portal changed, Archangel Michael held out his sword as if holding it open for her. Rebecca had taken a great risk in invoking trial by combat: The archangels would witness, but not intervene.

"You called me as your champion," the Templar said. "You do not have to put yourself in jeopardy again."

Rebecca shook her head. "This time, I fight at your side."

She pointed with a shaking hand to where Baphomet stood. The too-sweet mouth in that alarming face with its horned brow was dark with blood. If they lost, it would take her life, but it would devour the Templar's soul.

Brian de Bois-Guilbert turned to face the demon.

"Old friend," said Baphomet in a voice as subtle as a breeze. "My student."

"No friend to you," said de Bois-Guilbert.

"Clearly not, or you would not have failed," the demon said. "What a fool you were, to care for this withered female when you could have had all the houris of the East."

The Templar held up a hand to her. *Baphomet seeks to provoke us. Since you will fight at my side, lend me your strength.*

Rebecca nodded. Deliberately, she summoned up an old pain: giving her diamonds to Rowena, telling her she would never again wear jewels, hearing her victorious rival pity her unhappiness and beg her to stay, convert, and be her sister.

She had mastered that pain long ago, as she had mastered

the pain of her father's death, the pain of being part of a race against whom all other races' hands were turned.

Deliberately, she laughed in the demon's face.

Baphomet turned back to Brian de Bois-Guilbert. "So, you hide behind a woman's skirts? Are you a coward as well as a failure?"

Rebecca willed him the patience she had learned in a lifetime of being a stranger in a strange land: the bowed head, the humble answer, the quiet that cost one only false pride. It was a thing every Jew learned. To respond with violence was to court death.

Brian de Bois-Guilbert nodded. But then, he had never been a fool. He shrugged at the demon, refusing to be baited.

"Time was," Baphomet said, "when no one might use such a word as 'coward' to you and live."

"It is not cowardice to admit the truth," the Templar replied. "I failed in my own passions: darkness, desire, the excitement of death, the foolish wisdom of flesh, and wrath. I have atoned."

He sheathed his sword and began to walk forward. Baphomet blocked his path.

Around them swirled women, wealth, combat heady as wine. Brian de Bois-Guilbert's face, so passionate in life, changed not a whit. The air changed again: more women, wine deeper than heart's blood, rubies clustered in gold like pomegranate seeds.

Rebecca put her hands to her temples, sending her champion the discipline her life had taught her: modesty, veiled and silent; a woman standing in a window, preferring death to dishonor. It had not been easy. There had been years, after Ivanhoe's marriage, when her rebellious blood burned high. Night after night, she had waked, cooling her passion with prayer, fasting, and exhaustion until she won peace.

"Out of my way," the Templar told the demon.

Baphomet did not move.

Brian de Bois-Guilbert took another step. Now a lady, her face vivid in the Gascon features she shared with the Templar, stood before him, arms outstretched.

Rebecca thought of Ivanhoe, the last time she had seen him. *Your son is safe,* she whispered to her memories.

Brian de Bois-Guilbert stared at the lady whose loss had driven him to take rash vows as a Templar.

"You married another," he said. "It was your choice."

When she pressed closer, the Templar shook his head. "I loved another after you, and this time I loved true. Begone."

The vision turned upside down, disappearing with a scream and a puff of sulfur.

Again, the Templar turned to Baphomet.

"And now, my enemy," said Brian de Bois-Guilbert. "This game is over."

A step more would bring him to where the demon stood. He took it. And another.

And then, glancing at Rebecca as if for strength, Brian de Bois-Guilbert walked *through* the demon.

Baphomet shrieked, convulsed, metamorphosed into shapes that turned Rebecca sick, then disintegrated into a column of dust.

The dust swirled, suspended between earth and air. For a moment, it turned to face the Archangels, who looked away. Demons were outside the Mercy.

The first breeze of dawn touched the dust, scattering it over the field.

"One more service to perform," said Brian de Bois-Guilbert.

At his gesture, a ghostly horse—the very one she had seen the demon ride—approached. The Templar swung into the saddle.

"I shall lead this Hunt where its creatures can harm no one. At least for now."

He bowed profoundly. Already, his form was growing more and more wraithlike. But his eyes were still very real, very alive, and they sought hers with the old fire.

"Go with God," she said. Her knees gave way and she sank to the earth.

The Templar nodded to the Archangels. "Now, I can go free. But where I go, though there is no Christian nor Jew, there is also no giving nor taking in marriage. So grant me one more grace before I go. Let me say the words, though I have no right: Guard this lady well, for her worth is indeed far above rubies."

The Archangels inclined their stately heads, and vanished in the dawn.

Alone on her battlefield, Rebecca let herself sink onto the ground.

The rising sun filled the letters marking the Templar's grave with light so bright she could not bear to look upon it or anything else. She shut her eyes.

"Hear, O Israel," she whispered against the earth, "the Lord our God, the Lord is One."

The morning stars sang together, and the shouts of the sons of God engulfed her in their welcome.

INTERLUDE THREE

By the middle of the thirteenth century, the time of our previous story, the glory days of the Templars were already beginning to fade. By the end of the century, the Latin Kingdom had been lost—not due to Templar failings, but because of dynastic wranglings and the inability of the secular inhabitants to keep the peace.

Meanwhile, the Order had been building and expanding its infrastructure in Europe, all geared toward supplying arms and horses and the money to provide these—and, in the process, evolving financial procedures that were to form the foundation of modern banking practice. Though Templar possessions numbered in the thousands, scattered across France, Spain, the islands of Britain and Ireland, and parts of Italy and Germany, the knights who fought in the Holy Land never numbered more than in the hundreds. By far their larger success—though, eventually, it was to be their downfall—was the thoroughness with which they pursued their efforts to amass wealth to support their war efforts.

The loss of the Latin Kingdom was not the fault of the

Templars, though their political machinations no doubt contributed to the instability that brought an end to European presence in the Holy Land. But by the end of the thirteenth century, when most of those involved in the century or so of the war effort were shifting their focus back to Europe, the Order remained focused on their original purpose. Even after the final fall of Acre, when Jacques de Molay, the last and probably best known of the Temple's Grand Masters, was called back to France to meet with the pope, his main purpose was to convince pontiff and king that a new crusade should be launched, in yet another attempt to win back the Latin Kingdom. (By contrast, the Master of the Hospital was shifting the emphasis of *his* Order toward establishing a base of operations in the Mediterranean, with an eye toward eradicating the piracy that increasingly threatened Mediterranean shipping. The Teutonic Knights, another crusader order similar to the Temple and the Hospital, had already refocused their energies toward fighting the pagans of the North.)

October of 1307 marked the beginning of the end for the Templars, however. And one of the most persistent traditions surrounding that time has to do with the fate of the Templar fleet, which disappeared after the arrests and was never seen again. It intrigued Patricia Kennealy-Morrison, creator of the Keltiad series, who had never written anything shorter than epic-length when I approached her about writing a story for this volume.

"Templars in space," said I. "You've done such a fabulous job of taking the Celts into space, weaving in real earth history with the universe you've created. Could there maybe have been Templars there as well?"

Well, being a fan of Templar history, in part because of her membership in a modern-day incarnation of the Templar Order, she'd already been thinking about Templars in Space— or at least Templars in *her* space, her interstellar cosmos of

Keltia—for quite some time, and trying to figure out how she could ever manage to get them there. Added to this was a longtime fascination with the dashing James Douglas, who fought at Bannockburn and later tried to take Robert the Bruce's heart on crusade, and a growing suspicion that there might be an interesting point of overlap between the historical Templar fleet, which vanished mysteriously after the arrest of the Templars, and the ships of the Keltiad, which carried Patricia's Kelts off to the stars.

The Last Voyage

Patricia Kennealy-Morrison

A chill dark night in autumn, a whipping wind from off the land, out of the heart of sleeping France, an outflooding tide obedient to the reins of an unrisen moon. In the Atlantic port of La Rochelle, chancy starlight made a ghost parade of the eighteen ships, too ill-assorted to be called a fleet, leaving the harbor, strung out stern to prow, silent under sail and tow and muffled oar.

On the deck of the first and largest, a war galley which bore upon her side the name *Great Mary* and an icon of the Holy Mother at her bows, a young man leaned on the taffrail, staring out at the foaming water. Strongly built, tall and broad of frame, he was much, much younger than first glance made him appear—just turned twenty-one—and for that, the somberness of the handsome features and the tanned skin were all to blame. He had dark hair and a well-trimmed beard, and his alertness of bearing and posture proclaimed him warrior no less than the sword that hung at his side.

His name was James Douglas, and he was a knight of Scotland—*Sir* James, a title to carry proudly; more proudly still, close friend to the new-crowned King Robert, first of that name, called the Bruce. This night he was going home to Scotland for the second time in two years, having completed the mission on which his king had sent him to France—a mission that, though successful, had not been accomplished entirely according to plan. He was close wrapped above his mail in a thick dark cloak collared with the fur of a wolf; as the *Mary* slid past the mole and the east wind began to cut clean and cold from the distant Alps, he huddled the cloak closer, brushing his fingers over the weft as over a woman's hair, touching not wool but memories— sight of heathered hills, scent of burning leaves.

"Good Scots web," he said, no hint of apology in his tone for the wistful gesture. "Shield as well as shelter."

A snort of companionable agreement from his left. "And us still in need of both, I am thinking."

James nodded, knowing that the other—his even younger cousin Walter Stewart—understood both sentiment and situation.

And a good thing too, he thought, bracing himself as the galley set to the first big Atlantic rollers like a hunter to a fence. *For all our present peril, this is but one strand in a far graver weave strung upon a far greater loom. Before the weavers are done, the web spun here will come to cloak the world, and that we knew before ever we sailed from home. . . .*

Glancing over his shoulder at the little carrack that had brought him from Scotland and had just decanted him on France, James Douglas took a deep breath of the butter-warm Bay of Biscay air, and scanned the bustling quays of La Rochelle, chief Atlantic port of the Knights Templar. As his retainers made arrangements for horses and escort to take them the last stage of their journey, James thought back to the event, or not-yet event, that had sent him here.

Earlier in that tumultuous summer of 1307, Robert Bruce,

who now held the Scottish crown in both gauntleted hands—
as he had seized it the year before in despite of English
Edward—had been troubled by rumors blowing across
Europe like wicked winds, rumors concerning the Knights
Templar—rumors that Philip, the avaricious king of France,
and Clement his puppet pope were plotting the order's doom.
When those rumors began to buzz too loudly to ignore, even
in the midst of his own woes Bruce had thought to send James
Douglas—without whose sword-arm he would still be Earl of
Carrick, not King of Scots—to the Templar commandery in
Paris, where James had been received a few years past as a lay
knight, to seek out his brethren and, in Bruce's name and
Scotland's, to both ask a favor and offer one.

Which favor was the greater, the proffered or the sought, none
could say, at least not yet. But James had left Scotland at once,
a royal commission sewn into the lining of his cloak and his
cousin and four men-at-arms as all his tail. They had landed at
La Rochelle, and now the tiny company was hastening to Paris,
up beside the quiet blue line of the Loire. Half his errand was to
petition the warrior monks for funds and military guidance—
swords upon the field too, if it came to that; but the other half
would prove to be more important still, and come to be more
strangely accomplished than could ever have been thought.

Yet however urgent they might seem, or even are, such high
matters are never swiftly decided, and James found himself enjoying quiet days in Paris as the official envoy, however covert,
of the King of Scotland. A very different state from his first visit
to that city, and he was not unaware of the irony. As he walked
by the Seine one sunswept afternoon with Walter, he recounted
the tale of how, four years before, when he was scarce sixteen,
he had lived here adrift, too proud and too powerless to go
home. Little enough to return to: the English, who had executed
his father in their Tower at London, had seized the Douglas

patrimony and given it to one of their own; and there seemed vanishingly small chance of James ever winning it back.

With nowhere else to go, he had fled to France, to try to work things out, and, as he had written to his cousin with touching faith, "to see what help God may send me." But divine aid—working to more than mortal timeframe—was not swift to show itself. Angry, sad, often drunk in low company, more often hungry and houseless, James had wandered Paris, accepting hospitality where he felt he might do so honorably, or at least with as little dishonor as possible.

Then one day he had come across the Templar preceptory, a forbidding fortress on the Seine's right bank, in a marshy district near the royal palace, and his heart went out to it on sight. With his name and title for entrée, he had ventured the acquaintance of some Templar officers, who saw in the tall Scots youth if not exactly monk material then surely warrior metal, while he for his part had been glad and grateful of the training they bestowed.

Perhaps God had shown His hand at last, or maybe it was merely fate's usual trick of favoring the favored, but once lapped in the protection of the Templar mantle, James's luck had changed dramatically. His fellow countryman Bishop Lamberton, aghast to learn of the youth's plight, took him in as ward, so that between bishop and knights James had been cared for and educated, in lore and war alike; and with the inborn loyalty that would mark his name forever, he had vowed never to forget.

But just as he was settling into a not-comfortless exile's life in Paris, as many had done before him and would again after, the year 1306 had called him home. William Wallace had been executed in London—the Lion of the North butchered like a steer—and Robert Bruce had been first excommunicated by the pope and then defiantly crowned by his own Scots, in the wild, deep, ancient way at Scone. So James had returned to Scotland like an arrow to the gold, to be present at that king-making; and his Templar training and his hatred as a sword against the English made him more than welcome.

Indeed, he had gone straight into the inner circle of the new king—and also into the notice of every marriageable lass in the land, and many more who, if not weddable, were eagerly beddable. But such romancing was best left to the ballad-makers. For those who stood with Robert Bruce, there remained a kingdom to be secured, and James had found in Bruce not only a monarch's cause but a lifetime's friend.

As such, he rode by Bruce's side, and despite his youth was entrusted with the captaincy of many a raid; he did not fail. Not just in battle did he serve: he it was, when Bruce and a handful of dispirited followers were hiding in a cave in the western isles, who noticed a spider desperately trying to anchor its web; and though the tiny creature had failed twelve times running, yet on the thirteenth it succeeded. Thinking to cheer his king, James had made a parable of the incident— and Robert took the homely little tale so passionately to heart that, come spring, he roared out of the isles and back to the mainland newly revitalized for the fight.

And from that tiny web, victory had blossomed like the spring itself, with James reclaiming his father's castle in a raid that would become a byword for ferocity, and Bruce going steadily, doggedly on, with the cunning of a stag and the spider's own persistence, and Edward of England—who had called himself (and not without cause) the Hammer of the Scots—dead at Whitsuntide and hammered in his turn upon God's own anvil, a weakling son left behind him to rule in the South. And scarce had they all turned round and drawn one deep quiet breath than the rumors began—the rumors that, reaching a royal ear, had sparked this errand.

In good time was that spark set. No sooner had James arrived in Paris than the smolder of rumor became certainty's flame, and Bruce's fey Scots foreboding proved a true one. Though the knowledge was as yet shared by only a few, the Templars were doomed: very soon now, in all lands that bowed to the pope's rule, as the pope himself bowed to the rule of the French king, all knights of the Temple were to be arrested and bound over for trial as heretics.

James considered it as he and Walter walked again on the riverbank. *I have not told Walter the whole tale, not yet, but he is fitting things together—well, in the two minutes at a time he can spare from sighing for douce bonny Marjory Bruce....*

Now the younger man frowned, and with a deep breath turned to James.

"I have been thinking . . . Templar spycraft is the best in the world—surely the Order has known what is coming?"

"Oh aye," said James, staring across the river at the roofs and towers of the Sorbonne. "They have not been sleeping, they know fine—and they have been taking steps. I could not tell you before, but that is why Rob has sent us here. Since even the smallest bairn in Christendom knows how charges of heresy must end, for weeks now Templars have been fleeing the commanderies, clad not as knights but rough as any peasant. They have been driving wains or riding packhorse convoys or sailing riverboats down the Seine and the Loire, all of them heading to La Rochelle, hiding up in the town and the countryside roundabout."

Walter stopped dead upon the cobblestones, fixed his cousin with an almost accusing gaze.

"They are planning flight," he said, in the arrested undertone that is the polite disguise for a gasp, though none was near enough to overhear. "Philip and Clement—to keep the treasure, and themselves, out of their hands, the knights are bringing it to La Rochelle—to escape with it—to *Scotland*?"

"Nothing has been decided," James replied. "Well, if it has, it has not been revealed to overmany. But aye, Scotland it is;

Rob has promised it, since he and Clement are hardly on terms just now, and the chance is too good to miss. I have already offered it privily to the senior masters, who have so far said neither aye nor nay. But the treasure is safe stowed; and every craft moored at La Rochelle, or that can get there, has rutters for Scottish waters in its sea-chests."

"Because of us, and the word we bring—but, Jamie, surely they must say *aye*, how not! Yet Clement and Philip swear themselves blue-faced that none of this is about money, only heresy."

"Oh, it is never about money with those two, to hear them tell it—yet money is all that they have ever been about, or ever will be."

And that is the nub of it, the real reason hell is going to be loosed upon the Templars—money and power, as always, at the root of things, not this lying midden of trumped-up charges, sorcery and heresy and blasphemy and buggery.

Not saying that that last, at least, might not have sometimes chanced, and small care if it had. As a soldier and a young man, James knew well enough that those who profess to scorn the flesh are often the first to secretly indulge it—leave it to them too to make it more a sin than it was. But for the rest of it, no: and one had only to look at Templar history these past two hundred years—and to scan the account books of pope and king, noting particularly the huge debts owed to the Temple—to see it.

But though escape was planned, destination was uncertain. Since every Christian man, woman, child, and nation was forbidden to aid heretics, where on this earth might Templars go to find safe haven?

Then one midnight, at a secret, well-attended conclave in the order's chapterhouse, James Douglas caught the eye of the Grand Master, great Jacques de Molay himself—no more than a glinting glance, a tiny nod—and recognized the moment for which he had been sent; for which, perhaps, he had even been born.

Rising up from his wall-seat in the lovely stone-vaulted chamber, where he sat as lay knight of the order as well as royal envoy of Scotland, James made his offer for all to hear, speaking with the authority of his king and the warmth of his own heart the plan that he had been empowered to speak.

"Brothers, time has come to choose. Doom walks in France, and treachery in England, but in Scotland there is sanctuary. Philip's avarice cannot reach there, and Clement's writ does not now there run, and the King of Scots takes no heed of either. I set his offer before you of a secret refuge and a new life—look where he has set his royal word upon it."

He drew from his tunic breast the precious commission he had carried—a single piece of parchment with Bruce's seal affixed as king—and held it out, but no one made a move to take it, and after a moment he set it down behind him on his chair.

"And what payment does Robert Bruce seek of the Temple for so great a service done?" asked the Paris preceptor, after a fraught little silence and a swift glance at de Molay, who made no sign that anyone there could read.

"My lord the king," said James, a bit more sharply than he intended, "asks only that the Temple support him in his reign, as and if he should have need, and if it may be done without violence to vows. Anyone's vows. Beyond that, he asks no more than that Templars should survive, in Scotland if nowhere else."

"As excommunicates," muttered a blond Burgundian from a seat against the farther wall. "Like your king himself."

"But safe," said James evenly, "and with a fine chance to stay so. For the interdict will not last forever, and neither will Clement and Philip."

A good point. Silence hung heavy as incense in the chamber. No eye turned to James, and no gaze dared even flicker to the great central throne, where Jacques de Molay sat sunk in thought.

At last the Master of all the Temple stirred in his seat, and when he spoke more than a few heads snapped round at a strange new note they thought they heard in his voice. But the lined old face turned to James Douglas was gentle, suffused almost with light, though it could not be said that he smiled.

"No. No—my dear son—you have the right of it. They will not last—forever."

Not long thereafter, at the house near the Sorbonne where he and Walter were Temple guests, James was shaken awake one midnight to hear a grim message. Dressing swiftly, hearts hammering, they roused their retainers and gathered up their gear, and rode like the Wild Hunt itself to the Paris preceptory, for the message was as terrible as it was certain: On Friday the thirteenth day of October 1307—mere days hence—throughout France Philip's officers would open sealed orders; and when they did, the Temple would be cast in chains.

Yet, however passionately James besought them, Jacques de Molay and other high officers steadfastly refused to flee, knowing that their absence from Paris would alert Philip and deny escape to their brothers; and they were resolved to bide the issue, and to die for the Temple if such was their fate.

As surely it shall be, thought James, defeated at last, his best arguments in ruins and native prescience chilling his soul. *What could be done has been done, and now we must bide what may betide. Yet at least something lastingly Templar will be salvaged from the wreck. . . .*

But time was now. He and Walter knelt to receive the Master's blessing, felt the old strong hands upon their heads in benediction and valediction ("until the end of our lives or the end of our Order, whenever it shall please God that that should be"), all three of them knowing that the thing would play out as it must, and that whatever way it ran, God's purpose would be served.

Then the party mounted and rode off in twos and threes through the narrow choking back lanes, not to the great main gates of Paris but to lesser portals, where guards—persuaded, bribed, slain as necessary—let them pass in secret from the city; they would rejoin outside the walls, taking not the main road but a rough hidden track through deep forests. Not a few times the guards stood silently aside for them, porting arms in proud salute as they passed, honoring them for what they were, and had been.

And so it was that the last of the Templars—brothers and sergeants, men-at-arms and knights—rode out of Paris, and heard as they rode the gates of history clang shut behind them.

To their surprise, there was no pursuit on the roads to La Rochelle; then, as word spread behind them, much pursuit—arrows, too, three of which were kept from their destination in James's back only by the thickness of good Scots wool. They passed empty Templar outposts as they went—a glad sight, meaning safety for others—and picked up fresh mounts as and where they could.

They were days and nights on the way, riding hard and light, but in the end they could not have cut it much finer. Pounding into La Rochelle hours before Philip's officers were set to strike, they found the ships tugging at their anchors like hawks in jess. But the Templar captains, calm as sea eagles, dared wait for the outbound tide and last-minute stragglers, and the gamble well repaid. As *Great Mary* left harbor, she and her sisters were carrying six hundred men and a hundred horses, and as they went would pick up more, from secret places on empty rockbound coasts.

Now, safe in sea-darkness under filled sails, James sighed and stretched within his cloak, and beside him Walter smiled, knowing how his cousin fretted not only for their homeland but for action in this righteous cause. They passed the Isle of Ré, hove to briefly near Finisterre, and now were headed west, straight out to sea. France had vanished: by dawn the Templar fleet would have vanished also, into mystery and legend—and ultimately, some of it into the secret service of Scotland and the Bruce. Still, battle before journey's end was not so much likelihood as certainty, James reflected, so the adventures were far from over.

The thought cheered him, and he twisted round to look at the line: sleek hounds of the sea, coursing under the great autumn constellations that slowly heaved themselves over the horizon. If he strained his nightsight, he could just discern the movements of the mariner knights at their arcane tasks; the others had tucked themselves out of the way on deck, or were down in the hold looking after the horses. Destriers, trained war chargers, were far too valuable to waste, and the ships had taken on as many as could be safely boarded.

Suddenly James felt a fierce exaltation out of nowhere, a soul-surge and lift of spirit that caught him in his middle, and which owed nothing to the rise and fall of the billow. *This is the Templar fleet!* he thought exultantly, *and I am bringing it home, to Scotland and to my king—perhaps not as we had planned it, but even so. . . .*

He saw in his mind's eye the ships' names writ proud along their sides, gilt-lettered in Latin and English and French, saintly images gracing the prows—*Great Mary, Michael Archangel, Idumaea, Holy Wisdom, Magdalene, Arimathean,* and three others headed to Scotland, three more bound for sympathetic Baltic ports, where folk cared only for merchantry and let religion shift as it pleased. The remaining six had just turned south for Portugal, where refuge had also been offered, and every soul on every ship had been on deck to lift sword in what was almost certain to be final farewell.

Of the several hundred vessels that had comprised the mighty war and merchant navies of the Temple, these eighteen alone were free. Only half were war galleys; the others were graceful nefs, coaster cogges, river carracks that had seldom tasted salt. The main seafleet was far distant, plying the waters of the pilgrim routes as Templar vessels had done for two hundred years, ignorant of the doom that stood waiting for them on the quays of Europe when they should come again to land.

Though the need for flight had put their pride in pocket—Templars were forbidden by their rule to turn their backs on their enemies—one thing the knights had been as iron upon: each ship's mast streamed the Beauséant against the wind, the black-and-white Templar war flag. And a leaching sadness took James as exaltation died.

Very like this is the last voyage of the Templar fleet, the last time the Beauséant will ever fly so, a Templar flag over Templar ships of a Templar navy. . . . And to fly it now was, if not sheer madness, imprudence at best; but faith and honesty and something that could perhaps be called defiance had constrained them. *If it be indeed the last voyage, then at least it will not be sailed under false colors beneath the eye of God. . . .*

But it needed no vexillum to tell even the most casual observer that these were ships of the Temple: if anyone were to glimpse them, the hunt would be up. So driven by a strong clear-weather gale that set the sheets creaking like trodden-upon snow, the ships went in a great sweeping curve out of the Bay of Biscay and far out to sea. For several days they were out of sight of land, going up past Cornwall, rounding the Sullia isles, then briefly raising the southern Irish shore and on to the west and north. In all those days and nights they met no other ship, had not even a glimpse of distant sail.

Still, all knew that such luck, or grace, would hardly hold. There had been word of an English fleet stationed at Ayr to bar the Irish Sea against just such an escape, and a few ships of the MacDougals of Lorne, English allies, blocking the waters farther north. But neither the English nor their bought dogs of Lorne could have dreamed what course their Templar quarry was soon to take. . . .

Luck held longer than they dared hope, or perhaps it was that heaven dared not let so many warriors' prayers go unanswered. After the first week at sea, the mists and fogs of those western waters veiled them from pursuit—often from each other also, but there was no help for that. Still, even prayer cannot balk fate when God has planned otherwise. With the Templar ships on a long beat to the southeast and Scotland a low blue line against a daffodil dawn, the mists drew aside on a changing wind; and strung across the channel like a shield-wall in the sea was the English fleet.

Because of what followed, in after days James recalled little of that fight. Two ships were already tacking to make a noble rearguard stand, and he could see others diving back into the safety of the fog banks. But the *Holy Wisdom,* the *Michael,* and the *Mary* had been cut off by part of the English line, as neatly as wether lambs are cut from the flock by a working sheepdog, and James prepared himself for battle as the enemy ships plowed nearer.

I had never thought to die on aught but Scottish earth . . . still, I daresay a sword cuts the same on sea as on land. . . .

He drew, and saw his blade glitter as it had always done; he held it up to heaven as a cross, Templar fashion, and breathed a brief prayer before battle, as he always did—and then came something he had never seen before, and would never again forget, as long as he lived, and after. . . .

One moment all was as it was; after that, nothing was ever the same again. A sudden gigantic shadow fell upon sky and sea and ship, dimming the morning like some great dark wing. Then, parting the mist and cloud like the hand of God and blazing like the sun come down to earth, something silver and tremendous, something stronger than a thousand London Towers and vaster than Edinburgh's mighty rock, came settling in silent majesty through the clouds. The waves churned under a wind from all quarters at once; the three trapped Templar ships bobbed and jinked like seal pups caught in shore break.

Then, with a sound of ten thousand drums, the wild waters were drawn up like a road into the sky, summoned home, a billion raindrops suddenly returning to the clouds where they were born. Before James or anyone else could draw breath to shout or even pray, the galleys were drawn upward also, sailing up that broad glittering path, straight into the dark yawning belly of a ship from the stars.

Within the—*well, within whatever it is, in God's holy Name, that we* are *in, where are we, what has happened to the English ships, what has happened to us?*—James pulled himself upright from where his buckled knees had brought him. Clutching the gunwale for support, he looked wildly around, first for his sword, then for Walter and the others, who were clinging, equally dazed, to the rail nearby.

Then all of them stared drop-jawed at their surroundings, all thought of swords forgotten. *No sword ever forged—not Durendal, not Tizona, not Caliburn itself—would be any use against this. . . .*

They were in an enormous, well-lit, vast-vaulted chamber, roofed and walled and ceiled all of metal. The soft rosy light seemed to come from everywhere and nowhere, and though it was a far brighter and steadier light than any they had ever known, it did not hurt their eyes. The water was gone, and the English ships were nowhere to be seen. But the three Templar galleys hung—and this they could not, literally could not, believe—suspended and motionless in the air, twenty feet above the floor.

Though his heart was racing as never it had done in battle,

James was neither afraid nor ashamed; this was something so far out of his sphere that there was no point in either shame or terror.

I will save my fear for when I know there is something to be afraid of.... Surely there is a natural explanation, though what that might be I cannot think! This ship of the air is a made thing. It is not magic, it is merely some natural enginery and philosophy we do not know. Men created it, therefore men can understand it ... even if I do not, or at least not yet ... well, if they are men, and not angels, or folk from lands beyond the sky....

That last was a shrewder guess than he knew—though not than he would come to know. Then, putting paid to his wondering by opening up a whole new slate of questions, doors opened at one end of the chamber, and a knot of entirely human-looking men—and women!—came in. One who seemed in command spoke briefly, and several turned aside to do mysterious things at a glowing panel near the door. Whatever it was they did, James and the crews of the three ships found themselves no longer on their vessels but standing upon dry decking made of some unknown material sure to the foot. He mastered himself with an almost physical effort, and turned a level gaze on the newcomers.

They returned his stare with friendly interested curiosity, and no hostility that he could detect. *We are not prisoners, then....* To his eye they had a familiar look: tall men with warriors' builds, well-mustached as Scots or Irishers, some full-bearded as any Templar. But, however unchivalrous, James could not stop staring at the women. Long-haired as proper ladies should be, they were not merely unwimpled but clad as no proper lady had ever been in all the life of the world, garbed like the men in tight-fitting trews and doublets of dark green cloth. They moved not like decorous court madams but with a straight-backed stride and forthright stance, and they spoke to their male counterparts as equals, with easy laughter and comradeliness, even with command. For their part, they returned James's uncivil stare with serene expressions and a warmly appraising smile or two, attending to their work with the same swift assurance as the men.

"My sorrow to put such fear and confusion on you," came a calm voice then, "but we saw that quick action was needed, and we knew a little of your plight, as your thoughtspeech gave it us." Though the words were meant to soothe, the fact that they were in resonant Latin every bit as good as a churchman's, and Irish-accented Latin to boot, only unsettled the new arrivals even more. The voice's owner saw this too, and stepped forward smiling.

"We are folk of many different tongues, so Latin will serve us easiest and best—you do speak Latin?" Seeing nods all round: "So then! I am Connla mac Nessa vhic Dhau, captain of this ship. This is the *Cabarfeidh*. And as you have doubtless worked out by now, we are not from around here."

James found his voice. "Nay—aye—may I ask where— who—*how*?"

Connla mac Nessa—tall, brown-haired, blue-eyed— chuckled. "You may ask indeed! We are Kelts, folk of a distant realm called Keltia, here on a—yes, you may call it a visit."

Keltia . . . "We—I—have never heard of such a land."

"No, you would not have. This will take some time, sirs, give me a little sword-room here. . . . Well. Keltia. It is not a land, just so, but a world, not one world but many, under not one sun like this above us but seven different suns. Under the guidance of Saint Brendan the Astrogator, we left Erith— Earth, this planet now beneath us—in the year 453 by your reckoning, fleeing the intolerances of Patrick of Rome. After sailing the stars for two long years, we came to our new home, and called it Keltia.

"Now, Keltia is as far from this world as it would take light to travel in a thousand years; Brendan taught us the principles by which we can voyage in such craft as this, and greater ones, making the journey in a matter of weeks, or even days."

Connla saw the utter incomprehension on the faces turned to him like blank wondering flowers—*Slow and easy! They still believe the Earth is flat, do not affright them any more than you must!*—and spoke more gently still.

"I know how strange and fearful this must be, even to warriors. For now, may I know to whom *I* speak? We know already what you are, and why you are in such straits; it is why we have removed you from the peril, and now we must discuss what you wish to do next."

Easier that would be if I did not feel as ignorant as a pig and stupid as a noonday owl....

James glanced quickly at the Templar officers beside him, hesitant to usurp a privilege of honor, but the three captains indicated as one that they were more than willing to let him, as ranking noble and presumed man of the world—*whatever world that might be!*—return civilities. His mouth pulled down at one corner and his heart had not ceased to pound, but he bowed to the outworld commander as he would have bowed to his king, and his courtesy was returned.

"James Douglas, knight, captain of war to King Robert of Scotland, first of that name...." He introduced Walter Stewart and the senior Templars; more bows. *Truly, these Kelts have not lost the courtesy of our people by going to the stars....*

"A fellow countryman," said Connla, smiling. "My mother's kindred hail from beside the Gala Water, not far from Douglas lands, though my father's people are from Valentia, in the Irish west. Not they themselves, of course; both kindreds left Erith long ago, with the first immrama. But come...."

He drew James aside with him; Walter, not without a

desperate backward glance, went off with the other Templars, each of them escorted by a Keltic guide.

Or guard? James dismissed the thought even as it formed. *Nay, these are folk of honor . . .*

After walking down what seemed leagues of cool smooth-walled corridors, they turned aside into a small chamber, and for all his resolve to keep a stern demeanor James could not suppress a gasp. One whole wall was sparkling window, a huge crystal pane framing a view such as never man of Earth had seen. He found himself standing at the glass, if glass it was, with no memory of crossing the room, one hand raised as if to caress what he saw.

Scotland lay at his feet, the Highlands a bright white comb so near it seemed he could reach down and touch their snows, while England and Wales were swathes of misty green and Ireland a burnished shield upon the waters.

This is what the lands must look like to the eye of God. . . .

As he watched rapt, though he felt no motion, the ship rose higher still. *They can cross in an effortless instant what distance took us long painful weeks—and such farther distances as we cannot even reck of. . . .*

James sensed the silent presence of Connla behind him, standing away, patient, giving him time to take it in, but for all his best efforts his voice shook as he spoke—though only a little.

"Sir and captain, perhaps you would now of your grace speak of what I must know."

"As you will have it, and gladly will I tell," said Connla, motioning to a wide padded bench by the great window, and James gratefully sank down into it. Pouring a mether of ale from the keeve on a low table, Connla offered it to his guest with the proper formula, and the good bread and cheese and meat in the dish beside.

"Well, now. We know of the Templar Knights from our

return voyages—oh aye, we have had some dealings and en-
counters with your order, of varied natures and outcomes—
and as I said, we know also a little of your current straits. But
the whole tale will serve us best."

It took a long while, and much repetition and side-explain-
ing, for Connla mac Nessa to make all clear about Keltia, and
for James Douglas to make things clear in return. But at last
James sat back and shook his head—and still he could not tear
his gaze from the view below.

*Sailing among the stars, and round planets, and magic of
the Sidhefolk, and light as power. . . .*

"Your tale is more amazing than anything I have ever
heard, lord, it stands above the stories of Fionn and Roland
and Arthur himself. Yet I cannot deny the evidence of my own
eyes—this is beyond not belief but beyond *dis*belief. That you
dared leave Earth at all—"

"We thought we could do no other," said Connla quietly.
"Patrick was too close behind us, and we saw that the forbearance we had given him and his faith was not going to be given
us and ours in return." He fell silent a moment, then spread his
hands and shrugged, a gesture more eloquent than speech.

"So we left. Great Brendan and Nia his mother built us ships
to sail the overheavens, and found for us the road through the
stars—and our promised home among them. We have dwelled
there ever since." Looking straight at James: "And I make this
offer to you now: You and your fellows are welcome to join us
there, to live in peace and freedom as you choose."

*Eight hundred years they have been out there, out among the
stars. . . . eight hundred years! And on the world they left behind
them, no one knew, or if they did, they did not say—save perhaps
in wild bard's tales that none ever took for truth . . . all those
legends about ships that could sail over land or sea, and flaming swords that could cut through any thickness, and magic*

armor and crystal ships . . . who could have known? Or know-
ing, who could have spoken to be believed?

"We kept it that way," said Connla, seeing his expression and
knowing his thought—the incredulous half-laughing, half-angry
disbelief. "Not that we feared others would follow—the secret
of the shipmaking was ours alone—but we preferred not to
leave to Erithfolk a bitter gnawing knowledge of something they
could not have; it would have been too cruel.

"Those who discover the secret and the truth, we bring
away to Keltia; the rest must bide—at least for now. Your own
plight confirms it: Your folk still persecute one another for
that most utterly stupid of reasons—difference of faith, or
rather a cloak of faith spread over greed and lust for power.
Yet for their souls' sake, they must learn to let different be-
liefs, as the Highest did give them to different folk, dwell side
by side, and respect all gods as they respect their own."

James acknowledged the truth of the charge with a tight-
ened mouth and a curt nod. "When my brothers of the Paris
Temple served in Palestinia, they spoke with wise men—aye,
and wiser women!—of the Saracen folk, and they told me
those learned ones said the same, to the confoundment, or
worse, of their own priests, their *mullah*s.

"My own Church did great slaughter in France a hundred
years ago, against folk called Cathari. And those Cathari were
Christians, children as we are of the faith we claim the true
one. I flatter myself that I am a good son of the Church, but
even I see how readily that Church wreaks pain and blood and
death when such suits its purpose, on its own and on others—
the Jews, the Cathars, now the Templars; aye, and doubtless
more still in time to come. Ploys of worldly power and control, made in the name of Christ Jesus—dare I blaspheme to
say it, but I do *not* think that such is what he had in mind. But
you are not Christians at all."

"Indeed we are not!" came the amused answer. "We follow

the draoícht way: Eolas, the Knowing, Shan-vallachta, the
Old Way of God and Goddess—as our foremothers and fore-
fathers did, before ever the White Druid of the Tree was
brought by Patrick to conquer our lands. So we too have felt
the hand of Rome against us."

"But—"

Connla waved a dismissive hand. "Your Christ was a
mighty teacher sent by the One, the Great Creator of Being.
You yourselves say that he took man's form but he also bore
god's nature. Well, you are more right than you know; and he
is not the only one, god or man, who has ever done so, or ever
will. Avatars, such beings are called in eastern lands, easter
far than your Templar Outremer—Chin and Persia, Nihon and
Hind. We have no quarrel with him, only with what was made
of him once he was gone and could not prevent it.

"Others of your faith are in Keltia, you know," he added,
seeing James's trouble. "They are not many, but they are
there, and glad to be so; fine Kelts they are, too. If you come
with us, you will not be alone, and you may follow your faith
as you will—as, perhaps, it was meant to be followed and
never yet has been. The Celi Dé, we call them, the Clan of
God—they joined us and the Sidhefolk on the Great Immram,
the First Voyage, when Patrick drove the Old Ways out of Ireland and brought in new ways that even these sheep of his
own flock could not, and would not, thole. After, Patrick
called us serpents and snakes that the power of his new god
had driven from the land."

"To a realm beyond the pope's reach—"

"Oh, beyond the reach of Rome, right enough. But—as my
Celi Dé friends are always telling me—never beyond the
reach of God."

"Well, beyond the reach of Clement and Philip—that is more
than enough for me! But how can God have made one truth—
and so different a truth—for you, and another for ourselves?"

But Connla smiled gently, and declined the gambit. "Who dares put limits on the One? Or limits on the power of Goddess or God—oh aye, there is a Goddess, I promise you, maybe even you shall come to know Her. . . . That is the only true blasphemy, to think that there can be boundaries to the Highest's creation—and the only real sin is to act as if there are."

James rallied one time more, though he wanted to believe this impressive and immensely likeable stranger more than he could say. "Yet churchmen have ever said that any other way than Rome's is a lie."

"Every man banks the embers to his own loaf, when he can get away with it; that is only what churchmen *say*. What *is*, is a very different matter. And once even Rome said otherwise. I ask you: What you have seen here today, what I have told you—does it *feel* like a lie?"

"A lie?" James flung back his head. "No, by the splendor of Heaven! It feels like truth and freedom! And yet my way too feels like truth."

Connla's smile widened and warmed. "And we do not say that it is not! Nor would we. But—and this we *do* say—it is not true in the way you think that it is true. And that is a thing you may yet learn, if you come among us; or even if you do not.

"Still—" he added, rising from the window seat, and James rose with him, startled to see that the sun which had been high during the battle was now nearly set, they had talked for many hours—"you will have ample time to consider. We remain here at least three days, though at such a height and behind such a cloak that folk beneath cannot see us."

Reasonably, seeing James's dismay: "Your companions need time to rest and recover themselves before they can wisely choose their fate; you know that this is so. We will repair your vessels as well as your wounded; also we require some time for our own duties. You are our guests, free of this ship"—the implication being, though Connla was far too courteous to say it, that the Templars were no threat because they were far too ignorant to understand what they saw, and, James reflected, he was far from wrong to think so—"and you may go wherever you will and speak with whomever you please. I must leave you now, my duties call me; but I will join you again for the nightmeal, and any of my folk would gladly converse with any of you."

James looked up, all his longing and confusion and wariness and hope battling it out in his eyes, and he did not care if the other saw. "Truly?"

Connla mac Nessa vhic Dhau laughed outright. "Truly! There is very much still to learn and explain, on both sides—and brehon law still holds among us. Hospitality to the stranger does not change simply because it has gone out to the stars."

On the morning of the fourth day, in the chamber with the huge window-wall where he had spent his first hours aboard the *Cabarfeidh*, James Douglas waited for Connla mac Nessa. Presently he must give the Kelts an answer to their offer of sanctuary, by comparison to which his own original offer was as a rushdip to the sun. Over the past three days—and wondrous days they had been—he had talked to any Kelt who would have speech with him; then he had put the choices to the knights, honest enough to allow them to see his own feelings on the matter—though he also took care not to influence their decisions.

Indeed, all Templars who had voyaged to Scotland had now been given the choice: those on the three surviving ships—one ship, the smallest, had been captured, and two destroyed—as well as those on the *Cabarfeidh*. James had charged Connla and his officers, diffidently if firmly, with the unfairness of it, how it was not justice that only some of the fugitives should have this amazing chance; and the Kelts had at once agreed. So James and Connla had gone down to each vessel, spoken privately to each captain; then the captains and crews had been brought up to the Keltic ship, to see as the others had seen, and make the choice along with them.

Some Templars had been resolved from the first to have none of it. For them it was Scotland or nothing; others held the whole thing to be the undoubted work of Satan, and the Kelts must be devils or fallen angels, or at best the duped mortal minions of the prince of hell—at which James only shook his head and sighed.

Yet many more were afire to ride out on this new adventure, even though it was made very clear to them that they could never return to Earth, and that anything looking like crusading or missionary work among the Kelts, or any other race (*for there are other races,* James recalled, marveling anew, *and they not human at all!*), would not be tolerated. "Though tolerance is truly our way," Connla had said, "you will be the ones to whom that gift is extended, and we expect you to return the same. If you feel you cannot, speak now; for that will be the price of your freedom. If your pouch is not deep enough to pay, do not think to be buying in any market of ours."

Now Connla entered, an air of command wrapped about him like a cloak. Greeting James warmly, he ushered him into a larger chamber adjoining. At a long, polished stone table, the officers of the *Cabarfeidh* were seated, and all down the table's other side sat Walter Stewart and the captains and officers of the Templar galleys—who to a man looked intensely relieved at James's entrance.

There was a palpable feeling in the room, James noticed at once as he took the seat facing Connla across the table's length. *Not tenseness—more like the feeling on the night before a battle, when you know you are committed to the fight but cannot see what shape that fight may take. . . .*

"Well, now," said Connla mac Nessa easily, though the air of solemnity remained. "We have met, and we have spoken. Now it is time to decide." Swiftly he outlined the offer and its alternatives once again, so that all might be perfectly clear on the matter.

"There it is, then: sanctuary in Keltia for all who wish to go, peace and freedom within our laws to live and worship as you choose, or to be safely set down again in Scotland, beyond the reach of the English fleet.

"We may have overstepped ourselves in offering this to you, and I am sure our Queen will wish to discuss it with me when we get home," he added, though he did not seem much alarmed at the prospect. "But here, now, we give you the choice, and ask only that all of you, whether you stay or go, take oath to your god to keep our secret. The King of Scotland may know, and we will deem his oath as spoken; but none else."

He ceased, and his eyes sought James Douglas down the table's length. For his part, James glanced at Walter, then squared his shoulders and lifted his head to meet Connla's gaze.

Now I know how Jacques de Molay did feel, that night in the chapterhouse, and again the night we rode from Paris. . . .

"We have considered among ourselves, lord," said James then, "and taken advice of your own folk, and we accept. Not all of us will come, but most will. We know an adventure when we see one, and we thank you, either way, for what you have given us. Nor are we strangers to oathfast secrets: We will swear upon our swords; no oath is more sacred to us than that."

"But for yourself, lord?" asked a tall, vivid, russet-haired girl with the eyes of a mermaid and the carriage of a young stag, whom he had noticed on that first day in the landing bay—as he now knew to call it—and whom for some daft reason he had fought shy of approaching until just the day before. They had talked for hours, with that shining, bubbling eagerness that comes the first time a young couple meet, when they know that each is drawn to the other and that more than talk will come of it, and he had learned, to his chagrined but proud surprise, that she was second in command to mac Nessa himself.

*I think I would beggar my soul to buy such freedom, such a
life, for my folk and for myself—and beggar it still more to
have her in it—but . . .*

"Scotland is my home, lady," he said at last, looking
straight at her, letting her see his agony of choice, his divided
heart. "But this"—he raised both arms in an oddly solemn
gesture, looked round at the shining ship, the star maps on the
walls, the jeweled orrery depicting Keltia that stood in the
center of the table—"this too is mine. Only I did not know it
until now."

"Will you come, then?" said Connla mac Nessa softly.
"You and Keltia would go strong together, and I think we are
friends already."

James was silent a long time, and they respected his silence. "I will not, then," he said at last, and they could hear
what it cost him to say it. "Not now. Not yet. I must return to
my king, and help him in his work. I pray you understand,
though I am not sure I understand it myself. . . .

"But when that work is done, I will come, if I may, and call
you friend in Keltia, as I do here and now. Or perhaps I will
send my son to you, if ever I have one—a scion to graft a
Douglas slip on this distant rootstock."

He met the warm sympathy in Connla's eyes, and though
he dared not turn his head to look, he felt the keen sorrowing
disappointment in the girl's, and knew both in himself.

"We understand very well," said Connla mac Nessa, and
though he did not smile, it felt as though he had. "A hero's
choice, either way, and we honor it and you together; know
that the Name of Douglas will be a thousand times welcome
among us whenever and however it comes. And it shall."

On a stony beach on the ocean side of the Mull of Kintyre,
ankle-deep in cold kelpy surfwash that swirled round his
boots, James Douglas stood with lifted head, shading his eyes

against the sea-glitter off the hull of the *Cabarfeidh* as it hung a hundred feet above the waves.

Cabarfeidh—a title of their god, named for him as Templar ships are named for our own. But only look! Not beholding this, who could believe? Even seeing as I have seen, knowing what I know, still I am dumbfounded. . . .

He took an involuntary step back as, in total silence, the gigantic craft began to rise, then took three steps forward in uncontrollable longing, feeling his heart rise with the ship; laughed aloud as a thought struck him.

However will those English mariners begin *to explain what they think they saw?*

As the *Cabarfeidh* mounted higher, James lifted his sword in salute, and the others who stood with him on the strand instantly followed his example. Standing off from shore, reunited with their sister ships, the *Mary* and the *Michael* and the *Holy Wisdom* paid their respects to another sister: On each mast the Beauséant dipped in homage to the great craft above.

I do not know if they can see us, but we can surely see them, and I wish to make them proper farewell. Such things my brothers shall see and know! Things that might have been mine too: a life and love—but no. I have made the right choice—at least, the choice that is right for now—and maybe yet one of my line shall carry the Name of Douglas to the stars. . . .

He saw the ship unfurl her star-sails, and tears stung his eyes as the vast silvery sheets inclined and rippled in return salute. Then as he watched, the *Cabarfeidh,* accelerating from a standing start, vanished at the zenith on a trail of white fire; and when even that was gone, still he watched. Then he sighed, and turned about, and went inland with the knights who had watched with him, all of them as subdued and as awed as he, to find a horse to carry him to Stirling castle, where he would speak to his king, and with his friend.

*   *   *

"If it were anyone but you, Jamie, to tell me this . . ."

"I know. But it is. And it was so."

Robert Bruce leaned back in the carved wooden chair, his reddish hair tousled as ever and his keen glance fixed on the eager, glowing face of his young friend—the friend who had just told him the most fantastic tale he could ever have hoped to hear.

"A realm of the stars—a ship to sail the heavens—" He drank from the mether that had stood untouched at his elbow for the past two hours, shook his head, marveling anew. "How I would have liked to have been there. . . ."

"It would have amazed you."

"God's feet, as it does!" The king was silent; but the man's eyes sparkled at the thoughts passing through his mind. "New worlds, new suns—and all of them ruled by our blood! But once settled in their new home, in this Keltia"—he pronounced the unfamiliar name with care and wonder—"did they never think, or wish, to return?"

"Oh aye, and they have—but only to keep an eye on the home lands, and to take away those who longed to go and knew how to make contact. When first they left Earth, they pledged themselves never to interfere with Earth's problems; that pledge has not been broken, though it has a few times been bent. . . . We have sworn on our swords, as Templars and as knights, to keep their secret."

"As will I—it will not be the first secret we have kept, nor yet the last."

"Still, Rob, the errand was not bootless: many knights went, but many remained, all of them vowed to our need and your service."

"And may heaven reward them for it," murmured Robert Bruce, "and avenge them upon their betrayers."

"And protect our brothers where now they may be," said

James presently, "and those among whom they now dwell," and the king joined him in "Amen."

So the years went, and if Edward Longshanks, Hammer of the Scots, had pounded hard, the Scots now pounded his England even harder. Thanks to the balladeers, James had already gone into legend as the Black Douglas, as much for his ferocity in battle and border raid as for his dark handsomeness. As for Robert the Bruce, he had only settled the crown of Scotland more firmly upon his head.

Seven years after the Templars came to Argyll, three months after Jacques de Molay, dying in flames at a Paris stake, had summoned Clement the pope and Philip the king to join him before the year was out before the throne of God's judgement—as, eerily, they would come to do—on the morning of the twenty-fourth of June 1314, a clear warm Midsummer Day, King Robert Bruce, and Sir James Douglas, and Walter Stewart newly betrothed to Bruce's vibrant daughter Marjory, and all the force of the Scots with them, met the English armies below Stirling castle, for the second day of battle on a flat plain hard by a little stream called Bannockburn.

It was a desperate day for the Scots; for all their valor, several times the battle, and Scotland with it, seemed lost. Beneath his standard, Robert Bruce was silent, as if he waited for something and dared not say for what.

Then, as suddenly as if they had ridden out of the air, a force of mounted knights came over the ridge and reined in, looking down at the fight. They were cloaked in white, the crimson cross gone now from the breast of their mantles, but the war-horses they sat were full-boned Flemish destriers, and the bared swords in their hands bore the plain Templar hilt.

They were not many; but as one after another the English soldiers looked up to see them motionless against the sky, an ominous silence began to settle over the field, like the breath-caught stillness before the thunder cracks in the heights of heaven, and a whisper ran swift as fire along the lines.

Templars, the hissing fearing word went up as English swordarms faltered. *The Knights Templar are come to fight for Robert Bruce!*

And so they did; so great was their skill in battle, so feared the Templar name, that the day was carried for Scotland and its king.

And at last there came a time when the horrors were done. Though the mighty Temple had been broken, both France and papacy were stained with blood that would never be washed entirely clean. Many knights had perished, great and lesser alike; many more had survived, finding sanctuary in other orders and other lands, though no knights in Templardom had found sanctuary stranger than had those who sailed from France with Jamie Douglas.

But in Scotland, a different tale was told. Early in the reign of King Robert, in the far west of Argyll, a small village had taken root in remote Kintyre. It was called Kilmichael, Saint Michael's Church—so far had those newly settled there wished to sanctify their new home ground, by placing it in the protection of the prince and captain of heaven's forces. From many lands had they come: Scots, English, Welsh, Irishers, French, Burgundians. Knights still, by the pope's decree they were monks no longer; to ensure their survival past the present generation, they had set aside their vows of chastity to wed with the flower of Scots noblewomen—suitable matches having been carefully arranged by Elizabeth de Burgh, Bruce's formidable queen.

Now they were raising herds and tending crops and keeping mains as did any other Scot, those who came from foreign parts still learning the language and customs, all of them still praising God, if not, perhaps, his vicar on Earth who had brought them to this fate.

As the first village thrived and prospered, the knights spread out around Loch Fyne to found other settlements. Their ships were long gone—sunk, sold as merchant vessels, rotted away; the white mantles had felt the moth's tooth. But the long straight swords were still put to old uses: the knights kept the blades bright, raising them to strike in battle or to kneel before in prayer.

What their wives thought was never to be known. Doubtless they were glad of the strong arm their husbands brought to their homes and to their king, but none knows what else they may have felt. What those husbands brought to the marriage-bed—well, as onetime monks, belike the knights were no worse mates than other men of their time, perhaps even better. Still, there was not a woman in the tiny Templar settlements but knew that this life, and she herself, had not been the first and longed-for choice of her spouse; the Almighty Himself was her eternal and undefeated rival. Perhaps it rankled; perhaps each strove to make it up to the other—and to the children that came of them—out of duty or chivalry or loyalty, or even out of love. Who can know how it may have been for them; or knowing, who would say?

But for those cross-hilted swords, in time one final use: Traced on plain stone graveslabs, their images were set above the mortal remains of those who once had lived to serve as swords themselves. Monks though they had been, they were human also, and perhaps in the end they found they could not entirely forgive; so that, not caring to have upon their graves in Scotland the sign of the Church that had betrayed them in France, they still needed the sign of the One who had never failed them and had never forgotten them, as they had never failed or forgotten Him. . . .

*   *   *

And that day came when King Robert Bruce lay on his last bed, attended by his kindred and his captains and his friends. His queen had gone before him two years since, his daughter two years after Bannockburn; the child prince his son stood silent by. Yet none but Sir James Douglas heard the last words of the king, as Robert plucked with strengthless fingers at his friend's sleeve, and James bent low to hear.

"Take my heart to the holy land . . . Jamie . . . the blessed land . . . you know what land I mean. . . ."

And, though the others were much gratified by this surprising display of piety—the dying wish of Robert Bruce, that his heart go on pilgrimage to Jerusalem—knowing very well what land his king did mean, James kissed him on the brow, and knew also that he would obey.

The white light of Andalusia struck like a drawn sword through his closed eyelids. Never had James dreamed there could be such heat and dryness and brightness. Skin used to Scottish mists and cloud-veiled sun was drawn tight as a drumhead for the sun to pound upon, and his own head was the drum.

And it is but March! What must it be like in high summer? Palestinia itself can be no hotter or drier than this—how the Templars fought there all those years I cannot imagine.

"This" was the field of Tebas de Ardales, hard by Tebas castle. Sir James Douglas and Sir William Sinclair and the rest of their party found themselves on a battlefield that day, fighting against the Moors of Granada for the Christian king Alfonso of Castile, even as the Cid himself once had fought for another royal Castilian Alfonso, not so very long ago. . . .

Battle had not been part of their plan when they left Scotland. Reaching Spain, they had left their ship in Galicia, near the great pilgrim city of Santiago de Compostella, and come riding down through Castile. Receiving them at his court in

Burgos, King Alfonso had indicated he would be glad of their help against the emirs; bound by chivalry, they could do naught but oblige.

"It is in no way inconsonant with our errand," Sinclair had argued—he of the Roslin Sinclairs, an old Templar family that had its seat in that tiny Pentland town. "Our king commanded us to bear his heart into battle against the infidel, and here we have a chance to do so; he will approve and understand."

Indeed Rob would, and likely did, reflected James. *Though how my true errand is to be accomplished, and without the others twigging, I am sure I do not know. To get my king's heart to Keltia, as he did charge me. . . .*

All the long and weary way from Scotland—even as he had knelt in farewell beside Bruce's coffin, in the dimness of Dunfermline abbey church—James had cherished the hope that somehow the Kelts would know his need: that their science, or their magic, could find him wherever he might be; that the *Cabarfeidh* would once more shadow the skies, that he and Connla mac Nessa vhic Dhau might sail together to wars among the stars, his tall, bright-flashing lady greet him again under another sun, and so he had never wed another.

But hope had dimmed the souther they had gone. *A lad's hope at best . . . still, I did believe they would. And perhaps even yet they will. . . .*

On the field of Tebas, with clear eyes the Scots knights beheld the steel wall of Moorish cavalry, many times their own numbers, cutting them off from Alfonso's army. Then they looked at each other, and their thought was the same thought: *This is the fight that for us shall end all fights forever, we will not make it through this one alive. . . .* James found that he was fiercely glad, wondered if every soldier recognized the moment when it came at last for him.

If it cannot end the other way, then this is how it should end; if not that, then something else. For everything happens somewhere, as I have come to learn. . . .

On his right, Sinclair straightened in his deep war-saddle, raising his head, and the others kneed their horses closer so that they might hear his words.

"They will find his heart where we died for it, where we lie for it, and they will know that it went before us to the end. Belike they will return it to Scotland, enshrine it in some abbey. And I daresay that will serve. We have lived with and for a legend—now let us die for him as well, and live in legend forever like the heroes of old."

And James, looking at his friend's smiling, sunburned face, knew that Sinclair was no more afraid than he himself, nor regretful that this was the way it would finish. *It will serve indeed. . . .*

"Fitting it is that today is the observable day of our king's crowning, twenty-four years ago at Scone," said James. "A good day to die; indeed, a better day than most." He leaned from the saddle to grip Sinclair's arm, feeling the strong pressure of an answering clasp, and the old wolf-grin scythed across his face. "And if the Low Road is the way we must travel to get home, so be it. So long as the heart be right, no matter where the rest shall lie—no, nor the heart neither."

He reached within his mail, under his shirt, and drew out something on a leather cord, and seeing it Sinclair and the others instantly bared heads and crossed themselves. James held it up to the sun, and it flashed like a mirror in the slanting light of Spain: clasped in a fine gold lattice, a small silvery orb—the steel case, made of the blade of his own sword, that held the heart of Robert Bruce.

James kissed it, then passed it silently to Sinclair, who kissed it with equal reverence and passed it on, to Sir Simon of the Lee, to Sir William Keith, to the brother knights Sir Robert Logan and Sir Walter Logan and to all the rest. When each man had touched his lips to the royal reliquary, receiving it back James kissed it again, and spoke words to it that no one else did hear.

Then, standing in his stirrups, Sir James Douglas raised his arm above his head, and with all his strength he flung the little case from him, deep into the midst of the oncoming Saracen force. In the voice he used in battle shouting above the fight, his words rose over hoof-thunder as the charging destriers hit stride.

"Go first in the fight, brave heart, as thou hast ever done, and we shall follow as we ever did!"

And drew his sword, and did what he did best, and as he did there came—even as he had hoped and prayed—from high above him, out of the heart of the sun, a great and welcome shadow. . . .

Cool dimness within walls, voices eddying like rapids in a Highland stream. James tried to focus, but his glance was strangely misted, so instead he turned his attention to the one voice he could hear clearly—a man's voice, deep and pleasant, oddly familiar.

"You yourself trusted we would find you, wherever you might be. Surely you did not doubt! We are come to keep our promise, and to bring you home."

He felt his heart give a great leap within him, and he smiled faintly. "I knew that you would, Connla mac Nessa vhic Dhau," he whispered. "As for promises—did I not say that I would call you friend in Keltia? I shall do so now, if it is not too late."

And heard the smile in the answering voice, so close by him now as to sound within his head itself. *Everything happens somewhere; and no time is ever too late. . . .*

"My lord of Douglas—to whom does he speak?" asked one

of the Castilian doctors who stood by, helpless to stop the bleeding from five mortal wounds.

Through blinding tears Sinclair, himself near death where he lay on a pallet beside his friend, made him no answer; and then James spoke no word more, nor did he hear the words they spoke to him.

For he was not there. He was gone from them—gone from Spain, from the planet, from the world. Alive amid the heavens, he was back aboard the *Cabarfeidh,* outward bound. Surely no living man had seen such sights as now he saw: his home world shimmered blue and white behind him, Mars burned for him, Jupiter blazed, Saturn spun its shining rings. He seemed to be lying on a low couch, with a small port by his head that gave a view onto the deepness of space; there was a vague memory that he was wounded, and it was the death wound.

Too long a warrior not to know, and for all their skill and knowledge, even these starfolk cannot stop it. When the Low Road opens before you, there is naught to do but ride—the swiftest way to come to the true heart's home. But perhaps. . . .

He turned on his side—there was no pain now—and looked out at the bluefire net of stars streaming past. *Perhaps there will be time enough. For no time is too late. . . .*

Yet though he was dying, and he knew it, somehow he was also walking alive in Keltia, with Connla his friend; and riding over far green plains with his auburn-haired lass beside him, knee to knee on matched grays, she fair and brave in Douglas colors . . . and laughing in a cold Highland rain with Rob, and standing back to back with Walter, sword in hand, at Bannockburn, and in the chapterhouse at Paris, Templar brethren thronging round with joyful greetings, blessed Jacques de Molay rising from his throne to take him by the hand.

Truly, no time was too late: all times were one time, and at the same time no time at all, for a fair triple-mooned planet, the loveliest thing he had ever seen, was looming now out the tiny window. And it seemed to James that he would not be needing the ship any longer, and he floated down close to the surface of the world beneath.

His sight had miraculously lengthened; and though through the great welcoming shout in his ears he heard no other sound, he saw below, as the light began to grow and spread behind him, a white stone building on the shore of a shining sea loch; sensed the peace of the place, saw Templars in unfamiliar new blue robes walking and praying in cloister and garden. Then he caught his breath, and tears burned his eyes, for he saw, he *Saw.* . . .

The stone building had been raised in the form of a cross: not the cruel Latin cross nor yet the Templar cross but the suncross, the balanced Wheel, the circled equal-armed cross of the Celts and the Cathars and the Celi Dé and so many others—the symbol that points the four winds of the world and the four seasons of the year and the four elements of creation, and the four archangels and the four Forts of the Danaans and the Four Chief Treasures of Britain, and, ringing it round, the endless circle of Eternity that is the same for all and ever will be.

And seeing that—and knowing that though all was indeed one, that "All" was not the same—James was well content. Then his spirit pulled back to soar up into that burning heart of light and Light; and those presences he had loved and missed and longed for were there to greet him—and someone else, someone he seemed to know well, and was glad of meeting once again—or for the first time, he did not know and it did not matter in the slightest—was taking his hand and conducting him, with honor and solemnity joyous enough to break his heart, to a place, and a Presence, that he had known always and longer still. . . .

Next day in Tebas castle church they sang to holy Santiago a Mass for the repose of the soul of his namesake—a warrior's requiem, and a pilgrim's also. That night they boiled the bones clean for transport home, reverently lapping the smooth, strong whitenesses in thin leaves of lead, tenderly robing the skull in Douglas colors, sealing the grim long package with the cross of the Temple and the scallop shell badge of Compostella—*campo stella,* "the field of stars"—though they were never to know the full irony of that last.

Sinclair too, who had died in the night speaking the name of Bruce, received the same honors, and the other slain Scots as well, found on the battlefield in a ring of dead Moors and returned by the emirs, together with the little reliquary, to honor their courage and their end; and the flesh that had been cleansed away in water was solemnly buried in the earth where they did fall.

But the heart of Bruce was borne upon the bones of Douglas home again—a Crowned and Bloody Heart would grace the Douglas heraldry ever after—and laid to rest in Melrose Abbey, though strange tales sprang up that it did not long remain there, that on a wild night of storm and thunder it miraculously vanished in a flash of light, and was not seen again on Earth. James was laid to sleep forever at Saint Bride's church in Douglasdale, over the hills not so far away, with Bríd herself—long a Celtic goddess or ever she came to be a Christian saint—to keep watch over him, and to keep safe in death and the life-after he who had never once been safe in life.

On a world circling a star that astronomers call Delta Orionis, but which is named otherwise by those who dwell beneath its light, a bearded man in a dark blue robe girt with a plain longsword comes out of a low stone building. Standing on the foreshore of the sea loch, he glances keenly around him, as someone will quarter to all airts who has heard or sensed something but knows not what or where or who.

Finding nothing, he raises his gaze to the heavens, and the hilt of his sword with it, and kneels briefly. His lips move silently, in prayer or chant or blessing, then he rises again, a faint puzzled frown on his broad brow.

Surely someone called? Who is here?

But no one is to be seen—at least not by any sight short of Sight. Still, true to his oath of chivalry and the rule of his Order and the faith of the folk of his much-loved new homeland, he will not chance letting any traveller go unblessed or unprotected, still less a stranger on such a voyage, a pilgrim on the Low Road. . . .

He smiles now, and turns away, and speaks aloud—to whomever, or whatever, might be near enough, or have ear enough, or heart enough, to hear—in words of a prayer newly learned a benison from of old.

"May your journey thrive."

INTERLUDE FOUR

The story of Bruce's heart and how James Douglas tried to fulfill Bruce's dying request to take it on crusade is a tale beloved of most Scots. And I love the way Patricia melded this tale with her "Kelts in space" and the persistent tradition that fugitive Templars fled to Scotland after the arrest of the Templars in France, undoubtedly aboard some of those ships of the Templar fleet that remain unaccounted for. Further tradition contends that some of these fugitive Templars came to the aid of Bruce at Bannockburn, the definitive battle that finally won Scotland her independence and sealed the kingship of Robert the Bruce.

Our next story deals with preparations for that battle, in both the English and Scottish camps, and the role behind the scenes of young Robert of Troyes, who became squire to the Templar Friedrich von Hochheim in an earlier story in this series. Several tales are told about Bannockburn involving miracles of one sort or another—especially, how a fresh troop of white-mantled Templars came galloping in to reinforce Bruce at a critical point in the battle. This one combines aspects of that tale with speculation about a famous Scottish relic known as the *Brecbennoch* or, more popularly, the Monymusk reliquary, carried into battle that day by the Abbot of Arbroath to strengthen the Scottish forces.

Bones of Contention

Richard Woods

1

From his vantage point behind the arras, Gilbert Wayland surveyed nearly all of the royal study—especially the great table where most of the barons and earls sat, toying with jeweled goblets, occasionally sipping from them, tugging at their sleeves, or engaging in quiet banter. One sat alone in a window nook, despite the cold, for Langley, King Edward's favorite retreat, boasted the almost unimaginable luxury of glazing. Another figure stood near the cavernous fireplace, where a generous fire further kept the chill at bay. It was the week before Lent, still over four months before the armies of Edward Plantagenet and Robert Bruce were destined to meet before Stirling Castle to decide the fate of the Scottish nation.

By his reckoning Wayland had stood thus for more than an hour, but so far he felt little strain. Once, he had stood thus for half a day without moving.

There were as many Scots in the chamber as Englishmen. Among the latter, in addition to the Earl of Hereford and Gilbert of Clare—the young Earl of Gloucester and the king's nephew—Wayland recognized Sir Ingram de Umfraville, an English baron with extensive holdings in Scotland. Hugh Despenser the Elder, whose sway over the king was growing daily, stood with his back to the fire like a sleek grey cat.

Seated opposite the English barons were Sir John Comyn, Sir John Hastings, and Sir Alexander Seton—all Scots and partisans of the old king, John Balliol, still an exile in France. Edward had won them over with assurances that Balliol would be restored when the Bruce pretender was finally crushed.

Donald, the young Earl of Mar and Bruce's own ward, kept to himself in the nook, gazing into the distance where masons plied high wooden scaffolds, struggling to finish the huge priory Edward was erecting to entomb the body of his beloved Piers Gaveston, which lay waiting against the day at the Blackfriars' chapel in Oxford. Taken prisoner at Methven as a boy and brought to Westminster, Donald had grown increasingly devoted to the young king over the years. Gilbert marveled at Edward's power of allurement. And envied it.

For all his reputed inattentiveness to the business of ruling, Edward had played his game well. Scotland was divided in its loyalties, and if Edward lacked the support of all the barons of England, he could rely on some of the most powerful among them. He would need to.

A small door that led from the royal apartments flew open.

"My lords, the king!" old Hereford barked.

There was a scramble as chairs scraped back and the seated members of the assembly rose in unison.

Two men entered, one tall, fair, and unusually handsome, robed simply enough in russet and sapphire and a plain leather belt. Edward's tastes ran to the commonplace in the eyes of many of the court, but the Scots admired at least that aspect of his personality. His carefully trimmed hair and beard were blond, the wide-set eyes heavy-lidded, blue, and captivating.

Lithe and well-proportioned, he filled the room with his presence. Even Gilbert Wayland felt a slight constriction in his throat as Edward Plantagenet strode splendidly across the chamber, lightly gripping his companion's arm.

The young man at his side was slightly shorter, darkly handsome, extravagant in white leather and lilac, girded with a golden cincture and sporting the latest fashion in pointed shoes: crimson ones at that, furred with squirrel and banded with gold. He cast a quick glance around the room, smiled coolly at the gathered nobles, and, after the monarch took his place in the large carved chair at the end of the table, not far from the arras, seated himself at the king's right.

Despenser.

Gilbert Wayland frowned as the earls found seats around the table. He sensed that the king's new favorite, old Hugh's equally feline son, was as ambitious, no less cunning, and even more dangerous than the not-greatly-lamented Gaveston, especially with his father at the king's other ear. He wondered if Edward fully understood the peril of his tastes.

The king greeted his audience with unfeigned affability. They, in turn, murmured appreciation, trying not to sound annoyed at being kept waiting for much of the morning.

"Good sires," Edward continued, "allow me to be direct. You are, I am well aware, busy about many things, and fish and fowl await below to speed you on your journeys homeward. Matters of state may wait, but not cooks."

A polite ripple of laughter rose and fell as quickly as courtesy permitted.

"I am told that among his several virtues, the Bruce pretender is deeply devout. Is this not so, my lords?"

A puzzled silence greeted the king's unexpected remark.

"If murdering a man before Greyfriar's altar can be reckoned as devotion," John Comyn at last suggested sourly, "truly Bruce must be a holy saint of God."

"For which crime against your noble kinsman he was rightly excommunicated," Edward replied. "But is it nevertheless true that he has a surpassing reverence for saints and their . . . bones?"

"So it is said," young Alexander Seton remarked a little curtly. Surely, *this* could not be what they had been summoned to discuss. "Why do you ask, my lord?"

"Such traits say much about a man," the king replied. "And about his influence. When my revered sire removed the Stone of Destiny from the Abbey of Scone to Westminster, I am told it blighted the spirit of the whole community of Scotland."

"It did, my lord," John Hastings said. "And should it be returned, the entire community of Scotland would mark the gesture most gratefully."

"And so it shall be returned—and the Holy Rood as well—*when* we have done with the Bruce upstart and his followers."

The point was not missed. The grim old Earl of Hereford glanced sharply at Edward as if to confirm that he had heard correctly. But an appreciative murmur arose from the Scottish side of the table.

"In the nonce," the king continued in a jovial tone, "there *is* this little matter of the saints to deal with. For instance, I have heard that the Bruce is particularly fond of a famed shrine of Saint Columba that you Scots set great store by. Is this not so?"

"It is, my lord," Seton said. "It is called the *Brecbennoch*. When Iona fell to the Vikings four hundred years ago, the saint's bones were divided. One part was taken to Ireland. Because Columba is the patron of our nation, King Kenneth MacAlpin carried the other portion to Dunkeld in a small reliquary. When William the Lion founded the Abbey of St. Thomas in Aberbrothock a century ago, he entrusted the Brecbennoch to the abbots' keeping."

"Many Scots believe that if the Brecbennoch accompanies

them in battle, they are invincible," added the boy-earl, Donald of Mar.

The Earl of Gloucester snorted derisively. "It will require more than a saint's bones to defeat *this* army."

The king laughed and reached over to grip his nephew's arm. "True, Gilbert, this will be the greatest force ever mustered against the north—and you shall lead it."

At this, the Earl of Hereford flushed deeply and coughed his displeasure. Heedless, the king continued. "But sheer force is sometimes not enough. 'Not by power, nor by might,' as Holy Writ has it."

"But do you intend to . . . to *seize* the Brecbennoch?" Seton asked. The Scots eyed each other warily.

"Think on it, Alexander. Lacking the bones of Columba, the rebels' confidence will be greatly lessened. To that extent, our chances of a quick and easy victory will be proportionately enlarged. Do you not agree, de Bohun?"

"There may be wisdom in what you are proposing, sire." The Earl of Hereford's careful reply was taken by Edward as approval.

"And I shall return them safely, my friends—once Balliol has been restored and the highlands are peaceful again. That I swear to you."

Again, the Scottish barons looked to each other silently. In Edward surely lay their only hope of seeing John Balliol back on the throne of Alba and, more importantly, their holdings reinstated. But questions seemed to hang heavily in the air. Could they rely on this inconstant king who preferred thatching and ditching to statecraft, and the bed chamber to the battlefield? Could he even make good on his intention? And if the Brecbennoch also fell into English hands, could Scotland ever hope to be free again?

"How to you propose to . . . secure the relic, my liege?" Seton ventured. "I doubt if Abbot Bernard will simply hand it over, even if you ask politely. He is the Bruce's chancellor, after all."

"The Brecbennoch is not kept at Aberbrothock, in any event," John Comyn interjected. "It has been housed for generations at the Templar chapel in Forglen, in the far reaches of Buchan."

Wayland shifted his weight from one foot to another to restore circulation and forestall cramping. But he had noted Comyn's words carefully.

"As you would know well, Sir John," Edward acknowledged. "And the Templars are even less likely to deliver it up with a smile and curtsey. Do you think they are still there?"

Comyn shrugged. "At the moment, sire, that area is under control of the Bruce. Anything is possible, not least the comforting of fugitive heretics."

"Tell me, then, what does this great treasure of faith look like? Not the bones, but the box. Have you ever seen it?"

Wayland's attention, normally sharp as a throwing dagger, became even more acute as the Scots again exchanged sidelong glances.

"It is . . . a *box*, my lord," Comyn ventured a little awkwardly. "A . . . *small* box."

He cupped his hands together as if to enclose something about the size of a thrush's nest.

"That is not terribly helpful, my lord Comyn," Edward smiled. "I suspect it has some embellishment, a dab of color perhaps?"

"It is, ah, silver or gold, sire, with, er . . . decorations here and there."

"Well *done,* Sir John," Edward said mockingly. "I'm sure such vivid detail will prove most useful."

Comyn flushed and bowed, biting his tongue.

"We are not priests or scriveners, my liege," Seton offered dryly.

"No, of course not," the king replied with an amiable grin. "As fighting men, you should not be expected to note the particulars of a relic-box. But surely there must be a description of it somewhere?"

Once more, the Scots looked to each other in silence. Like guilty school boys, Wayland thought. Edward was playing his role well.

"Well," the king said after a moment of forced patience, "that will amount to a mere wrinkle in the fabric of calculation. Come Gilbert, show yourself!"

The barons suddenly noticed a dark figure standing beside the rich tapestry where no one had been seen a moment before. Instinctively, hands moved toward sword hilts. What they saw was a tall man clad in a tunic of such a deep crimson that it appeared almost black. His shirt, hose, and boots were truly black like his hair and, indeed, his eyes. The face was unlined and sharp-featured, not unpleasant to look on but less attractive than the youthful faces of most of the men in the room.

"Gilbert is my expert in the arts of disclosure and retrieval," the king explained. "I am confident he will acquit himself in this matter as he has in others."

Wayland bowed modestly. "I pray I will not disappoint your Majesty."

"Yes, do," the king retorted playfully. "That might help."

The young Despenser laughed out loud, but the other barons merely nodded politely as Wayland's bow deepened. Edward rose from his chair and the room rose with him. "Come, gentlemen, dinner awaits. Walk with me, Gilbert."

Wayland bowed again as the barons began to file out of the privy chamber. He smiled to himself, imagining Despenser's pout at being displaced from the king's side.

But Edward remained still and held Wayland back with a

gesture. "You will succeed, will you not?" he said in a low voice.

"Do not doubt it, Majesty. But there is the possibility that after today's exchanges the Bruce might get wind of our plans."

"A palpable risk, Gilbert, although I trust our Scots. And they have heard my vow to return the holy treasures to Scotland when this business is finished. Still, you must act quickly and decisively. What have you heard?"

"Sailors' rumors about a casket on board the *Sainte-Vierge* when it docked at Cromarty of Easter Ross in August. It was in the keeping of a beguine who sailed with the Templars from La Rochelle. She may have been of the household of the old king in France, although it would appear that she was also related to the House of Bruce in some way."

"They all seem to be cousins, even the ones that despise each other," Edward reflected. "Rather like us, actually. What became of her?"

"Disappeared, they say. Along with the *Sainte-Vierge*. But I have reason to think the casket was taken ashore at Cromarty."

"And was it this Brecbennoch?"

"Possibly. I, too, lack an accurate description of the reliquary. But one way or another, the Templar preceptory bears watching."

"Then by all means watch it. You are especially well-suited for such a task. Heaven must have guided my hand when I plucked you from the Tower."

Wayland bowed graciously, suppressing an ironic smile.

With a flick of his unsuitable workman's fingers, the king dismissed him and passed from the chamber. Through the doorway, Wayland could just see Hugh Despenser waiting languidly in the corridor.

2

The half-frozen turd hit the stall board with a resounding *thunk.*

"Sweet Saint Julien-the-Poor!" Robert muttered, "where have you led me? All I ever wanted was to serve the good Lord with the Poor Knights of Christ—now I am an outlaw, far from home in this horrible northern wilderness mucking horse-shit. I am hungry and cold and do not know what will become of me!"

He sniffed back a tear of self-pity and poked the rake at another smelly horse turd half-hidden in the straw covering the floor of Wahgemut's stall. The huge destrier stomped a rear leg and snorted in sympathy. All the Templars' horses were big and ate a lot, but at least their body heat created a little zone of comfort in the farming outpost at Forglen.

"At that speed, squire, you will need a whole day to clean one stall."

"Joseph!" Robert blurted, wiping his nose on the back of his coat sleeve. "I—I didn't see you there. . . ." His breath hung in the air for a moment before dispersing in the relative warmth of the stables.

"Obviously not, my young friend," the swarthy Turcopole said from the doorway. "Else I would have been bound to discipline you for insubordination."

"I'm—I'm truly sorry. It's just that . . ."

"You miss the mild winter of France," Joseph al-Kalim finished for him. "And you are unsure of your fate here in the harsh land of the Scots."

"Yes, but—"

"Keep silence," Joseph said, cutting him off. "Even when you pray to your saints. That will ensure that they and the All-merciful One alone will hear your complaints. In the meantime, I will speak to Sir Friedrich about your situation, and he may speak on your behalf to Sir Gideon. Now get to work with a will. It will help warm you."

The half-breed Templar sergeant left as silently as he had come, a dark shadow whose quiet demeanor belied his skills in combat as well as in surgery and physic. Abashed, Robert attacked the foul, steaming straw with renewed energy, if not enthusiasm.

Robert had been surprised in August to find himself standing on ground that moved with the same roll as had the decks of the *Sainte-Vierge,* that had so unnerved him when she set sail from La Rochelle in mid-July. As he stepped off the wooden wharf, he toppled and would have fallen had not a powerful hand steadied him.

It was that of Sir Antony of Ross, the middle son of the Earl of Ross, whose mission it had been to bring as many fugitive Templars as he could find to Scotland to bolster the woefully scant cavalry of Robert Bruce.

"There, my young friend," he said, "is the true treasure of the Temple."

Regaining his footing, Robert looked past the knight's finger where dozens of destriers, palfreys, and rouncies were walked slowly in improvised paddocks to accustom them once more to dry land. Their grooms and a number of squires soothed them with comforting words, frequently stroking their necks and withers.

Robert suddenly noticed several newcomers on the beach—four mounted men riding slowly toward them. One of them dismounted and approached Antony and Sir Friedrich of Hochheim, the big Saxon knight in whose service Robert had informally entered the ranks of the recently suppressed Knights Templar only a few weeks before. He was tall, with a fine red beard, blue eyes, and a bearing that imported a sense of high purpose. His tawny surcoat was emblazoned with a red lion rampant.

"Sir Robert Keith," Antony informed the others as he neared. "The Marischal of Scotland."

Keith clasped Antony's hand tightly and clapped him warmly on the shoulder. "Well done, my friend!"

Antony quickly introduced the Templars to Keith, who welcomed them on behalf of the king.

"We will soon be in sore need of mounts. Midsummer may seem like a distant shore, but there is much to accomplish ere we meet the English at Stirling Castle."

"And riders as well, I would suppose?" Friedrich responded with a hint of irony.

"Of course, but we have more men who can ride than we have horses," Keith explained, "especially destriers. Scotland is a mountainous country covered with forests and carselands. It is not horse-breeding country. Nor can it produce sufficient fodder for cavalry even a third the size of that Edward Plantagenet will bring north."

"We will be pressed hard to winter those we have now," Antony added. "And still others will be coming from France."

"At least two thousand mounted knights will answer Edward's call to arms," Keith resumed. "King Robert will be fortunate to field a quarter of that number. And there will be need of them even before that. As long as the English hold castles, we are to that extent vulnerable, especially to sorties. This war will be won on foot, but it cannot be won without mounts."

Over the following two days the Marischal, Sir Antony, and the Templar commanders devised a plan for dispersing the new arrivals, both horses and men, to fortified areas in the north and west, so as to distribute the burden of support as widely as possible. In June it would also facilitate moving the knights and their baggage to Stirling over Scotland's few and narrow roads. Fortunately, while Templar holdings were not numerous, they had not yet been handed over to the Hospitalers, since the papal decree disbanding the Order had not been promulgated in Scotland.

"If any benefit came from the pope's refusal to recognize Robert Bruce as king, perhaps it is that," Sir Antony jested. "You still have winter quarters."

Friedrich fixed him with his good, sapphire-hued eye. "From what I have heard of your northern reaches, I suspect that when the snow flies that will be a very good thing."

Friedrich and three younger knights—Girard Fitz Gilbert, Heralt de Châteauneuf, and Michael of Inbhear Mór—were assigned with their squires, horses, and grooms to the Forglen preceptory at Turriff, a fortified manor a few miles south of the small burgh of Banff on the northern coast of Buchan. The addition of so many men taxed the resources of the house to its limit, but despite the years of relative inaction since the fall of Acre, many Templars were still accustomed to austerity or even courted it.

One such was the Commander of the House, Sir Gideon Fraser, a grizzled Scot who had served many years in Outremer. His face was scarred even more than Friedrich's, and his left arm was missing from just above the elbow. Robert thought he must be almost sixty years of age, but he was on no account feeble. Surprisingly robust and agile, he sparred tellingly with his good arm, keeping pace with much younger men in the practice yard. Strict with discipline, he was nevertheless possessed of an amiable disposition. On a still day, his great laugh could be heard almost anywhere within the precincts.

Besides Fraser, there had been few Templars at Forglen— two old knights, Aubrey la Roche and Diego de Tolosa, tough veterans of the Crusades; the chaplain, Godfrey of Lille; and a toothless old serving brother named Simon d'Auteuil, who acted as cellarer, infirmarer, and cook. As the most experienced knight, Friedrich was appointed Turcoplier, in command of the sergeants and squires, to whose ranks Joseph and Robert had been added.

"The chapel houses the Sacrament of Christ's body, of course," Sir Gideon said as he led the new arrivals through the three-storied manor house. Stone and sturdy, it was neither a castle nor even a tower, but its walls were four feet thick at the base; and with window slots on the ground floor and stout oaken doors, it could be well-defended in a routine assault. It would not withstand a real siege, but there was not much likelihood it would have to, although, as the commander continued, "It also holds another treasure, one it has been the duty of this house to guard since the preceptory was built."

He guided them to one of the chapel's internal walls, where a worked metal door had been placed in the center. Robert could make out the figure hammered into the central panel, a robed man holding a staff and surrounded by sea birds wrought in a strange, cursive style.

Producing a key from his belt pouch, Sir Gideon unlocked the little door and opened it. He bowed profoundly and stepped back, revealing in the shallow niche a shining container about a hand's breadth in width and perhaps four fingers in height. The ends of the lid were tapered, creating the impression of a miniature gabled house or church. The front and sides were ornamented with animals etched in the same cursive style Robert had seen on the door and a few gemstones that glimmered dimly in the poor light of the chapel. Two large hinges fixed the lid to the container. The end of a short metal chain was attached to each.

"The *vexilium regis*," Gideon said, "the king's relic. In the Scots' tongue, it is called *brecbennoch*, 'the speckled one,' because of the pattern of the gold and silver overlay. It is ancient, having been brought to Dunkeld by King Kenneth MacAlpin over four hundred years ago."

"It is very beautiful," Robert said.

"The treasure it holds is far more precious," Gideon corrected him. "For it contains bones of Saint *Coluim Chille*— Colum of the Church. We hold it in trust for Sir Bernard Linton, the Abbot of Aberbrothock, who is the king's chancellor and *Deóradh*—the keeper of the holy relic. It will be taken from here to go before the army of Scotland in battle, like the Holy Ark of old. It is to that end that we guard it."

The knights, sergeants, and squires gazed on the ancient reliquary for a few moments, then Sir Gideon again bowed deeply, closed the door, and locked it. The company paid reverence to the sacred relic with a bow, genuflected before the altar, and filed out of the chapel in silence.

The Preceptory chapter was divided. Sir Friedrich argued that Robert should be received into the Order, which survived in Scotland only because Robert Bruce, who had been excommunicated for killing the Red Comyn at the Franciscan church in Dumfries, had refused to promulgate the edict of suppression. Fortunately for the rebel king and the people of Scotland, the Scots bishops had also evaded the papal decrees, barely avoiding a national interdict as they trod a narrow diplomatic path between the interests of the French-dominated papacy, the claims of Edward II of England, and the aspirations of Bruce and his loyal supporters. As a consequence several of them, including the heroic old Bishop Wishart of Glasgow, Bishop Lamberton, and the Abbot of Scone, were languishing in English prisons or French exile.

Other knights were opposed. "We do not know how long the Order can survive even here," Girard Fitz Gilbert pointed out. "How can we ask a young and promising scholar to pledge his life to an unsure cause?"

"He could profess his vows for a limited period," Friedrich replied. "It is commonly done with knights and sergeants."

"*Was* done," Sir Gideon corrected him. "Are you sure of his conviction and determination, even in the face of condemnation and proscription?"

"I am," Friedrich said with a finality that brooked no further opposition.

And so it happened. On the feast of St. Sebastian the Soldier, clad in a white tunic and belt, Robert approached and stood before Sir Gideon, who was seated in front of the altar in the chapel. Friedrich, Joseph, and the other knights and sergeants watched from their choir stalls.

"Robert of Troyes, are you willing to renounce the world?"

"I am," Robert said as steadily as he could muster.

"Are you willing to profess obedience to your lawful superior?" Gideon cautiously omitted the customary reference to the precept of the lord pope.

"I am."

"Are you willing to take upon yourself the way of life of our brothers?"

"I am."

"Then may God help and bless you."

During the recitation of the prescribed psalm, Robert unbuckled his belt and removed his tunic. Friedrich stepped forward and placed a used but serviceable habit over his shirt and hose, a loose-fitting black-hooded robe that he secured with a black leather belt. Then in the time-honored ritual of fealty, Robert knelt and placed his hands on that of the old commander lying open on the book of the Rule.

"I, Robert of Troyes, am willing and I promise to serve the Rule of the Knights of Christ and of His knighthood with the help of God for the reward of eternal life, so that from this day until three years hence I shall not be allowed to shake my neck free of the yoke of the Rule. And so that this petition of my profession may be firmly kept, I hand over this written document in the presence of the brothers, and with my hand I place it at the foot of the altar, which is consecrated in honor of almighty God and of the blessed Mary and all the saints. And henceforth I promise obedience to God and this house, and to live without property, and to maintain chastity, and firmly to keep the way of life of the brothers of the house of the Knights of Christ."

Robert then rose, as did the Commander. Both proceeded to the front of the altar, where Robert signed the parchment testifying to his promise of obedience. Then, he stretched his arms out and lay forward on the altar stone.

"Receive me, Lord, in accordance with Thy word and let me live," he prayed.

"And may Thou not confound me in my hope," the assembly chorused.

"The Lord is my light," Robert rasped in a rush of fear and joy.

"The Lord is the protector of my life," the others responded.

Gideon's great voice rose above the others. "Lord have mercy upon us!"

"Christ have mercy upon us!" Robert and his brothers replied.

"Lord have mercy upon us," the old commander concluded more quietly. Then he intoned the Lord's Prayer, after which he clasped Robert in a great bear hug, kissed him on both cheeks, and turned him to face the others.

"Let us pray," he said. "Receive, we beseech Thee, O Lord, this Thy servant fleeing to Thee from the tempests of this world and the snares of the devil, so that having been received by Thee he may happily enjoy both protection in the present world and reward in the world to come: through Christ our Lord."

"Amen!" the knights and sergeants replied.

Then as one man, they genuflected with a crash and filed mutely out of the chapel.

3

In the weeks that followed, despite days of howling wind and biting sheets of snow, Robert found the daily routine at the preceptory oddly comforting. And soon winter storms and darkness slowly gave way to ever-longer days, fairer skies, and occasional thaws. Weather permitting, Joseph resumed instructing Robert in the arts of combat and the detailed rules of the Poor Knights of Christ when he was not exercising or grooming the horses.

Late one afternoon in the waning days of winter, a weary rider struck the bell at the gate from the saddle of his winded palfrey.

"Sir Malcolm, the son of Thomas of Monymusk," old Simon told Robert as they watched the young knight cross the courtyard with Sir Gideon a few minutes after his arrival and disappear into the house. "Their holdings also belong to the Abbey of Aberbrothock, where the king's chancellor is abbot. He'll be well-informed."

Malcolm's news was welcome. Robert Bruce's brilliant lieutenant, the Black Douglas, had taken the castle of Roxburgh in February. Then, just days earlier, the Earl of Moray had captured Edinburgh itself. True to the young king's promise to rid Scotland of the English presence, each castle had been razed to the ground to prevent recapture. Now only Stirling and Berwick remained of the fortresses that could be of value to the English invaders.

"Scotland is free from the Forth to Cape Wrath," Gideon Fraser explained later that day in the chapter room. "But we must also remain on guard. Not all Scots are partisans of the Bruce. Not far from here, the Earl of Buchan had his castle at Kinedar—he who was cousin to the Red Comyn slain by Bruce at Dumfries, and a supporter of John Balliol. Men still speak angrily of the harrying of Buchan. And in Banff and Elgin, there are still those who would fight to restore the Toom Tabard. Caution is warranted."

"It means 'The Empty Surcoat,'" Father Godfrey whispered to Friedrich and Robert. "Old Balliol was made king by Edward Longshanks, then unmade by him and sent away to France to wither away in idleness and tears. He was never truly King of Scots."

Early the following morning, after Lauds and a brief meeting with Sir Gideon, Malcolm of Monymusk returned the way he had come on a fresh mount, and the preceptory resumed its orderly routine.

Several times as he went about his work in the days that followed, Robert noticed Brother Simon lurking around the stables or sheds, occasionally gazing towards the woods or fields as if looking for someone. He had heard some of the knights claim the old man's wits had been addled by age and long service in the hot sun of Outremer.

"*Non!*" a young groom named Yves whispered to Robert in the stables. "He feels that we are being watched. He told me that."

"And do you believe him?"

"*Mais oui!*" Only a few years older than Robert, Yves was born in a village near Sens, not far from Troyes. The familiar twang was comforting. "He sometimes knows things before they come to pass, and speaks of things he has not learned by his five wits."

"*Un sorcier?*" Robert wondered under his breath and crossed himself.

"*Pas du tout,*" whispered the groom. "*Un prophet! Frère* Simon was blessed with the Sight when he visited the Holy Sepulchre in Jerusalem. I swear by holy Jesus!"

The next day as Robert returned from exercising Näscher in the newly snow-dusted pen, he caught sight of Simon, wrapped in a tattered old *garnache,* laboring over something just outside the precinct of the manor house itself. He slipped into the porch and paused to watch as, with a sharpened stick, the decrepit serving brother etched a shallow curving trench through the thin layer of snow into the earth beneath. If he continued the arc, Robert realized, it would eventually encompass the entire building.

Simon passed Robert's hiding place a few moments later, unaware or uncaring that he was being observed while he scratched the thin orbit. ". . . and ward off all powers of evil, whatever they may be," he muttered, "or whence they come."

Robert watched him continue his circuit right over the paving stones outside the kitchen entrance.

"Hark that you do not break the circle," Joseph said quietly from behind.

"*Mon Dieu!*" Robert gasped, spinning around. "You gave me a fright."

"You might have cause to fear, young friend. Our old serving brother seems to have found it necessary to invoke powerful support against someone—or something—that lurks beyond the preceptory."

"Is it a charm then? Surely such things—"

"Are better not mentioned again, squire. Do you understand?"

"Yes," Robert said penitently. "I understand."

"And try to grow an eye in the back of your head," Joseph

added very softly. "Or otherwise protect your back. It might save your life."

That night, Robert found it difficult to sleep. And when the matins bell sounded and he rose to join the warrior monks in prayer, he purposely pressed close to one of the window slots through which he could peer down into the yard below. For an instant, he was sure he saw a faint, rose-hued arc pulsating through the film of snow. With a shudder, he crossed himself and moved along swiftly to the chapel.

A few days later as Robert passed Simon in the chapel corridor, he moved to the side, partly in awe, partly in fear. The old brother swerved quickly, brushed against him and pinched his arm sharply.

"Do not doubt!" he whispered hoarsely as Robert froze to the spot. "I have seen you fulfilling a great and arduous quest. But it will cost you! Yes, cost you much."

He went on his way as if nothing had happened, leaving Robert gaping after him in wonder and a feeling of mild terror.

Snow fell occasionally over the next ten days. Each time, Robert noticed, Simon's circuit was carefully reinscribed. He didn't see the glowing ring again, but he entertained no doubts that whatever barrier Simon had raised, whatever he had raised it against, and whatever power surged through it were all still in place.

Then, the Wednesday after Palm Sunday, just before Lauds, Sir Diego of Tolosa was discovered dead, the grip of a throwing dagger jutting up from his breastbone. His body lay near a side entrance, where the door stood slightly ajar in the early morning darkness.

"He must have surprised a thief who had entered the house unobserved," Sir Gideon concluded when he addressed the stunned community at Prime. "Whatever the killer was searching for, he appears to have failed in his quest, for nothing is missing."

"The shrine!" Robert blurted out.

"*Nothing* has been disturbed," Sir Gideon repeated firmly. "The *vexilium regis* is secure in its niche. But," he added before turning to the assignments of the day, "be on your guard at all times."

On the Tuesday of Holy Week, when the blue-bells and squills were already blossoming bravely in the glens against the dull bracken and still-slumbering heather of early April, another messenger made his way from Balantrodoch to Turiff. Under a threadbare brown cloak, he wore the black surcoat of a Templar sergeant. The tolling of the chapel bell soon summoned the cohort from the stables and fields. From Sir Gideon's grim countenance, Robert knew the news this time had not been welcome.

"On the fourteenth of the Kalends of April," the commander began in a flat voice, "the Master, Sir James of Molay, repudiated all accusations of infamy against himself and the Order and was burned alive by order of King Philip of France. With him died Sir Geoffrey of Charnay. Sir Hugh of Pairaud and Sir Geoffrey of Gonneville were condemned to perpetual confinement."

Fraser's words echoed eerily in the breathless silence of the chapel. Then, one by one, the Templars sank to their knees, murmuring prayers for the mercy of God on behalf of their martyred leaders.

Father Godfrey sang a requiem mass the following morning. For while Scotland might still lie under the threat of interdict, to the discomfiture of the pope in Avignon, the Scots bishops recognized neither the threat nor the excommunication of Robert Bruce. Nor did any advert to the condemnation of the Templars.

"Such matters are of no consequence in the eyes of God or good King Robert," Friedrich grumbled. "And here, at least, we have made our peace with the church."

Nevertheless, the clouds of mourning for the Master and, indeed, for the Order did not lift then or, indeed, ever.

As the chill rains of April gave way to warmer, brighter days, more news came to the preceptory. On the Kalends of May, when golden coltsfoot and hawkweed were in full flower and the bees began to awaken, a report tied to the leg of a pigeon arrived from Aberbrothock—Pope Clement had died three weeks before in Avignon.

"Struck down for the murder of our brothers," Friedrich rumbled, striking his fist against the chapel rail. "Sir James is avenged."

Sir Gideon glared at him, then ordered prayers for the soul of their spiritual enemy.

"His fate, like ours, is indeed in the hands of God," old Simon whispered from behind. "Pray that the new pope will be merciful and just."

"If he is also French, it is unlikely he will be either," Friedrich replied.

4

The sixth day of May, 1314, dawned clear. Sunlight gleamed coldly off the cross atop the chapel tower in the little glen of Turriff. According to the proscription of the papal bull issued after the Council of Vienne two years earlier, any fugitive Templar who had not surrendered to the local bishop by sundown that day was subject to death at the stake if ever apprehended. The Scottish bishops had shown no interest in promulgating the decree, however, or even referring to it.

Elsewhere, Templars had joined other military orders or were pensioned off. Some went to ground. But in Scotland, they went about the business of the day under the covert protection of the Bishop of Moray and other Bruce partisans. They prepared for war.

On the first Wednesday after Pentecost, still more than three weeks before the appointed day of battle, Sir Gideon summoned Friedrich to his chamber.

"The final mustering of King Robert's forces has begun in the forest of Torwood, three miles south of Stirling Castle. At Easter, King Edward advanced from York to Newcastle. The baggage train alone, it is said, stretched for twenty miles. The English will move to Berwick before the Ides of June, and from there enter Scotland east of Edinburgh. Shortly, the garrison here will join King Robert's muster. First, however, the Brecbennoch must be delivered to Abbot Bernard at Aberbrothock. I have selected you to safeguard it."

Friedrich was surprised. "I, Sir Gideon? It is a great honor, but I am still a stranger in this land."

"This mission is not without danger, as Sir Diego learned to his sorrow. I can ill spare you, but the others are either aged or much less experienced in combat. After you deliver the relic to the Chancellor, you will escort him to Torwood, where the rest of us will join you in a fortnight. And have no misgivings about a guide—one has been provided. He should arrive with his aides by nightfall. Be prepared to leave at first light with your squire and man-at-arms."

Friedrich stiffened and bowed his head. "As you command."

He quickly found Joseph and Robert and ordered them to prepare for departure with all their baggage in good order for the long ride to Stirling. Although the battle itself was still weeks away, Robert felt his pulse race as, under Joseph's strict tutelage, he assembled and inspected weapons, armor, harness, and supplies.

Any doubts Friedrich might have had about a guide were dispelled just before Vespers, when the clanging of the bell brought Simon trotting to open the gate.

"Sir Antony!" Robert shouted, coming up rapidly behind the old brother. Friedrich was not far behind.

"Aye, Robert," the Scot shouted back, ducking under the lintel as he rode into the yard astride his ash-gray palfrey, Stoirmeil. "Niall and Alisdair as well. My noble father has loaned us to the Templars once again!"

5

It was still dark the next morning when Father Godfrey removed the precious reliquary from its niche and placed it on the altar.

"Mighty Lord and Merciful Saviour," he prayed, "through the heavenly intercession of our father Columba, we pray Thee to deliver this land from the scourge of the enemy. May Thy holy saint march before us like a pillar of fire. By his prayers may Thy servants be protected in battle. Like the Ark of Thy Covenant, may his sacred bones safeguard our freedom. Deliver us, Lord our God, from all evil, strengthen us to fight all Thine enemies, and preserve us in Thy service."

The response of the preceptory trembled the rafters.

Moments later, as the cobbled yard blushed under the first rays of dawn, the little band set out for the great abbey of St. Thomas Becket. Friedrich and Antony were well-armored, if not in full battle gear. The knights' destriers, Wahgemut and Confadh, followed in the train behind Robert and Niall, who had donned leather cuirasses and wide-brimmed helmets. Alisdair led two sumpter horses packed with great helms, swords-of-war, and battle-axes as well as sufficient supplies for the long journey to Torwood. Friedrich himself bore the Brecbennoch, strapped around his neck by cords of twined leather.

The road soon led them past the fields and meadows of Turriff village into the thick forest that for over a hundred miles skirted the great central highlands called the Mounth. From Fyvie, they would pass on to Meldrum. By nightfall, they would reach the safety of the preceptory at Maryculter. The journey to Aberbrothock would require another two days.

Eddies of ground mist swirled around the horses' hooves as the dark shadows of the forest closed around them. Robert felt grateful for the old *garnache* Simon had given him just before they left. Sleeveless and well-worn, it was still warm enough to fend off the mist and clammy coldness of the still morning air.

An hour into their journey, Friedrich suddenly called the company to a halt. The trunk of a great pine lay over the path ahead. Instinctively, the knights loosened their swords in their scabbards. Alerted by the tension he felt in the warriors, Robert unslung the arbalest he had attached to his saddle and prodded his mount slowly forward, halting a few paces behind Friedrich and Antony, well out of the way of the span of their swords.

A lone rider ambled slowly into the road from the shadowy pines on the right. Heavily cloaked, he threw back his hood, revealing a mail coif. But he appeared to be only lightly armed.

"Who are you, messire, and why do you bar our passage?" Friedrich demanded in French.

"My name is Gilbert Wayland," the rider replied smoothly. "A Christian far from home in the service of the king."

"Which king?" Sir Antony called out.

"Why, King Edward, of course," Wayland smiled amiably.

"My business is with you, Sir Friedrich, or rather, with what you are carrying to Aberbrothock."

Friedrich unhooked his hand-axe. "Ambuscade!" he called to the others.

The forest rustled and snapped. Nearly a score of well-armed men emerged and ranged themselves around the Templars. Some had arbalests, others halberds, billhooks, and spears. The rest held swords and clubs.

"I refer to the *Brecbennoch,* Sir Knight," the rider continued. "I mean to have it, whether you deliver it to me of your own volition or I take it from your dead body."

Nervously Robert calculated the odds of overcoming a force almost four times larger than their number. And these were no peasant bandits as in the forest of Thivars. But he also knew that it was forbidden for a Templar knight to retreat except under the most overwhelming circumstances.

"I cannot surrender the reliquary to you," Friedrich said bluntly. "You will have to take it from me. That will not be easy, I assure you."

Wayland nudged his horse slowly forward. Friedrich held Näscher still, working the haft of his axe through his gauntlet.

"Easier, perhaps, than you think."

With a quick flick of his left wrist, Wayland hurled a small dagger he had held concealed in his sleeve. Friedrich did not flinch, for he quickly realized that the blade had not been thrown at him.

Well-aimed, it struck Robert in the throat, just above the collar of his hauberk.

As Robert toppled from his mount with a strangled cry, Friedrich attacked with a roar, swinging his axe in a deadly arc. Wayland held, then pulled clear at the last moment. Friedrich attempted to wheel Näscher around, but found himself blocked by the trunk of the pine and then grappled by one of the billhooks.

Näscher reared back, pulling the attacker off his feet. Friedrich dislodged the billhook with a backhanded swipe of his axe, as a second and third reached toward his neck and shoulders. Bolts whizzed past. In the distance, he heard Antony and Niall shouting, and the cry of wounded men.

Fighting to dislodge another hook, Friedrich felt Näscher sink suddenly beneath him with a scream of agony. In a dizzying whirl, the palfrey crashed to the ground, pinning Friedrich by the leg. Dazed, he felt himself netted and dragged off his still-thrashing mount. Näscher's shrieks were stilled when one of the ambushers slashed his throat with a misericorde.

Still roaring, Friedrich struggled to get to his feet, but he could neither stand nor move his arms, now bound with cords over the net. He steeled himself for the killing thrust, commending his soul to God and Christ and the Blessed Mary, half-cursing himself for bringing Robert to his death, praying for him, for Joseph—and suddenly realized that his prayers were taking too long. He should be dead by now, by Our Lady's sweet veil!

He opened his sound eye and tried to get the other to work behind the fold of tough flesh that obstructed it. The din of battle had ceased. He lurched as he was dragged by the heels down the road.

He was dropped at the black-booted feet of Gilbert Wayland, who gazed down at him with mild contempt or what might have been amusement.

"Foolish courage, Sir Templar," the Englishman said. "And now, please, the relic. I haven't all day to dicker with you."

The netting was pulled away from his head and shoulders, but Friedrich was aware that a half-dozen sword-points hovered within striking distance.

"If you simply hand it over, I will release you and your company," Wayland went on. "Your deaths would profit no one. You might even be able to save your squire."

As he was pulled to a sitting position, Friedrich glanced around. He saw Joseph sitting on the ground holding his arm, surrounded by men with spears and swords. Antony and Niall stood nearby, battered and bound. Robert lay on the ground near them, groaning weakly.

Alive, then!

"In exchange for the *Brecbennoch,* Sir Friedrich, I will give you the antidote. Without it, your squire will surely die. Slowly, I regret, and in great pain."

"Poison?"

The Englishman examined the dagger he had retrieved from Robert's throat, then wiped it on a white cloth. "A useful precaution."

Wayland sniffed the cloth, tucked it into his darkly crimson doublet, and sheathed the dagger in his arm-scabbard. A half-apologetic smile flitted across his face. He flipped open his belt pouch and withdrew a phial that he held up to the chill morning light. It shimmered with a deep green luster.

"This will undo the toxin. Act quickly."

"Release me," Friedrich said.

"Unbind his arms," Wayland ordered.

Two of his guards cut through the ropes. Friedrich found the thong at his neck and retrieved the reliquary from within his mantle.

"How can I be sure the remedy will work?" Friedrich asked, struggling to his feet.

"How do I know that the relic is genuine?" Wayland retorted. "At some point, Sir Knight, we have to trust each other."

Friedrich snorted his disgust. "Swear by the Blood of Jesu that the antidote is true."

"I so swear," Wayland replied in a low, mocking voice. "I was once a priest of Holy Church, Sir Knight. Even of the Temple. I would not jeopardize my soul by swearing falsely."

"You are a traitor and priest of hell," Friedrich growled, holding out the little box. "Now let us go."

Calmly, Wayland opened the reliquary, unwrapped the red velvet bindings, and examined the small bones they protected. Satisfied, he replaced the bones in the casket and signaled to his men. They strapped the corpses of three of his henchmen to sumpter mules, and without further conversation, the company melted into the forest.

Ignoring his own wounds, Joseph cleaned the tear in Robert's throat with wine from a skin he produced from his supplies, and bound it lightly under a cold poultice.

"The blade did not sever the great vessels or the windpipe," he told Friedrich with relief. "He will not bleed to death. But harm has been done. If he lives, he may never speak again."

He sniffed the contents of the phial, touched the tip of his finger to the lip of the little bottle, then tasted it.

"It may indeed save him," he said after a moment's reflection. "*Insh'Allah*—if God so wills!"

He retrieved a goblet from the supplies and sloshed wine into it, adding what was in the phial. Quickly mixing the liquids, he lifted the cup to Robert's bloodless lips and slowly poured the contents into his mouth. Pressing gently on the poultice, he stroked the young man's throat. "Swallow," he whispered. "Swallow."

Robert's eyelids fluttered briefly and went still. He moaned but did not cough up the solution.

They found Alisdair a few yards into the forest, unconscious but alive. He had suffered a head wound and broken arm. Only Näscher had been lost, and in his heart, Friedrich grieved the palfrey as he would a companion-at-arms.

Silently, the Templar band retraced their way to the preceptory. Now astride the great chestnut destrier Wahgemut, Friedrich carried Robert in his arms as one would cradle a child. The youth had not regained consciousness, and blood still seeped from beneath the poultice. A year ago, Friedrich reflected, had Robert died he would have sworn to search out the renegade Templar priest and kill him. Now, he was astonished to find that the lust for vengeance no longer inflamed his soul. He prayed only that his young friend would live.

6

Simon hurried to admit them when Antony tolled the bell sharply at the entrance gate. Apprised of the situation, he quickly transformed a cell into an infirmary with the addition of an extra candle, a second blanket, and a basin.

They were soon joined by Sir Gideon. Retiring to the courtyard, Friedrich and Antony recounted the ambush.

"Do you think the boy will recover?" Sir Gideon wondered.

"As God is merciful and the English whoreson did not lie, he might. But we have failed. My sin is great, Sir Gideon. I traded Robert's life for the *Brecbennoch*. It is I who deserve to die."

"You did not fail, Friedrich. None of you did. Nor have you sinned. Come, let me explain."

"A ruse!" Friedrich exploded in the commander's quarters. Both he and Antony had sprung to their feet when the gnarled Templar told them of the deception.

"Sit down. And replace the chairs, please," Gideon said patiently. "I would not willingly place you under penance for unruliness."

Damping his fury, the Saxon knight stood the chair he had overturned back on its legs, but neither he nor Antony found it possible to sit. So Gideon stood as well.

"I deeply regret the injury done to Robert. But for the ploy to succeed, it was necessary that everyone believe that the

Brecbennoch was with you—especially Gilbert Wayland. I was under instructions from the royal chancellor himself. You are too guileless to be a good spy, Friedrich. I will not ask you to forgive me, for you were under obedience and at no time did I state that you were bearing the true relic of Columba."

"That is well, Sir Gideon, for if Robert dies, I might find it difficult to forgive you."

"Is the relic still here, then?" Antony demanded.

"Sir Malcolm removed it to Monymusk more than two months ago. By now, it is safely in the hands of Abbot Bernard, who is already with the king. It will lead the Scots in battle."

"And the English?" Friedrich queried. "When will they discover they have been deceived?"

"In God's own time, my friend. And in God's way."

Two days later the preceptory was vacant except for Robert and old Simon. Even one-armed Sir Gideon had gone south with Friedrich, Joseph, Antony, and the other knights and sergeants to join the army of King Robert at Torwood, near the little river known as the Burn of Bannock. There the fate of Scotland would be decided. Greatly outnumbered by the troops and cavalry of Edward of England, the Scots would find the aid of the Templars and their horses critical, that of the *Brecbennoch* decisive.

"God, Columba, and Saint Fillan will fight on Scotland's behalf, *prabanach*—dear young one," the old nurse whispered close to Robert's ear. "You will not see battle there, but you have helped secure victory. Rest now and recover."

He placed his hand lightly on Robert's brow, content to find it warm, but not feverish. The heathen Turcopole had said the antidote should counteract the poison, but the wound itself was severe and might yet claim his life, especially if putrefaction set in. Best to be watchful. Muttering his prayers, the old man snuffed out the candle and went about his chores.

Although he could not speak nor raise or turn his head without causing searing pain, Robert's mind was alert and active. Perhaps too active.

"Kindly Saint Maurice," he moaned somewhere deep within, "you were a soldier and a martyr and have great influence in the court of heaven. Please do not let me die just yet. I am young and have much living to do."

At first the darkened room remained empty as well as silent. Not even the echo of his own voice was detectable, for in truth no sound had escaped his lips for days. And he only gradually became conscious of the white-robed figure sitting on the edge of his cot.

Regrettably, he looked nothing like Saint Maurice. His beard was long and white except for a few dark strands just at the corners of his mouth. He had a staff in his left hand. Although his dress was unfamiliar and the cut of his tonsure very strange, he was evidently a monk.

"Yes, I am a monk." The old fellow's French was astonishingly good, very much like Robert's own.

"Am I dying, then?" Best to get these matters out in the open, as his father used to say. Robert suddenly wondered if Friedrich would be able to get word to his parents. A wave of regret washed up on the shores of his otherwise pious reflections. And he had been doing so well. . . .

His embarrassing relapse into self-pity was interrupted by a friendly pat on the foot. "You still have a long journey ahead, my son. Now you must rest. You will need all your strength in the days to come."

He must have dozed for a few minutes, for when Robert opened his eyes again—or thought he did—the light in the room had shifted. The shadows were darker and two other figures stood behind the aged monk. One he did not recognize—an elderly knight wearing a white surcoat emblazoned with the red cross of the Temple; his eyes were blue. The other he knew well. His heart swelled when she smiled at him.

"Yvette," he said silently. "It is good to see you again."

It sounded stupid, but it was the first thought that came to mind.

"Come, Father Columba," the white-bearded knight said. "We must leave now."

"Yes, yes, Sir Jacques," the monk replied a little testily.

The old man smoothed his beard and started to raise himself from his perch on the corner of Robert's cot. He was helped to his feet by the equally venerable knight.

"Know that the army of Scotland has won the day," the old warrior said. "Your friends live, although much blood has been shed. The English king is in rout, only narrowly escaping capture himself."

"Have I been ill so long?" Robert asked. "The appointed day was weeks hence when we left for the abbey."

"In your world, only five days have passed," the monk explained. "But have no fear. It will happen as Sir Jacques has said. In God's eyes, it has already happened. And the little box with those curious bones will be returned soon," he added with a wink. "I think they're an old fox's bones, but I may be wrong."

"Your sacrifice was not in vain, Robert of Troyes," Jacques de Molay concluded. "Even though you did not will it, you accepted that possibility when you vowed obedience within the Order of the Poor Knights of Christ. Be comforted in that."

The abbot raised his hand in benediction. "And now rest."

Somewhere nearby a dove's wings fluttered.

"Don't forget," de Molay cautioned.

"Hmm? Oh, yes!" Colum of the Church halted and returned to the side of the cot. "You will need your voice, *prabanach.*"

He placed his right hand over the wound on Robert's throat. At first, it caused a twinge of pain. Then Robert felt a sense of cool and blessed relief.

"There," Columba said. "Now go to sleep."

And he did. As his eyes closed, the last thing Robert saw was the great glowing sign the old man carved into the living air—a flaming, roseate cross that for some time after hovered brightly in the gathering darkness.

Historical note

Although known in later centuries as Turriff Hospital, in 1179 the Knights Templar were granted land at Forglen parish for a second Scottish base. For some time after the suppression of the Order in 1312, Knights Hospitaller and Templars shared quarters in Scotland, and in some instances it seems probable that certain Templar properties were never fully turned over to the Hospitallers.

Although both his cavalry and foot soldiers were greatly outnumbered by English forces, Robert Bruce's brilliant triumph at the Battle of Bannockburn, on June 23–24, 1314, secured Scottish independence and assured Bruce's eventual recognition by the pope and King Edward III as the true King of Scotland. Legends that Knights Templar fought on the side of the Scottish host appear to date back almost to the battle itself.

On the eve of the battle, Sir Alexander Seton, a cousin of Bruce, defected to the Scots, disgusted by the disorder, favoritism, and lack of planning among the English. His presence contributed significantly to the Scots' morale and subsequent victory.

Among the flower of English knighthood killed at Bannockburn were Sir John Hastings, Sir John Comyn, Sir Henry de Bohun—the Earl of Hereford's son—and the king's brave cousin, young Gilbert of Clare. Sir Ingram de Umfraville and the elder De Bohun were captured at Bothwell and later ransomed in exchange for Robert Bruce's sister, the Countess of Fife, and Bishop Wishart, among other prisoners. Donald of Mar returned to Scotland after Edward II was deposed. Sir Ingram de Umfraville, at first reconciled to Bruce, later renounced his possessions in Scotland and returned to England for good. Following Edward's capture by Roger Mortimer and Queen Isabella, both Despensers were brutally executed, and Edward himself was most likely murdered at Berkeley Castle in 1327, although reports that he was rescued and escaped to the Continent continue to intrigue historians.

The *Brecbennoch,* now known as the Monymusk Reliquary, can be seen in the Museum of Antiquities in Edinburgh. Most likely crafted in Ireland, it is a small rectangular wooden casket four inches long and about three inches high, overlaid with gold and silver, semi-precious stones, and worked in animal figures and the dots that give it its Gaelic name. For centuries, it was guarded by the Clan Connell, later known as the House of Fife. In 1211 King William the Lion entrusted the Brecbennoch to the abbot of the Benedictine monastery he founded at Aberbrothock (later shortened to Arbroath), also granting to the abbey the lands of Forglen in Buchan, "given to God and to Saint Columba and to the Brecbennoch," in return for the services of the relic-bearer or *Deóradh,* the origin of the family name Dewer or Dewar. Six months after the battle of Bannockburn, Bernard de Linton, the Abbot of Arbroath, granted hereditary custody of the Brecbennoch to Sir Malcolm de Monymusk on condition that he and his heirs performed in his name the service of *Deóradh* whenever need arose.

INTERLUDE FIVE

Relics were exceedingly important during the period of the existence of the Order of the Temple. Indeed, the Temple is known to have possessed many of them, notably the True Cross and possibly the Holy Shroud. The relic then regarded as the True Cross was burned after its capture by Saladin; the Shroud, which may have been in the keeping of a Templar family for a time, may be the one now known as the Shroud of Turin—which may or may not be the burial cloth in which Christ was wrapped before being laid in the tomb for three days.

But there were other relics, of greater or lesser importance and potency, not all of them benign. Our next story, which sees a return of the redoubtable William of Occam, deals with another such relic.

Occam's Treasure

Robert Reginald

They came for us at the hour of the wolf, that time in the darkest part of the night when the Shrouded One stretches forth his shriveled hand and snatches up the souls of those wavering at the boundary 'twixt life and death, while their bodies are yet quivering with their last gasp of air.

The papal soldiers burst their way into the Monastery of Saint Anaclète in Avignon, not even attempting to secure the permission of Father Superior Pontien, and rousted us from our cells, no more than half awake. They dragged us into the warm night air, and escorted us forthwith to the Palais des Papes, a large complex of buildings covering the south end of that crag which is called the Rocher des Doms, high above the city.

His Holiness, Pope John XXII, who scarcely deserved such an appellation, was waiting for us on his golden throne.

"So, Friar William, we find your overall demeanor as obstinate as it ever was," the old man whined.

In the year since our last meeting, the pope had developed a slight tremor in his left hand, or so it seemed to me.

"And you, Brother Thaddæus," he continued, turning in my

direction, "do you still have in your possession that ugly sack-
cloth you showed me last year?"

He was referring, of course, to the Holy Burial Shroud of
our Lord and Savior, Jesus Christ.

"I do, Holiness," I responded.

"Hmm," the pontiff replied.

Then he said nothing for many minutes, leaving us standing there before him, his eyes glazing over in reflection or fa-
tigue or something else entirely. Not much more than a
twelvemonth ago, in the year of Our Lord 1324, we had
played a game of cat and mouse with the pope over the Templar treasure, and had come away from that confrontation
with at least a stalemate. The much-touted wealth of that mil-
itant order of religious knights had turned out to be the Holy
Burial Shroud of Our Lord Jesus Christ, over which we had
been granted temporary custodianship by the new secret
Grand Master of the Templars. Ever since then, we had been
confined under house arrest in the papal town of Avignon, forbidden to venture outside the small city-state on the pain of
instant excommunication and death.

"We have need of you again," the pope finally stated, in a
voice that was barely audible. "Our nephew, Boson Comte de
la Bâteau, has been foully murdered this past fortnight."

"This is tragic news, Holiness," my dear master replied,
"but what has it to do with us? I would be happy to say a mass
for the repose of his soul, but I see nothing else we can do."

The pontiff motioned to an aide, who stepped forward and
put something in Fra William's hand.

"These were found on the body of the deceased," the pope
continued, "or rather, within the corpus itself, resting on his
tongue."

I watched as my master unwrapped an old coin from a
piece of papyrus. A large numeral "IV" was inked on the scrap
of paper. I didn't recognize the ruler on the disk.

"Was this the first such incident, Holiness?" Fra William inquired.

Again we waited while the Holy Father framed his next response.

"No," he finally admitted. "There have been three previous killings, all of them involving individuals directly connected to us."

"What else has happened?" my teacher asked. "You've received something further, haven't you?"

The old man shifted on his throne and sighed, then nodded to his associate, Father Johad, who passed another document to Fra William. My master took a moment to review the letter, and showed it to me. It read:

To Ioannes XXII, who calls himself Pope:

Jacques de Molay, Master of the Order of the Knights of the Temple of Solomon, reaches out from his grave to accuse you, Jacques Duèse, of heresy, murder, bribery, simony, and other crimes and misdemeanors unbecoming a prince of the Church, in that you schemed and manipulated and purchased your way onto the chair of Saint Peter. For these actions, he condemns you in the name of Jesus Christ to eternal damnation, unless you renounce your titles, offices, and emoluments, and become as a little child, without possessions, sees, or purse.

He gives you until Michaelmas of this year to abdicate your throne and acknowledge the poverty of Jesus Christ and his followers. For every week that you delay, one of those connected to you shall render the ultimate penalty for your obstinacy. Should you fail to renounce the papacy by the date indicated, the power to do so shall be wrenched from your filth-covered hands.

Maître Jacques de Molay
Les Chevaliers Nouveaux du Temple

The pope coughed very loudly and cleared his throat.

"If we yield to such persuasion," he said, "we establish a precedent that others may employ against our successors; should we not abdicate within the next four months, many more of our dearly beloved associates may meet a fate wholly undeserved by them; in either case we shall be made the harlequin of the Christian world, fit for nothing but mockery by those we attempt to guide, for we have no doubt that these rogues will very shortly make public their actions against us. Our rule shall fail, and the thrice-damned Templars shall once again be re-established in their seats of power."

"We are Franciscans, not men of action," Fra William noted. "The temporal authorities are certainly capable of dealing with such matters far better than we."

"So one might presume," the pope sighed, "but the matter has proved more troublesome than we expected. We have dispatched several individuals and squads of papal guards to investigate these crimes, Fra William. The bodies of one such group were discovered several weeks ago in the Tournal District, blasted by some foul magic of Satan himself. So what are we to do?"

Then he began crying most piteously, a high thin sound, like that of a young girl who has just been thwarted in love.

My master waited until the pontiff had regained some control over himself, before saying: "You have three options, Holiness. You can acquiesce to the demands of these renegades. You can take no action, and let God sort out the consequences. You can fight back. You must realize, however, that should you opt for the latter course, whoever is behind this storm of terror may well escalate the price that you ultimately pay for the resolution of this mystery."

"We understand this perfectly well, Fra William," the pope responded. "Do not treat us like some six-year-old waif. We want *you* to find these resurgent Templars. Identify those responsible for these crimes, and we will take care of the rest. We shall give you letters granting you and your companion access into any house in France. Father Arlan d'Esprit, our trusted associate, shall be our eyes and ears in this matter."

I could tell from his manner that Fra William was not much pleased with these proceedings, but truth to tell, he had very little choice in the matter.

"I shall need access to all of the reports collected on the previous deaths," my master indicated.

"Father Johad will provide these to you, as well as the coins and notes found on the others," came the reply.

"What about the bodies of the victims?" Fra William asked.

"They were consigned unto the earth," the pontiff indicated.

"Can they be exhumed?" my teacher wanted to know.

The pope put his hand up to his mouth and chewed on the mottled web of skin between the thumb and forefinger.

"Is this truly necessary?" he asked.

"Do you wish this mystery to be solved?" came the retort.

The pontiff sighed a second time.

"Very well," he stated, turning to his aide. "Père Johad," he ordered, "draw up the appropriate order."

"Yes, Holiness," the priest said, bowing low.

Then we were released to return to our lodgings.

It was now the hour of the dove.

My illustrious master, the *Doctor Invincibilis* Father William of Occam, of the Order of Friars Minor, was primarily known at this time not for the rich philosophical tomes which he was to pen during his long exile in Germania, but as an *investigator veritatis,* or seeker after truth. Beginning with the terrible murders at Exeter College in the year 1320, in which Father Occam proved that the treacherous Master Morbinus had very slyly poisoned three of his fellow *magistri* in order to better his own position, my teacher's fame had spread rapidly through certain circles in England; and during the ensuing years, before he was abruptly summoned to the chair of Saint Peter, he was often called upon to resolve questions of life and death.

It was during these years that I first heard him develop that logical principle which became known even during his own lifetime as "Occam's Razor," which holds that "what can be done with fewer assumptions is done in vain with more."

As we broke our fast back at the abbey, I asked him about our meeting with the pope.

"I think, young Thaddæus," he stated, "that our Holy Father did not really want to give us this task, but felt that he had no choice in the matter. Things have advanced too rapidly, and his position is now seriously threatened."

"But who would attack the Holy Church?" I asked.

"*Papa* John has made many personal enemies," my master emphasized, "who would delight in his fall from grace, including the Emperor Ludwig and our own Father Superior."

Then he took the coin that had been removed from Count Boson's mouth, and held it up to the light, turning it over once or twice.

"Most curious," he said, placing it on the bench in front of us.

I had never seen anything quite like it. The bright silver disk was a little larger than my thumb. On the obverse, it featured the bust of a clean-shaven man of perhaps thirty-five, his curly hair bisected over the crown of his head by a narrow band of cloth, the two ties of which draped down the nape of his neck. The portrait was framed by a fillet border.

The reverse of the coin bore the image of a seated, bearded

man holding the small figure of a standing woman in his right hand, and a floor-length staff in his left. She was offering him something. The *tableau* was framed on either side by two lines of large type, written in a language that I did not understand, whose letters consisted of a series of interconnected dots.

"What do you think?" my master asked.

"Well," I said, "the king on the front, if that's what he is, has a large, hooked nose and a protruding chin."

Father William smiled slightly and shook his head.

I tried again. "Although the coin looks newly minted," I indicated, "the style is not modern, and I suspect it may be much older than it appears."

"Very good," my teacher responded, "what else?"

"The inscription uses non-Roman characters," I observed. "If we knew the language in which it was written, we might be able to identify the time and place more accurately."

"Excellent!" he stated. "Why do you think this determination is important?"

"If the other three coins are similar to this," I noted, "then the killer might be sending some hidden message by placing these artifacts in the victims' mouths."

"Yes," Occam agreed. "How shall we determine whence these derive?"

"I . . ." I paused for a moment. "I don't know, master."

That afternoon we again made our way to the Rocher des Doms to meet with Fathers Johad and Arlan d'Esprit. The former was a clean-shaven man of about fifty, clad in the red robes of the Order of Saint Blaise, while his companion was perhaps twenty years his junior, tall and straight and bearded—and a fellow Franciscan!

Laid out on a small table before them were the implements from the earlier murders: three coins, three scraps of papyrus marked with Roman numerals—two of them badly discolored—and a bronze stiletto. It was immediately apparent that all four deaths were connected.

"These tokens and papers," my master inquired, "all were found in the victims' mouths?"

"Yes," Johad indicated.

"Tell me about them," Father William ordered.

"The first death occurred a month ago," Johad continued. "Bishop Thoune, in town to visit the pope, was dining in the refectory of Saint Jude's, when he began gagging and collapsed onto the floor. They thought he had choked on something, but when they pried opened his jaws, all they found were these . . . things.

"The second victim was Sieur Phocion Duèse de La Pacaudière. He had come to Avignon to pay his respects to his papal cousin, but was stabbed to death one night while frequenting a certain establishment on the Rue des Putains. The coin and note were discovered while his body was being prepared for shipment back to his manor.

"The third incident involved Monsignor Lezay, a major advisor to His Holiness, who was beaten to death on the Rue Fortunée. Count Boson was hit on the head while walking through Avignon."

"All of these deaths occurred in town?" my master indicated.

"Indeed," Father Arlan responded.

"Well, then," Father William stated, "if three of the victims resided outside Avignon, how did the killer know their schedules while they were here?"

The other two exchanged glances and shrugged. They had no idea.

"Where was the demand note left?" Father William asked.

"In the alms box of the cathedral," Johad stated.

My master rubbed his chin and frowned.

"Which of the bodies were sent home for burial?" he asked.

"All but Lezay's," came the reply, "which was interred at the Monastery of Saint Herbin."

"Then that's the one we shall exhume," Father William indicated, "on the morrow."

"It shall be done, Father Occam," Johad stated.

After the two priests departed, my master put the implements into his purse, and indicated on our way out that we would make another stop.

"There is a man," he stated, "who may be able to tell us something about these artifacts."

We wound our way down a number of narrow streets into an older section of town, finally entering the Rue David.

"What is this place?" I inquired, looking at a curiously shaped emblem of a star embedded on one door.

"The Jewish quarter," he replied, knocking on the small round window of an adjoining building.

"Yesss?" someone answered within.

"Occamus Magus to see Yehuda ben Sion," my teacher stated.

"One moment."

Then the door cracked open, and a short, middle-aged man with a long, graying beard peeped out. He wore a red skullcap pressed into his straggly black hair.

"Come in, come in!" he cackled. "How good to see you again, Frère Occam."

He gave my master a kiss on both cheeks, and then beckoned us inside.

The shop, for such it was, was strangely outfitted. On one wall hung the dried skins, heads, and entrails of mostly unidentifiable animals. On another I saw jars of roots and herbs and powders and other things. On the third were large crystals and curiously shaped jewels and twisted silver implements. On the fourth were hung various garments and hats, all of them oddly cut and decorated. I could smell incense burning somewhere, but couldn't place the fragrance.

The Jew took us back into a second room, obviously his workshop, with a long table set against one wall. We perched ourselves on several wooden chairs.

"What can I do for you, my friend?" Yehuda inquired.

Father William removed the four coins from his pouch, and laid them on the table. The shopkeeper pulled out an oblong piece of cut glass from a drawer, and ran it over the artifacts, moving the thing back and forth as he peered at them.

"What is that?" I asked.

"It makes my vision wax stronger," the man replied. "You will understand, my boy, when you get older.

"These are very unusual pieces, very old, ben Occam," he went on. "The lettering is Greek, but of a style I have never encountered before. These dots on the back—very curious indeed. The inscription reads, '*Basileós Philippou Epiphanous Philadelphou,*' or in your tongue, 'From the King Philip,' the—uh—how do you say? 'coming-to-light,' no, the better word is 'famous,' 'the one who is devoted to his brother.' I have seen a similar coin of the great King Alexander; I know that his father was named Philip, and also his half-brother, so perhaps it is one of these. I will make the usual inquiries for you. If I may retain these for a day or two?"

"Of course," my friend noted, discreetly leaving a copper on the bench.

"Thank you, ben Occam," ben Sion responded, "you are very good to me."

"No more than you deserve, old soul," Father William stated.

Then they kissed again, and we headed back to the abbey.

"Who was that?" I asked my teacher.

"An acquaintance from my Oxford days," he responded. "He did me a favor once, and when the pogrom of 1306 threatened his family, I ensured their safe passage out of the country."

"But he must be a magician," I stated. "If the authorities knew . . ."

"They know," Occam sighed, "but they tolerate him and his countrymen, because they provide services no one else would render.

"Now," he continued, "we need to examine the facts of this case. Four men have been killed, all of them with ties to *Papa* John. We must ask the obvious question, *cui bono?* That is, whose benefit would be served by the resignation or disgrace of the pontiff?"

"There are many such possibilities," I indicated, "including the remnants of the Templars and those other religious orders who have been attacked by this pope and his predecessor, *Papa* Clemens."

"There may also be personal reasons involved," my master stated, "such as revenge, greed, lust for power. All of these things may prompt a man to murder. We know too little at this point to speculate overmuch. Tomorrow we must begin looking into the crimes themselves. Let us pray to God for guidance, that He will show us the way."

And so we knelt down on that hard stone floor, lending our muted voices to the Lord, and then went off to bed.

In the morning we joined the pontiff's two aides at Saint Herbin's Abbey, just outside the city walls, where two workmen had already begun excavating the tomb of Monsignor Lezay. Soon they reached the coffin, and employed ropes to haul it out of the ground.

"Ooh!" one of them exclaimed, when the lid came off.

The stench was overpowering, and I ran behind another monument to void my breakfast.

Father William, however, merely tied a rag around his

nose, and began poking and prodding the remains. At one point he even asked the laborers to rotate the corpse, while I looked on from a distance—a great distance!

Then he was finished, and exchanged a few words with the two priests, before motioning me to follow.

"What did you find?" I asked.

"He was indeed beaten before he died, although whether those injuries actually caused his death, I cannot tell. There was a crude cross cut into his chest. Similar marks were apparently found on the other bodies as well, in one case etched into the forehead."

"What does it mean?" I queried.

"The murderer wants us to think that the Templars were responsible," he indicated. "But these scratches are not firm evidence of any such connection."

"Where do we go next?" I inquired.

"We look into the background of Lezay, and the circumstances of his passing."

Already he was hurrying out of the cemetery.

"Come, Thaddæus," he shouted, "time's a-wasting."

On the Rue Fortunée in the Bélon District, we began questioning residents, shopmen, even passers-by, about the crime.

"I knew this Lezay," an apothecary named Rocambole stated. "He came here often to buy his powders. But I was closed when he was killed. It's just not safe staying open after dark."

"When was the last time you saw him?" my master pressed.

"Well, let me see," the proprietor mused, "you know, I think it was the same day that he died. He was with another man. Now that I think about it, there was something strange about the companion. Oh yes, I remember: He was dressed as a working man, yet I caught a glimpse of the pectoral cross on his chest, and he talked and acted just like a clergyman. You see a lot of people in my business, and you get so's you can pick them out, if you know what I mean."

"What did they discuss?" Father William inquired.

"Can't say that I really paid that much attention," Rocambole replied, "except . . . well, they had an argument just as they were leaving. The other man, he said to Lezay, 'You'll do it!' and the monsignor, he kept shaking his head, 'No.' That's all I know."

As we left the shopkeeper's establishment, we brushed by a man entering the place, and he abruptly pressed something into my left hand. I turned to give it back, but Father William grabbed the elbow of my right arm and muscled me out into the street. We marched another block before he asked me to show him the thing. It was a small, rolled scrap of paper, which, when unravelled, said, "*Vendidit hic auro patriam,*" or, "This man sold his country for gold."

"Now *that's* very interesting," was all my master would say, before stuffing the message in his purse.

That afternoon we visited Saint Jude's Church, and spoke to the priest there, Father Ursus, a florid man in his mid-thirties. He told us that Bishop Thoune had been staying with him during his visit to Avignon.

"What was his business with the pope?" Father William asked.

"I'd rather not say," the pudgy priest indicated.

"I have the authority of the Holy Father in this matter," my master noted. "If you wish, I can get confirmation from the papal offices."

"No, that won't be necessary," Ursus responded. "I think it had something to do with your order, actually."

"Indeed?"

"Yes, Bishop Thoune was reporting on the activities of Michael de Cesena, your Father General, operating under the pope's direct instructions," the priest said.

"The Holy Father asked the bishop to spy on our leader?" I interjected.

"Well, yes," he said.

"Why?" Father William inquired.

"As you know," the cleric replied, "Cesena has been criticized for stating that Jesus and his followers owned no property of their own, thereby implying that the Catholic Church and its clergy should follow His example. These views have been deemed heretical by *Papa* John and his cardinals, and so the pope asked Bishop Thoune to, shall we say, watch over the Father General."

"Do you know what he was going to recommend to *Papa* John?"

"No," the priest proclaimed. "He died the day before his audience, and never told me."

He knew nothing else. My master thanked the priest, and we returned to Saint Anaclète's for supper and prayers.

We found our way back to the Jewish shopkeeper the next morning.

"Ah, my very good friend, I have news for you," he chortled, dragging us back into his workroom. "These silver coins, they show the image of King Philip of Syria, surnamed Philadelphus, who died about fourteen hundred years ago."

"Before the time of Christ," my master interjected.

"As you say," Yehuda replied. "But there is something very interesting about these pieces. When the Romans annexed Syria, twenty years after Philip's death, they kept on minting these coins for another fifty years or so, using the same images. They called them tetradrachms, and they were widely employed by the moneychangers."

"How strange, to keep a dead king's face on a Roman coin," Father William mused. "They were common?"

"In Syria, Israel, Mesopotamia," came the response. "Common then, uncommon now."

The shopkeeper reluctantly handed the four coins back to Father Occam, and then added: "I've heard that the Emperor Ludwig will soon name his own pope."

"Making a pope and having him accepted are two different things," Father William noted. "Thank you, old friend."

We were heading back to the center of town when a papal guard approached us.

"Are you Occam?" he inquired.

When my master nodded, the soldier ordered, "Come at once."

We followed him to the Papal Palace, where we were immediately taken to the pope.

"Father Johad is dead!" he gasped, holding out his palm.

On it was a fifth coin, cousin to the other pieces in our possession, and a scrap of papyrus labelled with the number v.

Father William took both pieces, and put them in his purse with the rest.

"Arlan!" the pope yelled quite loudly, and the aide came rushing into the chamber.

"Yes, Holiness," d'Esprit mumbled.

"I want them arrested," came the order, "Jews, gypsies, former members of the Templars, the leaders of the other military orders, all of them. I want them interned by sunset. Round up the usual suspects, and then begin the interrogations at once."

When Father Arlan failed to respond as quickly as the pontiff desired, John shouted: "*Now!* Or you'll be added to the list yourself."

"As you say, Holiness," the aide gushed, hurrying from the room.

"Where are my murderers, Occam?" the pope demanded.

"I'll have them for you within the week," my master indicated, "but first I must view the body of Father Johad."

"Oh, very well," the pontiff grumbled. "Out!"

"I've never seen him like this," Arlan said, motioning to us frantically as we exited the room. "He's going to do himself an injury."

The priest led us to the adjoining cathedral, and thence to a side altar. The body of Johad le Physe sprawled next to a prie-Dieu. A papal guard stood at attention nearby.

"He's not been moved?" Father William inquired.

"No," Arlan noted, "save to inspect his mouth."

My master motioned me to approach. Father Johad's head was lying in a pool of congealed blood. His throat had been sliced.

"What strikes you about this scene?" Father William asked me.

"There's no sign of a struggle, sir," I responded.

"Thus?"

"He either knew his attacker and wasn't afraid of him, or didn't hear him approach."

"Walk over there twenty paces," my master ordered, "and then back again."

As I did so, my sandals made a clop-clop-clop sound on the hard stone floor. But when I removed them, and tried again, there was very little racket.

"I've seen enough," Father William indicated.

Then he turned to the aide: "I would like a pass to the dungeons."

"Whatever for?" Father Arlan responded.

"I want to visit someone there," my master replied.

Then we departed.

That afternoon, we visited a certain Madame Joyaue on the Rue des Putains. I had never been to this kind of establishment before, and was abashed by the accouterments. Several of the female denizens made rude remarks.

"Ignore them," Father William ordered, before we were escorted back to the owner's private office.

"We don't see too many monks here," Joyaue noted. "Bishops, yes, even some cardinals on occasion, but not your sort."

"We haven't any money," came the laconic reply.

"Maybe that's why. What do you want, Father?"

"Sieur Phocion, cousin of His Holiness," Father William said.

"We don't use names here," the madame snickered.

"He was murdered here last month," my master stated, "stabbed, I believe."

"Why should I tell you anything?" she asked.

"Because I carry the pope's authority," he noted, "and if you don't, I'll have you expelled from Avignon."

"Oh, very well," Joyaue grunted. "He was a guest during his visit to our fair city. Of course, we gave him every consideration."

"Of course."

"Amalie found him with a knife in his back."

My master was puzzled. "But aren't the activities here usually carried out with the joint participation of both parties?"

"He liked to watch."

"What?" I asked.

"He liked to watch other people being, ummm, active, as you say. From an adjoining room, peering through a peephole."

"Oh."

"Who else was present then?" Father William asked.

"I have no idea. You think we keep a roster? Ha!"

"Is there any other way into your establishment except the front?"

"Of course," she replied. "The demoiselles enter through the back door, and there's also an escape route in case we're raided."

"Then anyone could have come and gone unannounced and unnoticed," my master said.

We thanked the proprietress for her assistance, and returned to the abbey.

That evening, after collecting our passes from the papal chancellery, we visited the dungeons beneath the civil palace in the center of town. Father William first sought out the cell of Yehuda ben Sion.

"I'm sorry, old friend," he said.

"It's those coins," the Jew responded, "they're accursed."

"How?" my master wanted to know.

"They have a stink about them," the shopkeeper hissed. "You have the implements. Look for yourself, and you shall see."

Then he retreated into himself, moaning about his fate.

Father William next asked the guards to show us the supposed Templars, all six of them, but when he saw them, indicated that he would speak with just one. We waited until the prisoner was isolated before introducing ourselves.

"I know you," the middle-aged man noted.

There was something familiar about the voice. Then it came to me: it was the Grand Master of the Hidden Temple, the masked individual with whom we had dealt a year earlier, when we'd been loaned the Holy Shroud.

"I know *you!*" I stated, and whispered the particulars in my master's ear.

"I thought so," Father William iterated.

"Perhaps you already know too much," the Templar said.

"On the contrary," Father William replied. "Abide me most carefully, good sir. I must have answers that only you can supply, or we may all soon find ourselves in very warm circumstances."

"I cannot reveal any secrets which are bound by oath," the grand master indicated.

"Then tell me whatever you can," my master requested. "Did you or your brethren have anything to do with these murders?"

"No."

"Do you know who perpetrated these crimes?"

"No."

"A year ago, you gave us the Shroud, for which the Templar Order was acting as custodian," Father William noted. "But you also mentioned other ancient 'treasures' that had been removed from Acre when that city fell to the Muslims in 1291. Is this correct?"

There was a pause while the man considered his response.

"Yes," he finally agreed.

"Were any of these taken by *Papa* Clemens and King Philip when they attacked the Templars in 1307?"

Another hesitation, another reluctant, "Yes."

"Can you tell me anything about these artifacts?"

"Not unless you uncover them first," the Templar indicated. "Be very careful, Father Occam. If handled incorrectly, even the Shroud of Our Lord can have a most potent effect on those whose hearts are not pure."

"Thank you for your forbearance," Father William stated. "May God bless both you and your order."

"And you also," came the reply.

When we were leaving, I asked my master if he knew who the Templar really was.

"His name?" Father William said. "I choose not to investigate such matters. Sometimes, friend Thaddæus, it is better to be ignorant of certain realities."

I pondered this response all the way back to the monastery.

*   *   *

The next morning, we sought out Father Arlan again, to gain further insight into the pope's late cousin, Count Boson.

"According to Father Johad's notes," the priest told us, "Boson had been delegated the task of investigating the murders, and had reported to Papa John that an underground remnant of the Templars was at fault. However, although he had the name of a man he thought was involved in the plot, he wanted to capture the leaders, and so asked permission to continue the search. The pope agreed."

"Do you have any record regarding the suspect's identity?" my master inquired.

"Boson just called him '*le prêtre,*' or 'the priest.'"

"What about the count's background?" Father William asked. "What can you tell us?"

D'Esprit thought for a moment. "Boson honorably served both the king and the pope, the latter from his accession nine years ago."

"The king in question was the late Philip the Fourth?"

"Yes, the very one who suppressed the Templars. Actually, now that I think about it, I believe that the count reported directly to Minister Nogaret during those years."

"Ah," was Father William's only comment. "How long did Boson work for the king?"

"I don't know exactly, sir. He did tell me in March that his service for the pope now exceeded his time with King Philip, so perhaps eight or nine years."

"When did *Papa* John ask him to investigate these murders?"

"Why, from the very first case. He was present, you know, when Bishop Thoune died, and so it was only natural that the pontiff would request his assistance, him being a relative and all."

My master pondered this, and then said: "Relate the circumstances of Count Boson's passing."

"He had taken a six-squad of papal guards, as he had done several times before, to arrest someone in the Tournal District," Father Arlan stated. "Father Johad's notes do not indicate specifically who was implicated. The bodies of the count and his men were found in a crumbling house on the Rue des Chèvres, partially buried under a wall that had collapsed onto them."

"I thought there was some kind of deviltry at work," Father William noted.

"There were strange markings chalked on one of the intact walls of the structure."

"Nothing else?"

"No."

"Very well," my master indicated. "Thank you for your help."

But as we turned to go, he stopped and spoke again: "One additional question, if you please. Father Johad was a Blaisean. What about Bishop Thoune and Monsignor Lezay?"

"Dominicans, both," the priest replied.

As we walked back through the city to the monastery, I said, "I don't understand why the clerics' affiliations should be important."

"They are and they aren't," he noted, "depending on one's perspective."

His answer didn't much elucidate matters.

When we reached our cells, Father William directed me to pack up the Holy Shroud and the ancient speculum, a most useful magical tool. I asked him where we were going, and he just said, "Tournal."

The latter section of Avignon was dirty and mean, being occupied by the lowest level of the social strata. Even so, the grim men existing there quickly gave way before the equally grave mien of Friar Occam, and we had only to question two of the natives before being directed to the place where Count Boson had perished. We pulled open the worn wooden door of the house and carefully entered the decaying structure.

"Put the Shroud over your shoulders, Thaddæus," he ordered, and I complied. We could see dried brown patches on some of the fallen bricks.

Father William gave me the speculum and lit a candle. The implement was round in shape and polished to a supernally bright sheen, looking almost green at times. I could not read the runes inscribed on its back. He had me sit in the dirt with my legs crossed under my body, the speculum held upright with its convex side towards me. Then he propped the light upright on a brick a few feet away, gradually adjusting its length to and fro until he reached the proper distance.

"Hold steady now," he said, and mumbled a few words under his breath.

Suddenly I felt the metal vibrate between my hands, and the candlelight seemed to concentrate right at the center of the device, throwing a beam of bright light towards the place where the wall had once stood. Then the bricks jumped from the floor into their former places again—my master whispered in my ear, "Neither speak nor move, Thaddæus"—and I witnessed the ghostly images of seven men fighting with an eighth, all falling down when the wall shook and tumbled 'round them. Then the becloaked image of a ninth individual entered the room, examined the scene, and exited.

I gasped and the light vanished, the speculum tumbling from my limp hands.

"Are you all right?" Father William inquired.

"Yes," I managed to say, "just give me a moment. What was that?"

"An image out of the past," came the reply. "And now, I think, I know enough."

We packed the magical implement and Shroud back in their cases, and I strapped the packs onto my back.

I was surprised to see the light so dim when we finally exited the ruined house.

"How long have we been inside?" I queried.

"Long enough," my master responded.

As we emerged from the alley, a large man suddenly blocked our way, and I heard the rustling of other steps just behind us.

"What mischief is this?" Father William shouted.

"Your death," the man stated, pulling out a knife.

The ruffian lashed out with the edge of the blade, but Father William hit him with his hand, and the stiletto went bouncing away into the gutter.

"Damn you," the man shouted, reaching out with his two large hands. Behind me someone grabbed my shoulder. There was a bright flash and a scream. I heard a shout of "My hand! My hand!" and then the thud of someone falling.

I briefly turned around, but a third attacker was already fleeing, and the one who had accosted me was holding his burned limb, rolling and moaning in the muck of the alleyway. The first man was still lashing out at Father William, but then he too fell to the ground, unconscious. My master quickly searched him, and pulled from his purse a sixth coin and a scrap of parchment marked VI.

"*Voilà!*" he stated.

Then we went home to Saint Anaclète's, where I secured the Shroud in its resting place. Friar Occam sent a note to the papal chancellery, requesting a meeting with the pontiff on the morrow. Then he went out by himself for a few hours, while I fell into bed, totally exhausted. I think he returned in the early evening.

*   *   *

His Holiness was his usual acerbic self, being flanked on this occasion by his new chief assistant, Father Arlan, and several of the papal guards.

"Well, what do you have?" he questioned.

"You asked me to investigate the murder of your nephew, Count Boson, and several other individuals associated with you," Father William replied.

"Yes? Yes?"

"I have some answers for you, which you may or may not wish to hear," my master continued, "but first, you must give me your solemn promise that you will immediately release any of those arrested by your guards this past week, who are innocent of these crimes."

"Perhaps they're guilty of something else," the pontiff indicated.

"Perhaps we're all guilty of something in the eyes of the Lord," Father William noted, "but that is for God to decide, not man. You will release them, or I will tell you nothing."

"Very well," *Papa* John reluctantly agreed, "I do so promise. All of the prisoners except those actually charged with these crimes shall be freed by sunset today."

My master nodded his head, and thought for a moment how best to begin his presentation.

"This puzzle has been one of the most difficult that I have yet encountered," he stated, "involving five victims, or eleven if we count your guards, and several murderers."

"Several?" the pope queried.

"Indeed," Father William agreed, "and we must examine each crime separately to arrive at the best possible solution.

"First, we have Bishop Thoune, who mysteriously choked to death at a dinner given in his honor at Saint Jude's Church. Curiously, at least one other victim, Count Boson, attended this celebration. Who else was present at this function, Father Arlan?"

The priest was taken aback by this sudden interrogatory.

"W-well," he stammered, "I think Monsignor Lezay was there, and perhaps Father Johad, too."

"Bishop Thoune choked on something. What happened then?"

"We all rushed to help him, and someone called for a physician. It was chaos, utter chaos," the aide responded.

"Think carefully, now. Who reached the body first?"

"Uh, well, it was Monsignor Lezay," Arlan stated.

"Who else gathered with him around the *corpus*?" Father William pressed.

"I think . . . well, Count Boson, myself, Father Johad, Sieur Phocion . . . why, they're all dead, all except me!"

"Yes," my master noted, "all of the future victims were present. We know that Thoune was poisoned, and the pertinent question, of course, is why. Holiness, I believe that you had given him a task to undertake on your behalf."

"He was asked to monitor the political activities of Father General Cesena," the pontiff responded.

"Indeed," my master agreed, "and this initially misled me, as I briefly considered the possibility that a Franciscan had been responsible for the bishop's murder. Thoune might have been preparing to report something scurrilous about the order at the audience with you scheduled for the very next day. But then I considered the reality of the situation: What could he possibly have learned about Cesena that wasn't already general knowledge? The Father Superior is a public figure; his opinions are well known.

"No, it had to be something else, something potentially dire to one or more of the individuals already present at the dinner. I think that Bishop Thoune accidentally uncovered someone in your entourage, Holiness, who was selling information about the papal court to a third party, possibly the Emperor Ludwig, your avowed enemy."

"What!" the pope exclaimed. "This is preposterous! Who could it be?"

"Actually, it was Monsignor Lezay," Father William said.

"But he was one of the victims," I protested, unable to contain myself.

"Indeed," my master agreed, "but that in itself is not an impediment. We have just heard how the monsignor was the first person to reach Thoune. I had already noticed that the parchment taken from the bishop's mouth was the only one not discolored by saliva. Lezay displayed to his frantic audience the scrap and coin that he had supposedly removed from his victim's mouth, but they had never actually been there."

"Yes, he was the one who found them," d'Esprit admitted.

"Also, I discovered yesterday that Lezay's background is completely unknown. I researched him in the Papal Archives, but found nothing in his file beyond the date that he first joined the Dominicans, less than a year after the dissolution of the Templars. I could tell by the creases in the folder that many more documents had once been included therein, but everything else had been removed. I suspect that as a young man Lezay had joined the Templars, perhaps as a squire. When King Philip attacked and suppressed the order in 1307, Lezay escaped by changing his name and affiliation, as did so many others."

"I knew the Templars were involved!" the pope exclaimed.

"Philip's nefarious minister, Nogaret, coordinated the assault on the Temple," my master went on. "Their goal was the seizure of the vaunted Templar treasure, which we now know consisted mainly of various religious artifacts from the time of Christ, which have little monetary value. But was the Shroud the Templars' entire trove? I think not. I believe that Nogaret found something else in the Paris Temple, and gave it to the king, who perished along with *Papa* Clemens in 1314, just months after they had burned Jacques de Molay.

"Somehow, this confiscated treasure found its way back into a collection of church documents and materials relating to the Templars. Naturally, when Lezay joined the Papal Chancellery, he became curious about the risk that its files posed to him, and so he investigated and purged his own. At the same time, he found something completely unexpected in the archives—the Templar treasure—and he removed it.

"And then, when he realized last month that Thoune's pending report to the pope posed a direct threat to himself, he killed the bishop, using one of the powders that he purchased from an apothecary on the Rue Fortunée. Someone at that shop, another phantom murderer, gave me a slip of paper that said, *Vendidit hic auro patriam*—'This man sold his country for gold'—in a blatant attempt to throw suspicion on Lezay, but it was nothing but the truth.

"Lezay himself used an artifact from the Templar treasure to place blame on the long-suppressed order, thinking that someone from the old regime might well recognize the piece. His ploy proved more successful than he ever could have anticipated.

"Count Boson was also present at the dinner for Bishop Thoune. Boson had been a runner for Nogaret in his early years, and had seen the coins then, perhaps even handled them. He immediately recognized the one from Thoune's mouth, and asked you, Holiness, to allow him to investigate the crime, which he believed was connected to the Templars."

"Then, why was Sieur Phocion killed?" the pontiff asked.

"That puzzled me for a long time," Father William admitted, "but I finally decided that Lezay murdered him merely to throw Boson off the scent. Two such deaths, plus a demand that Your Holiness resign, constituted a major conspiracy against the papacy, instead of something accomplished primarily for personal benefit."

"Then who killed Lezay?" Father Arlan inquired.

"Count Boson, of course. He was a better investigator than anyone knew, including himself. He suspected everyone, not just the Templars, and had Lezay's quarters secretly searched. Of course, as soon as he found the artifacts, he knew the name of the killer. He decided to pressure Lezay into revealing his accomplices, but the man proved obstinate. The beating perhaps went too far, and then the count was left with a body to hide. Thus, he maintained the fiction of a Templar conspiracy by putting another of the coins into Lezay's mouth.

"However, Lezay's partner and fellow spy wasn't sure whether or not his friend had betrayed him, and so he lured Boson and his men into a trap, rigging an old wall to collapse upon them. He stole the coins, and continued the fiction of a Templar conspiracy."

"What about Father Johad?" the pontiff asked.

"He was beginning to ask uncomfortable questions about Count Boson's investigation, having inherited the man's notes, and came to believe, or at least hint, that something about the scenario was just not right. He communicated that suspicion to the wrong person, thereby signing his own death warrant."

"And who was this accomplice?" Father d'Esprit pressed.

"Why, that would be you," my master stated. "Father Johad knew his murderer intimately, and never felt any anxiety about being alone with him. It was, I might say, a serious lapse of judgment."

"Seize him!" the pontiff ordered.

"But . . . but," the man sputtered, as the guards grabbed his arms and hauled him away.

"He will reveal everything by the time my interrogators

have finished with him," the pope said. "Now, then, Father Occam, what exactly was this treasure?"

"The thirty pieces of silver paid to Judas Iscariot for the betrayal of Our Lord Jesus Christ," Father William replied. "It taints everyone who touches it, being accursed by God for all time. The Templars found the cache in Jerusalem, and hid it away from the world, hoping to limit its influence, but it destroyed them in the end, as it destroyed King Philip, Pope Clement, Monsignor Lezay, Father Arlan, and many, many others. I will search d'Esprit's possessions and find the rest of the coins, and then secrete the treasure somewhere safe. With Your Holiness's permission, of course."

"As you say," he ordered. "Now go and leave me in peace, Father Occam."

"And the prisoners?" my master posed.

"They will be released this afternoon, as promised," the pontiff indicated. "This audience is over."

"What will you do with them?" Father William asked.

We were talking with the Grand Master of the hidden Templar Order, who had never given us his name, knowing that it was safer for us both if we did not know.

Laid out on a table in front of us were thirty shiny tetradrachms of King Philip Philadelphus, looking as new as the day they had been minted. The Master slowly put them into a leather satchel, and frowned.

"When we left Acre for the last time in Ninety-one, after the Muslims had taken the Holy Land," he indicated, "one of our brethren dumped the coins into the sea, thinking that the curse of the thirty pieces of silver had destroyed our final strongholds in Palestine. Several months later a fisherman on Cyprus cut open the belly of a shark and found the trove. After being plagued with continual ill luck, he donated the lot to the Templars.

"We cannot give the coins away, knowing what they will do to others. They cannot be lost or discarded, without returning to us again. So, I do not have an answer to your question."

"Perhaps I can offer a solution," my master stated.

He motioned me to come forward. I was once again carrying the Holy Shroud of Our Lord Jesus Christ. I removed the cloth and wrapped it carefully around my right hand and arm. Then I leaned forward and picked up one of the coins out of its container.

I felt a surge of energy, and heard a sizzling sound as the metal began to pop and melt and boil away. Thirty times I accomplished this deed. Thirty times we said a prayer for the repose of the souls of those who had been tainted by these accursed coins.

When the last of them was gone, I carefully folded up the Shroud and handed it back to the leader of the Templar Order.

"I believe this is yours, sir," I indicated.

"I believe you're right," he responded, smiling at us for the very first time.

INTERLUDE SIX

Rumors of a Templar survival persist to this day. Many say that the origins of Freemasonry—or at least its public surfacing—are inextricably intertwined with the Templars. Some researchers go so far as to quote long lists of grand masters after the death of Jacques de Molay. One of the lists derives from a document known as the Larmenius Charter, in which de Molay nominates as his successor one John Mark Larmenius, a Palestinian-born Templar left behind in Cyprus when de Molay set out for that fateful journey to Paris in 1306. The Larmenius Charter was first surfaced in 1804 by a Frenchman called Bernard-Raymond Fabré-Palaprat, who used it as the basis to validate a non-Masonic neo-Templar organization still extant. Though internal evidence suggests that the document is a later forgery, might it be possible that, despite the "evidence," the document has another story to tell?

Stella Maris

Scott MacMillan

The small signals room of the submarine was slowly fill-ing with water. Sinclair had no idea how long they'd been on the bottom; it could have been a few hours, or even a day. All he knew for certain was that they'd been on a reconnaissance run along the Turkish coast when there had been a loud bang accompanied by a shuddering groan as the sub rolled heavily to port and began to slide down by the stern.

As the boat slammed stern-first into the sea-bed, he'd been thrown backward against one of the bulkheads and knocked unconscious. As he slowly came to, sprawled in nearly a foot of water, he knew they were in trouble—nose-up at a thirty-degree angle, the whole craft listing crazily to the port side, and with only a few lights still on. Struggling to his feet, he could hear the panicked shouts of the crew and smell the raw diesel fuel that was pouring through the inner hull from rup-tured fuel lines in the engine room.

Moving down the narrow gangway was impossible. Sea-men pushed and clawed their way forward toward the bow in a desperate struggle to outrun death as the C46 slowly filled with water. Wedged in the signals room, Sinclair waited for the blind panic to subside. Once the crew had gained the temporary haven of the forward torpedo room, he shoved himself out into the gangway and cautiously worked his way aft toward the sub's control room.

Amidships, the stern-end of the control room was already under several feet of black, oily water. Lieutenant Compton-Hall was face-down on the deck, one corner of the upturned chart table driven into the back of his head. The helmsman was slumped over his wheel, his labored breathing coming in ragged gasps.

Shaking his head, Sinclair moved to the small desk bolted to the bulkhead and found the submarine's log, opened it, and took a pencil from his pocket to make a final entry: *14 March 1914—HMS* Mohle *struck by unknown surface craft two miles off coast of Turkey.* He paused for a moment as the bow of the ship began to slowly settle. *All souls lost.* He looked up at the ship's clock, and continued the log entry. *1200 hrs/ Lt. Alistair Sinclair, RN.*

Having made the final entry, he tore a blank page from the back of the log book and wrote a brief note to his wife and still-to-be-born child. With the water now over his knees, Sinclair folded the note and placed it in the breast pocket of his coat. From an overhead bin he pulled out a lifejacket and set it on the desk. He then carefully wrapped the log in its waterproof oilskin pouch and tied it securely to the front of the lifejacket.

Satisfied that the log was secure, he put on the lifejacket and turned toward the conning tower. As an afterthought, he went back to the desk and, using a key attached to his belt by a gold chain, unlocked the small drawer under the writing surface. Inside was a Webley service revolver. He hesitated for a moment, then stuffed the revolver in his pocket. Shooting, he had decided, was preferable to drowning.

The submarine gave a final lurch and settled onto the floor of the Sea of Marmara, a giant cloud of mud swirling up to veil its death throes from all but the eyes of God. Inside HMS *Mohle*, Sinclair was pitched forward and only barely managed to grab hold of the conning tower ladder before the lights went out. The distant screams of the crew were drowned in the roar of the sea as it flooded into the ship.

The conning tower was nothing more than a wide metal pipe containing a ladder that led to a hatch opening onto the bridge deck, outside the submarine. His plan was to climb to the hatch, open it, and float to the surface where, hopefully, his body and the submarine's log would be recovered. Somewhere, between leaving the submarine and reaching the surface, he would place the barrel of his revolver in his mouth and pull the trigger. . . .

Clinging to the ladder, surrounded by the dark silence of the lifeless vessel, Sinclair tried to remember what he had been told about escaping from a downed submarine. He had to wait until the water had filled the conning tower, then turn the lock and push up on the hatch.

Not that it mattered. By his own estimate, the ship had settled in at least 250 feet of water. Perceived wisdom was that anything over a hundred feet was the realm of Davy Jones. But he had to try.

Shivering, with the cold sea water nearly to his neck, he struggled to reach above his head to the wheel that would undog the hatch. It spun easily in his hands, the well-greased gears withdrawing the bolts that secured the hatch in its down-and-locked position. In the few seconds that remained, as the water rose to his neck, he took a final deep breath, filling his lungs with what little air remained in the bubble trapped above him, then pushed.

The hatch swung outward on its hinges in a final burst of air bubbles, and Sinclair found himself outside the HMS *Mohle*. Holding his breath, he heaved himself clear of the bridge deck-railing and began rising toward the surface, but too slowly. As the submarine receded beneath him, he fumbled for the revolver, but the life vest and log book now were blocking its access.

In a panic he tore at the life vest, trying to get at the gun, his lungs beginning to burn in his chest. Frantic, he could feel the fire as a great, white-hot light building up behind his eyes. He was drowning, and he knew it. His silent scream was carried away on a flotilla of silver-green bubbles that raced ahead of him toward the surface of the sea. With dimming vision, he watched in awe as they sped toward heaven. Then everything slowly went black.

"Where?" asked the man with the iron-grey beard, who was obviously in command of the ship.

"Over there, sir, just off the starboard side." The sailor pointed to something floating in the water about fifty yards distant.

"Send someone out and, if he's alive, haul him aboard."

"Swim, sir?" The sailor looked incredulous.

"Have we another boat?"

"No, sir, but—"

"Then put your best man in the water, give him a rope, and haul them both in," the bearded man said. Then, as an afterthought, "Either dead or alive."

Turning, he walked back to the command deck and dropped down into his heavily carved chair. Running powerful hands through his thick grey hair, he shook his head.

Why, he thought as the sailors scurried on the cramped deck to carry out his orders, *why is it that sailors can't swim?* It was as alien a concept to him as the thought of a knight who couldn't ride a horse.

"Well?" he bellowed. "What's the delay?"

"I'm sorry, sir, but no one can swim that far," came the sailor's sheepish reply.

"Sweet Mary!" he exclaimed. "Piers? Piers! Get yourself on deck right now!"

A moment later, a well-built young man in his early twenties came sliding down from the rigging.

"Sir?"

"Piers, there appears to be a man in the water." The bearded man pointed in the vague direction of where he supposed the man to be. "Over there. Can you bring him in?"

"Yes, Sir Charles." And without another word, Piers stripped naked, mounted the top railing and, with a quick scan of the sea, dove into the water.

Sir Charles watched as the swimmer cut through the water with a series of powerful strokes until, finally, he reached the floating man. With a wave of his arm, Piers signaled the ship and began to swim back with the man in tow. When both had been hauled aboard, Piers was handed a rough blanket and a cup of wine to ward off the chill of the sea while the seamen clustered around the other man just pulled from the water. Though unconscious, the half-drowned man was breathing, but his appearance was most unusual.

"Stand back!" Sir Charles barked, and the sailors fell back as if pushed by a giant hand.

"You and you." He pointed to two sailors. "Take him below."

As the sailors scrambled to obey the order, Sir Charles walked over to where Piers was pulling on his loose-fitting shirt.

"Follow them down," he said, "and see that they don't steal

anything. Once they've left, strip him and lay everything out for my inspection. I'll be down directly."

Piers nodded as he cinched up his belt and adjusted his dagger. "You two," he called to the pair carrying the unconscious man. "Take him to my cabin."

Below decks, the two sailors heaved their charge onto a narrow cot pushed up against one wall near Piers's hammock. One of them, a short, swarthy fellow with heavily scarred hands, started to reach into the man's pocket, but Piers's voice stopped him cold.

"Theft is punished by cutting off the hand," came the warning from just outside the door. "But in your case I'll also geld you like a pack horse."

"I was just—"

"And liars have their tongues cut out," Piers finished. "Now, get out."

The men left, and Piers closed the door. Turning back, he looked at the man he'd pulled from the sea, then set about stripping off the odd-looking clothing as ordered.

On deck, beneath his blue-striped canopy, Sir Charles stood beside his chair and brooded. Thirty years at sea had taught him that sailors were a superstitious lot at the best of times, and he wondered how much longer he could rely on them to obey his commands. Finding that man in the sea would be regarded as an omen. Bringing him on board might have been a mistake. If anything went wrong . . .

Feigning indifference, he made his way below decks to see what he could learn.

In Piers's tiny cabin, Alistair Sinclair lay naked on a cot, shivering beneath a blanket. On a small table bolted to one bulkhead, his possessions were spread out for inspection, his wet clothes somewhat folded and stacked on the deck. On a chest at the foot of the cot was the life vest with the log still tied to it.

"Well?" Sir Charles asked.

"Not much, but what there is, is very interesting." Piers spread out some coins on the table. "Only a few coppers, some silver—and four gold. But look at this." He handed Sir Charles one of the gold coins. "Look how finely struck it is." Sir Charles studied the coin closely. "I've never seen any like it."

"Nor have I," Sir Charles admitted, handing back the coin.

"And there's this," Piers continued, holding up Sinclair's pocket watch. "It appears to be a very small clock."

Sir Charles slowly let out his breath as he stared in frank amazement at Sinclair's gold half-hunter, then drew his brows together in a frown. "Tell me more."

"I don't know what this is," Piers said, indicating the life vest, "but his clothes, although very strange, are exceedingly well made. And he wears a lot of them. Boots, stockings, undergarments, a shirt, some sort of knit jerkin—and over all of that, this." He indicated Sinclair's uniform jacket and trousers. "He wears more clothes than most possess."

Sir Charles folded his arms, deep in thought. "Throw the boy back in the sea," he said after a time.

Inwardly Piers bristled at the word "boy." The man he had rescued looked to be his own age and Piers, although not a knight, did not consider himself to be a boy.

"I think, sir, he is a nobleman," Piers replied.

"Why so?"

Piers wondered how the best naval commander in the world could sometimes fail to grasp the obvious.

"Well," he began, "aside from his clothes, and the gold and silver coins in his pockets—oh yes, and the clock—he has a gold ring on his left hand—I couldn't get it off—bearing a coat of arms. . . ."

For the first time Sir Charles turned to actually look at Sinclair.

". . . and he is fit. Very fit. As well fed and well muscled as any noble in Christendom."

Sir Charles drew back the blanket and looked at Sinclair.

"Odd. No scars." He bent down and inspected Sinclair's hand. "Not the hands of a knight, but not the hands of a laborer, either. Maybe he's a priest." He looked at the signet ring on Sinclair's little finger, said nothing, and drew the blanket back over him.

"And, Sir Charles, there is this." Piers reached under Sinclair's uniform jacket and drew out his revolver. "I think it may be a weapon."

Sir Charles took the Webley revolver from Piers and turned it over in his hands several times before gripping it by its chequered walnut stocks.

"Hmm. A weapon. Well, it's heavy enough, although I don't see how it could do much damage." He handed the revolver back to Piers. "Still, best not to let him have it if he comes around."

A rattling cough from Sinclair interrupted Sir Charles.

"Will he survive?" Sir Charles asked.

"He's swallowed a lot of water. There is a chill on him, and his face feels as if it is on fire," Piers said.

"Is he going to live or die?" Sir Charles asked again.

"I don't know," said Piers. "I really don't know."

"Then I'd better tell Larmenius," said Sir Charles, turning his broad shoulders to step through the narrow doorway.

Back on deck, Sir Charles paused to gaze up at the aft castle rising above him. Around him, the sailors went about their work—grudgingly it seemed, almost as if they would prefer capture by Algerian pirates to continuing their voyage.

He looked up at the rigging. *Well,* he thought, *with no*

lookout on the mast, they would be fair game for any ship that sighted them.

Then with a shrug he climbed the ladder up to the castle deck.

It had been four years since Sir Charles and six of his brother knights had sailed their galleys from Cyprus to Greece. During that time much had happened, including the perfidious betrayal of his beloved Order by an avaricious king and a spineless, captive pope. Even though suppressed, and in some kingdoms hunted, the Order of the Temple was far from dead. Although their traditional lines of communications were interrupted, Sir Charles still received excellent intelligence about the fate of his Brothers, as well as regular reports as to the condition of their imprisoned Grand Master, Jacques de Molay.

The latest news concerning the Grand Master had reached Sir Charles only a week previously, brought to him by the redoubtable Piers.

It had been a moonless night when Piers's sleek vessel had bumped against the side of the Templar galley as it lay at anchor off the western coast of Cyprus. Neither of the lookouts saw the boat as it drew into the lee of the galley, nor did they see it a few moments later when a dozen men in black turbans strained at the oars and the vessel silently regained the open sea.

If Piers had been an assassin intent upon taking Sir Charles's life, he could have sent him to the Almighty and slipped away long before any alarm was raised. Instead, once he had gained the knight's cabin, he lightly twisted the old warrior's big toe and suppressed a laugh as Sir Charles awakened with a roar.

"By the Holy Saints—"

"No, sir," Piers interrupted. "By way of the fastest boat on

Mare Nostrum. With this." He handed Sir Charles a leather tube, its strap and buckle sealed with wax impressed with the sigil of the pope's chamberlain.

Now fully awake, Sir Charles took the tube to a low table where an oil lamp of Eastern design gave off faint light. Pulling a second closer, he lit it, then placed the two of them next to each other. Behind them he positioned a well-polished silver mirror and, by adjusting it on its stand, managed to reflect enough light to read by. Breaking the seals on the tube, he pulled off its cap and from within withdrew a single page of carefully rolled vellum.

In the pale light cast by the lamps he could make out the coded cyphers written in a neat chancery hand. Twenty years on the deck of a galley had taught Sir Charles to read the Templar fleet code as easily as he could read his own native language. More complex than the simple code used to communicate with the land-based commanderies of the Order, there had been a time when perhaps a dozen Templars commanding the galleys might have unlocked its message without the aid of a key. Now . . .

Rather than dwell on the unpleasant, Sir Charles focused his attention on the neatly drawn symbols carefully arranged on the vellum. The news wasn't good. De Molay, fearing for the life of the Order, had secretly named his successor. It was only a matter of time before he would retract his confession and suffer the consequences. Once de Molay was dead, the signal would be given for the remnants of the Order to rise up and turn their fury on the King of France.

Turning the thin goatskin over, Sir Charles held it to the light and, starting at the right hand bottom corner, began to read right to left, bottom to top, lining up letters on either side. Unlike the news of de Molay, this message was written in a code known only to Charles and the other six renegade commanders. Despite the mass of figures, numbers, and letters on the front of the vellum, this coded message contained only two words: *pac ni.*

Smiling grimly, Sir Charles set aside the vellum and picked up the cap of the tube from where it had fallen from the table onto the deck. Using the point of his bodkin, he carefully unpicked the stitches around the top of the cap. There, carefully pressed between two pieces of thick bull hide, he found a second message. Written on ivory-colored silk, the same fine chancery hand instructed him to proceed to the North coast of Cyprus, there to take on a passenger. That the second message was written in Arabic did not surprise Sir Charles at all. Such was not the case when he first saw his passenger two days later.

Ioannes Marcus Larmenius, Preceptor of Cyprus, stood dramatically at the end of the pier, armor polished, the scarlet Templar cross emblazoned across the whole of his white silk surcoat, his right hand resting on the pommel of a great two-handed sword. Behind him was a mountain of baggage attended to by several slaves in red and white turbans. Nearby, more slaves in red and white turbans looked after several well-fed horses belonging to their master. To those assembled on the dock, Larmenius appeared the very model of the perfect knight.

He was, in Sir Charles's opinion, the most detestable runt in the bad litter that had become the minor nobility of the Kingdom of Jerusalem. Short of stature, effete of manner, with squinting blue eyes, his parents had bought him a place in the Order of the Temple, conniving to have him knighted on the day before he took his first vows of profession. This he did in the presence of his mother, various snot-nosed relatives, and several members of the clergy whose moral integrity was questionable, at best. Sir Charles had been present, and from the moment he first saw Larmenius, he disliked him intensely.

Larmenius, for his part, equally detested the sight of Sir Charles, but for an entirely different reason. He could never be certain that at some less-than-propitious moment, Sir Charles wouldn't recognize him as the young lad, shirt up, he had surprised with Brother Emil in the choir of Saint Saviour's church, some twenty-five years previous. In truth, Sir Charles had so focused his fury on pummelling Brother Emil into the Next World that he hadn't paid the slightest attention to who was with the hapless religious—Larmenius, after all, wasn't exactly facing Sir Charles when discovered—or how the boy managed to escape by crawling through the choir stalls and dashing out into the street beyond. Still, Larmenius didn't know this, so he had gone to great pains to distance himself from Sir Charles whenever he was in close proximity.

This mutual dislike, added to the orders Larmenius had handed Sir Charles when he boarded the galley, did nothing now to hasten Sir Charles on his way to report having pulled the stranger from the sea. He smiled as he climbed the stairs to the castle deck, as the ship rolled on a light swell. Ensconced in the two small rooms that made up the solar of the aft castle, Larmenius would feel each roll of the ship magnified tenfold. Sir Charles allowed himself a quiet chuckle.

Serves him right, he thought. *Nothing like a touch of sea sickness to put one of these Lords of the Levant in their place.*

Outside Larmenius's door, he could hear the combined sounds of moaning and retching, followed by the sort of screeching curses usually associated with bawdy women in taverns. With a deep breath, he knocked on the door, then entered.

Even with the shutters latched back from the arrow slits, the tiny room was dark and thick with the odor of stale vomit. Barely visible in the gloom, Larmenius hung over the side of his bed in the corner of the room. Kneeling next to him was one of his slaves, holding a large copper basin. The ship rolled, Larmenius heaved, and the slave did his best to keep the basin in position. All things considered, he did his job tolerably well.

"Brother Larmenius," Sir Charles said.

"What?" said Larmenius, as he regarded the older knight through watery eyes.

"We sighted a man floating in the water." A moan interrupted Sir Charles, and for a moment, it looked as if the basin might be required again. "I had Piers bring him on board."

"So?" Larmenius propped himself up on one elbow. "I feel like I'm dying, and you come in here to tell me about some half-drowned sailor. Get out, and throw the man back into the sea."

"I think you should see him first," Sir Charles said. "Although he's strangely dressed, I think he's a nobleman."

"Strangely dressed? Like those Genoans with their hats and—" He threw himself over the side of his bed and, to the relief of his slave, merely belched. "God, I am dying. . . . All right, bring him here."

"I can't," Sir Charles replied. "He's unconscious, and burning with fever. Piers doesn't think he'll live."

Larmenius puked. "*He* might not live? What about me? Sweet *Jesu!* If this nobleman lives, bring him here." He propped himself up again. "If he dies before I do, throw him back to the fishes. Now get out."

Back on the deck, Sir Charles stood on the gallery, both hands on the railing, and watched the sailors, wondering which one of them would betray them to the Algerian pirates, or lead the others in a mutiny. One thing was certain. He doubted very much that any of them would willingly sail where Larmenius's orders would take them. And, until the

Preceptor of Cyprus was able to command the ship, all Sir Charles could do was lie at anchor.

"Well?" Sir Charles asked as he came into the cabin.

"It's been three days," Piers replied. "He rambles a bit when the fever takes him. Sounds something like English, but not as we speak it."

"Might he be a Scot?"

"Possibly. I've never met one."

"Well, I have. Uncouth lot of ruffians, gave old Longshanks more war and less pleasure than any people on earth." He looked at Piers. "Do you suppose he'll live?"

"I was about to ask the same about our Preceptor. I haven't seen him since he came on board."

The man let out a low groan, and Piers turned to place another damp cloth on his forehead.

"Don't worry, he'll survive," Sir Charles said. "And apparently, so will this one."

"I think his name may be Sinclair," Piers said, leaning closer as their patient opened his eyes.

The sound of his name focused the reviving Sinclair, and a momentary look of bewilderment came to his eyes.

"Where am I?" he said in a weak voice. Mustering what strength he had, he tried to sit up, but fell back on the bed.

Piers immediately put his arm around Sinclair's shoulders and helped him into a seated position. "Just take it easy," he said. "You've swallowed half the ocean."

For a moment Sinclair stared at the two strange men next to his bed, then said in halting, school-boy French, "*Vous êtes Français?*"

"The question, sir, is where are you from?" Sir Charles asked.

Sinclair understood the rough Norman-French, and replied, "Edinburgh," before collapsing back on his bed.

Great, thought Sir Charles. *A Scot.*

Piers, on the other hand, seemed delighted at the opportunity of meeting an uncouth ruffian from Scotland. "I do believe he's going to make it," he said with a smile.

"Yes," said Sir Charles. "As soon as he can talk, find out what you can, then we'll take him to the Preceptor." He started to leave, then turned back. "Assuming, of course, that the Preceptor will be seen."

When Sinclair next came to, Piers was sitting next to him.

"Here," he said, lifting a spoon from a bowl of thick stew, "eat this." Sinclair did as he was told, and by that afternoon was well enough to feed himself.

"So," Piers said, as Sinclair mopped up the last of the stew with a chunk of bread, "would you mind telling me how you came to be adrift in the sea?"

"My ship went down," Sinclair said as he handed Piers his bowl. "Would you—mind handing me my clothes, please?"

Piers set down the bowl and reached to where Sinclair's clothes were neatly stacked on a chest by the door, setting them on the foot of the bed. "So what happened?" he asked.

"We were rammed by another ship," Sinclair said as he began to dress. "I was below deck, and we went down almost immediately. I can remember opening a hatch to get out, and then I was swallowed up by the sea." He tugged on his trousers. "The next thing I knew," he indicated the tiny cabin with his chin, "I was here."

"I see," Piers said. "And where did you come from?"

"We sailed from England about a month ago. My ship was part of a larger fleet sailing to Egypt and Palestine." Sinclair finished tying his shoes. "Now, if you don't mind, can I ask you a few questions?"

"Not at all," Piers replied.

"For starters, what sort of ship is this?" Sinclair pulled his thick turtle-necked sweater over his head. "Some kind of fishing vessel?"

Piers gave him a wry smile. "You are on what may well be the last galley under command of the Military Order of the Poor Soldiers of Christ of Jerusalem."

"A galley, you say." Sinclair smoothed back his hair, looking confused.

"That's right. Although there's no one to man the sweeps. The crew can only just manage her under sail, which puts us at a real disadvantage in a fight." Piers stood up and went to the door. "Perhaps you'd like to meet the captain?"

On deck, Sinclair was stunned by what he saw. The galley was squat, and broad at the beam. The decks were low, with the sweeps—long, broad-bladed oars—lashed together amidships. Both the bow and stern were adorned with what looked, for all the world, to be two miniature wooden castles, complete with arrow slits and fluttering pennons. On the deck below, several deeply tanned men in red and white turbans were quietly grooming horses while more than a dozen of the crew idly looked on.

As Sinclair took it all in, a large man with close-cropped iron-grey hair and a shaggy beard came up the stairs leading to the half deck. Without so much as a glance at Sinclair, he went over to Piers, who was still in the doorway.

"Well," asked Sir Charles, "what have you found out?"

Piers quickly recounted Sinclair's version of events, and then added, "Oh yes. His name is Alistair Sinclair and you were right, he's a Scot."

"What tongue does he speak?" Sir Charles asked.

"French and English dialects, mostly. He's easy enough to understand, if you pay attention."

"Well, let's hope the Preceptor can pay attention long enough to decide what he wants to do." Turning to Sinclair, Sir Charles beckoned to him. "Come with me."

One of Larmenius's red and white turbaned slaves stood just outside the low door of the aft castle. At the approach of Sir Charles and Piers with a stranger, the slave blocked the door with one muscular arm. The tuft of hair under the arm was blond, and the slave's eyes a deep blue. When he spoke, his words were accented not by the lisping whisper of the Arab, but by the more guttural sounds of a European.

"You are to wait until my master is ready," he said.

Inside the aft castle, the Preceptor's two rooms were as austere as those of any other Templar, with three exceptions. On the floor was a pale-blue silk prayer rug. Above it hung a lamp of Byzantine gold work, set with colored glass oculi that cast splotches of red, blue, and green onto the walls of the small room. Directly below the lamp was a reliquary, also of gold, its sides pierced by arabesques forming a grill through which could be seen a glimpse of the object of adoration.

Larmenius was kneeling on the prayer rug, facing the shrine, his head bowed onto the soft blue silk, when the muffled voice of the slave outside his door interrupted his devotions. Rising slowly from the rug, he carefully placed the reliquary into an olive-wood box, then placed it in a small chest next to the door. Rolling up the prayer rug, he set that in the chest next to the olive-wood box. Satisfied that all was right, he closed the lid of the chest before opening the door.

Outside, the slave continued to bar the door with his arm, moving it only when his master spoke.

"Ah, Sir Charles. You have brought a guest." And with a gracious gesture, he bade them to enter. Sinclair entered with the others, ducking to avoid cracking his head on the low door. Once they were in the small chamber, Larmenius drew up a low chair and sat down. For a moment he regarded Sinclair, then:

"Tell me, Master . . ." he glanced at Piers.

"Sinclair," Piers offered.

"Tell me, Master Sinclair, can you read and write?"

"Yes," Sinclair said. "I can."

"Latin?" Larmenius asked.

"No, only English and some French," Sinclair answered.

"Excellent," Larmenius said. "I'll put you to work copying my letters immediately." He rose from the low chair, stepped between Sir Charles and Piers, and opened the door onto the deck. "Now if you two will leave us, we have work to do." And with a flip of his wrist, he indicated they were to leave.

Once they were alone in the room, Larmenius went to his chest and took out a quill and inkhorn and also a neatly folded leather wallet. Opening the wallet, he removed a folded letter and several sheets of finely prepared vellum. These he laid on a small oak table secured to the wall beneath one of the arrow slits. Sinclair, seeing what was required, brought over the chair and settled in at the desk.

"Now," began Larmenius, "here is what I want you to do." He unfolded the letter and smoothed it out on the desk. "I want you to copy this exactly, letter for letter, word for word, and line for line. Do you understand?"

Sinclair nodded.

"Good. Except I want you to make one little change." He pointed to the letter. "Do you see where it says *Conrad von Regensberg*?"

Again Sinclair nodded.

"I want you to write this name instead," and from the wallet he pulled a scrap of parchment on which was written *Ioannes Marcus Larmenius* and handed it to Sinclair. "Do you think you can do that?"

Sinclair studied the letter and the slip of parchment for several seconds, then said, "It won't fit."

"What do you mean, it won't fit?" Larmenius's voice had gone up in pitch, if not volume.

"This name," Sinclair held up the scrap of parchment, "won't fit." He pointed at the name on the letter. "See? Too many letters."

Larmenius studied the two names, then took the pen and wrote *Marcus de Larmenius* on the scrap of parchment. "There," he said. "Use that, instead."

With a shrug, Sinclair began the tedious work of copying the letter.

On deck, Piers and Sir Charles had moved out of hearing range of the slave before talking.

"What do you make of that?" Sir Charles said with a jerk of his head toward the aft castle.

"I don't know," Piers said. "These legates are pretty much a law unto themselves."

"True enough, but that doesn't explain why he didn't ask you to copy the letters," the older man continued.

"Because I can read and write Latin," Piers said.

"But, what would Larmenius have to hide from you?" Sir Charles asked.

"Not from me," Piers said. "From the king."

Sir Charles's brow knitted into a deep frown. What Piers said was true enough. Only cats have nine lives, and if he were ever to fall into the hands of the King of France, it was certain that the king's torturers would extract every last bit of information from Piers before he ended up on a pyre, or was dumped into the Seine.

That's why Piers, a *courier avant,* could never know the content of the messages he delivered. Torture him they might, kill him they most certainly would, but the king would never learn the secret of his mission. Larmenius was another kind of cat. He was a legate.

Legates were the last real link that the remnants of the Order of the Temple had with the Pope in Avignon. Working through a network of intermediaries, legates were able to communicate by *couriers avant* with the papal court, as well as send messages to fugitive Templars. While their exact number was not known—some said it to be as many as nine, while others believed it to be only three—the legates wielded immense power, as they controlled the treasury of the order. Even though most of the income of the Templars had been stopped, the actual wealth they had accumulated was such that the legates could buy—or sell—kingdoms, or ransom a pope.

While held captive of the French king, the pope had been coerced into betraying the Templars, and while some had died and some been absorbed into other orders, a few, like Sir Charles and Piers, had remained loyal to both the pope and their order. Taking to the hills like brigands, and to the sea like corsairs, over the years since the mass arrests in France, these fugitive Templars had conceived many a bold plan, one of which now met with the pope's favor.

Simply put, twenty-five knights were going to capture the pope as he set out for Paris. Riding hell for leather, they would make for the coast, and there the pope would be put aboard Sir Charles's galley. With a full crew filled out by the escorting Templars, the galley then would make for Ostia on the Italian coast, where, still guarded by Templars, the pope would be placed on a barge that would carry him up the Tiber to Rome, safely beyond the reach of the French king. If they were successful, the pope would pardon the Templars and reconstitute the order. With the Templar army his to command, and their treasure his to dispose of, the pope would be able to assert his paramountcy over all the secular rulers in Christendom. If the plot failed, and they were caught by the king, the pope could claim to have been taken by force of arms and made to act against his will. The Templars would suffer the consequences.

The whole plan had been conceived in secrecy, and as Sir Charles knew, secrecy was a coin whose reverse side was treachery. Now he was sailing his galley to France to rescue the pope, and in so doing, he tossed Fortuna's coin, not knowing if it would land with treachery facing up.

With a shrug, he descended the steps down to the main deck and settled into his captain's chair beneath its blue and white striped canopy.

Piers watched Sir Charles descend the stairs, then idly turned his attention to the slaves that had accompanied Larmenius when he boarded the galley a week previous. Mostly, they were lounging on the deck and looking attentive, and avoiding the sailors at their work.

Piers guessed that they were, for the most part, in their late twenties or early thirties, only slightly older than himself. Well-muscled and deeply tanned, only one of the them, shorter than the rest, appeared to be of Eastern origin: swarthy, with the thick, stocky build of a mason. The others Piers took to be Europeans, probably captured as children, sold as slaves, and raised to become Mamelukes. In that, at least, his own life had not been greatly different than theirs, for he, too, had been raised to become what he was—or what he was meant to have been.

Over the past hundred years or so, his family had given the Templars donations of land, and provided both men-at-arms and knights, when needed. As the youngest boy of five children, it had been decided that Piers would become a Templar, as had his cousin and a distant uncle. So, in addition to the usual skills taught to the sons of the English nobility, Piers had been schooled in reading and writing, as well as in mathematics. These skills, his father thought, would assure Piers rapid advancement in the Order.

But all of this careful planning had come to naught. When Piers was fifteen, two dreadful things had happened. His father, one of the barons who opposed the extravagance of King Edward, was killed in a skirmish with the king's army. That same year, the Order of the Temple was suppressed in England, and Piers, too young yet to be knighted and make his vows to the Temple, had found himself without a purpose.

Unlike many younger sons, Piers had some land—a demi-manor which was his, free of enfeoffment. The land was worked by vassals, and for a while Piers had toyed with the idea of working the land himself. In fact, he recalled, if his sister Avril hadn't teased him about becoming "Piers the plowman," he probably would have settled down to farming.

Instead, he had headed down to Oxford and, for several years, continued his studies until, late one evening, as he was about to wade across the River Cherwell and set out on the road to London, he had come by chance upon two fugitive Templars hiding in the rushes. Within weeks, he and the Templars had made it to the comparative safety of Spain.

Piers had lived the next three years in a state of constant adventure, proving himself to be not only intelligent, but highly resourceful. In the shadowy world that was all that remained of the once mighty Templar empire, his courage and loyalty had quickly marked him out as one of the trusted ones. And so, when the time had come, he was the one chosen to carry the message that would rally the knights to the pope's rescue.

Now, he could not say precisely why he had become uneasy. Perhaps it was the Mamelukes, idling on the decks: a potential danger, if Larmenius had some secret plan of his own. He wondered what it was that Larmenius was having Sinclair copy. Hoisting himself up onto the aft deck, he settled himself next to some of the coils of thick rope stored there and reclined to wait, eyes closed against the Mediterranean sun.

In Larmenius's quarters, Sinclair finished the first copy of the letter.

"How is this?" he asked, passing the copy to the other side of the table.

Larmenius took the copy and carefully compared it to the original. "Excellent," he said, then set the original letter on a smoldering brazier in the corner of the room. He watched as it began to curl up and slowly burn. "Now do another," he said, handing the copy back to Sinclair.

"Perhaps tomorrow," Sinclair said.

"Tomorrow?" Larmenius's voice arched. "Excuse me, Master Sinclair, but I don't believe that is your decision to make."

"No, it's your decision. If you want a copy as good as that, I'll start in on it tomorrow," Sinclair said.

"I see," said Larmenius. "The choice is between good and fast. Well in that case," he smiled at Sinclair, "one of my Mamelukes will bring you here in the morning. Now get out."

Sinclair had no more than stepped out onto the deck when Piers called out to him. Sinclair looked around to see where the voice had come from.

"Up here," said Piers, sitting up between the ropes so that Sinclair could see him. "I thought you'd never finish."

"I've more to do tomorrow," Sinclair said as he climbed up toward where Piers sat. He stuck his hand out. "Give us a hand, will you?"

Piers grabbed Sinclair's hand and helped to pull him onto the topmost deck. "So what has our high and mighty lord of the Levant got you doing?" he asked.

"Making exact—and I mean *exact*—copies of a letter." From his vantage point high up in the stern, Sinclair cast a practiced eye over the whole of the ship. "She could take more sail," he said.

"Probably. Why do you suppose he's having you make those copies?" Piers asked.

"Probably because he can't write," said Sinclair.

"No," said Piers. "He can write." He looked at Sinclair for a long moment. "It's just that he doesn't want the copies in his handwriting."

Sinclair stared out to sea and let Piers's words sink in. "I suppose, then, that when I'm finished, he'll have no further use for me?"

"I think that about sums it up," Piers said.

"And why tell me this?" Sinclair asked.

"I don't know," Piers said. "Maybe it's because, having pulled you from the sea, I feel responsible for you."

"Well then, maybe you can tell me who this is." He handed Piers the scrap of vellum that Larmenius had written his name on.

Piers glanced at the name on the vellum. "Larmenius is your friend with the letters. Why?"

"Because he had me substitute this name for another one in the letter I'm copying," Sinclair said.

"Do you remember the other name?"

"Not really. It was German, I think."

"Could it have been Conrad von Regensberg?" Piers asked.

"Yes, that's it. How did you know?"

"Because Regensberg is the titular head of the order as long as the Grand Master is held captive by King Philip. If anything were to happen to the Grand Master, Regensberg would automatically succeed him."

"So, where's Regensberg?" Sinclair asked.

"It doesn't matter," Piers said, avoiding the question. "If Larmenius gets the pope to issue a new bull of foundation for the Order . . ." his voice trailed off.

"And you think that's why I've been asked to make the copies?" Sinclair said. "So that Larmenius can become head of the Order?"

Before Piers could answer, the door to Larmenius's quarters opened, and he stepped out onto the deck.

"Sir Charles," he called.

"Aye," came the reply.

"I need to see you."

With a silent groan, Sir Charles pushed himself out of his chair and climbed the stairs to the aft castle where Larmenius stood waiting.

"How many days sailing to Marseilles?"

"In this weather?" Sir Charles eyed the almost cloudless sky. "Not more than four days—probably three, if the wind freshens."

A quick smile flashed across Larmenius's face. "Good. Slip the anchor, and let us get on with it."

"All hands to the rigging!" Sir Charles bellowed. "Make ready to sail!"

Below, the order was repeated and the crew moved into action, hauling up the anchor and scrambling up rigging. Larmenius watched for a time, then turned and went back into his quarters. When they were underway, Piers left Sinclair and dropped from the top of the aft castle onto the gallery, then made his way down to the deck where Sir Charles stood. Marseilles was no more than a day's ride from Avignon—and the pope.

From his vantage point in the galley's stern, Sinclair watched as the crew went about its work. During his naval training at Dartmouth, he had spent six months on board one of His Majesty's ships with sail, so he could appreciate what was going on. Although no way as efficient as "proper sailors," as Lord Jellicoe had termed them, the galley's crew brought her under sail with little in the way of wasted motion. Larmenius's slaves stayed out of the way and merely watched, though at least they did not get in the way. After a while, when the ship had settled into what appeared to be their set course, at least for a while, Sinclair retired to his cabin to puzzle out what had happened in the past few days. It was very nearly dark when Piers came in and swung himself up into his hammock.

"Hungry?" he asked, as Sinclair stirred in the cot opposite him.

"Yes," he said through a yawn.

"I thought you might be. Here." Piers handed him half a chicken. "I've got some wine, too."

"Thank you," Sinclair said, as he tore the leg from the chicken.

The room was quiet for several minutes, then both men spoke at the same time.

"Sorry," said Piers. "You were about to say?"

"Oh. I was going to ask you where your home is, that's all."

"My home. Well, I suppose you could say that my home is here on this galley," Piers said. "For the time being."

"You must live somewhere, Piers," Sinclair said, before taking another bite of the chicken.

"Not really. My family is in England, but my home is wherever the Templars send me."

"The Templars." Sinclair's tone held notes of disbelief and bewilderment and despair. "I'm sorry, you were going to say something before I cut across you," he said.

"Well, I was wondering if you had given any thought to how you were going to get home. That's all," said Piers.

"Well," said Sinclair. "I've given it a lot of thought, but I don't think I'm going to make it back to Scotland."

"Why not?"

"It's a little hard to explain. Let's just say that I wouldn't know how to get home even if I knew where I am." Sinclair took another bite of his chicken. "Did you say you had some wine?"

Piers handed the bottle to Sinclair in the dark. "Got it?"

"Thanks." Sinclair took a drink of the musty red wine.

"Well," said Piers, "in two or three days we'll be off the coast of France, some little way west of Marseilles. There's a fishing village there, where we have to meet someone." He put his hand out into the darkness. "Wine?"

He waved his hand about until he felt the bottle Sinclair held out to him. "Sir Charles thinks that you should leave the galley then," he said, before taking a drink. "Provided you are still alive. Here," he passed the bottle back in the darkness.

The moon moved from behind a cloud, and a thin sliver of light lanced across the cabin from the arrow slit. It was enough for the two men to just make out one another.

"That's a comforting thought." Sinclair took another drink from the bottle and set it on the deck. "And where do I go from there?"

Piers sat up in his hammock, swinging his legs over the side, and reached behind his head to untie a leather thong that passed around his neck. Dangling from the thong, glinting in the faint light, was a silver cross in the shape of a star. He handed it to Sinclair.

"Here. Take this," he said.

Sinclair sat up on his cot and took the cross from Piers's outstretched hand.

"What is it?"

"It's called *Stella Maris*. Sailors believe that it will always guide you home. Show it to any sailor, tell him where you are going, and he'll do his best to help you get there."

Outside, the moon had moved behind a cloud again, and Piers was swallowed up in darkness. "It has never failed me."

Sinclair tied the leather thong around his neck. "Thank you."

The next morning the seas were rough, with a wind driving up out of the east. With the March winds came a chill, and Sinclair found himself pulling on his uniform jacket to keep warm.

"Going to Larmenius's cabin?" Piers asked from his hammock.

"Yes, although it's probably too rough to do any copying," Sinclair replied as he smoothed the front of his jacket.

"Then you'd better take this." Piers reached above his hammock and withdrew Sinclair's Webley from between the overhead beams. "Here," and he tossed Sinclair the gun.

"I thought I'd lost this in the water," Sinclair said as Piers dropped to the deck from his hammock.

"If you don't mind my asking," Piers said, "how does that work?"

"I'll show you," said Sinclair. He opened the revolver and dumped the bullets into his hand, then snapped the gun closed again. "Here," he said, and offered the gun butt first to Piers.

Piers took the revolver and held it awkwardly in his left hand, unsure what to do with it.

"Now," said Sinclair, as he adjusted the gun in Piers's hand, "put your finger here, like so." He placed Piers' index finger on the trigger. "And pull."

Piers pulled the trigger, and the hammer of the Webley rose, then snapped down on an empty chamber.

"Try it again," Sinclair said.

Piers pulled the trigger another half dozen times. "Is that all it does?" he asked.

"No," replied Sinclair. "When it's loaded with these," he held up a bullet, "it goes off with a bang, and this lead bit here hits your enemy hard enough to wound or kill him."

"Can I try it?" asked Piers.

Just then the door was opened by one of Larmenius's Mamelukes.

"Come," he said, pointing at Sinclair.

"Your shooting lesson will have to wait, I'm afraid," Sinclair said. And with a wave he followed after Larmenius's slave.

The table in Larmenius's room was ready for Sinclair when he arrived, with parchment, inkhorn, and pen set out below the copy of the document that Sinclair had made the day before. Larmenius was lying on his bed in the corner of the room, obviously discomfited by the motion of the galley as she rode out the heavy winds and rough sea.

"Can you work in this weather, Master Sinclair?" Larmenius asked.

"I'm willing to try," was his reply.

"My lord!" Larmenius shot back. "You will address me as 'my lord' when you speak to me."

"I'll do no such thing," Sinclair said in an even voice. "I'm an officer in the Royal Navy, not your flunky. Sir."

"I do beg your pardon," Larmenius said stiffly. "I wasn't aware of that." He said nothing as Sinclair settled at the little table and took up his pen. After a little while, he ventured another conversational gambit.

"This weather," he began, "is both a curse and a blessing."

"Really, sir?" said Sinclair, as he tried to write while the deck pitched below him. "In what way?"

"Well, the wind will have us off the coast of France ahead of schedule, which is a blessing," Larmenius replied.

Well, thought Sinclair, *Piers was right about that. France, and from there . . .*

"Damn!" he said, as a drop of ink fell from the pen onto the parchment.

"A problem?" Larmenius asked.

"Ink dripped," said Sinclair, as he carefully blotted it up with the cuff of his jacket, a trick he had learned at the Royal Naval College—had it only been eight years ago? "Nothing serious, sir."

"What are you called in the Royal Navy, Master Sinclair?" Larmenius asked.

"Lieutenant Sinclair, sir," came the reply.

"Well, Lieutenant Sinclair, as I was saying, the wind is both a blessing and a curse. The curse is that I will need two more copies of this letter before we reach France." Larmenius paused for several seconds, but Sinclair made no reply. "I know this is very tiring work, but I wondered if I might persuade you," Larmenius clapped his hands and a Mameluke entered from the adjoining room, "to complete all of the copies before we complete our journey?"

With a gesture from Larmenius, the slave placed a small red leather bag drawn closed with tasselled green cords on the corner of the table where Sinclair was working. "I thought thirty golden bezants might speed you on your way to Scotland?"

"I'll do my best, sir." Sinclair didn't look up from his work. "And thank you."

With the aid of his Mameluke, Larmenius got to his feet and wove his way into the adjoining room, leaving Sinclair to continue his task. Outside, the wind was dying down and Sinclair could feel the galley becoming more steady beneath him. According to his pocket watch, it was almost ten o'clock. He would have light enough to work by until five, at least. That gave him seven hours to make two copies—more than enough time to complete the task.

The problem was, as soon as he had finished the final copy, Larmenius would in all likelihood have him killed, and his body dropped over the side. For a moment Sinclair allowed himself the luxury of being angry at himself for having left his pistol with Piers. Then, realizing that self-pity would get him nowhere, he returned his attention to his task. And as he worked, carefully copying the letter, he slowly hit upon a plan.

He had copied nearly all of the document when he stood up and stretched, arching his back and flexing his fingers. With several shrugs of his shoulders, he pushed back the low-backed chair he had been sitting on, and walked over to the door.

His hand was no more than on the latch when the Mameluke with Larmenius darted forward and pinned Sinclair's arms to his side.

"Stay," he said.

"Excuse me, sir," Sinclair called out to Larmenius. "But even your horses need to be fed."

"You are hungry?" Larmenius asked.

"Yes, I am. Would you like me to bring you back some cold

mutton?" Sinclair tried to shrug off the grip of the Mameluke, but failed.

What little color remained in Larmenius's face drained away. "Cold mutton . . ." A shudder ran through his body. "Let him go," he ordered, and the Mameluke released Sinclair.

"I'll be back presently, sir," Sinclair said, and then he was out the door.

Sir Charles was on the top deck supervising the loading of more sail when Sinclair approached him.

"Excuse me, Sir Charles, but when do you think we'll reach Marseilles?" he asked.

Sir Charles's eyes never left the sail. "We won't."

"Won't what?" Sinclair replied. "I don't understand."

"We're passing Marseilles." Sir Charles gave Sinclair a quick look. "But if you can swim, we will be there before nightfall."

Sinclair knitted his brow.

"Don't worry," Sir Charles said, in a lower voice. "Either Piers or I will tell you when to jump." And with that he returned his attention to the sail.

Sinclair nodded his thanks and made his way below deck to the cabin he shared with Piers. He had planned to enlist Piers's help in carrying out his escape, but the young man was nowhere to be seen. That being the case, all Sinclair could do was load his revolver, put it in his pocket, climb into his life-jacket, and wait for the signal to go over the side. That, and hope that they would be close enough to land that he could swim to the shore. What he'd do once he reached Marseilles—well, that would have to be decided later.

As Sinclair stood lost in thought, the Mameluke who had been with Larmenius stepped into the room, and for a moment Sinclair thought that he was to be killed on the spot. The Mameluke made no hostile move, but stood a menacing few feet away from Sinclair, watching him intently.

With as casual an air as possible, Sinclair reached over to

the chest next to his bed and picked up the half-eaten carcass of the chicken he had been given the night before. Looking around on the floor, he found the unfinished bottle of wine and, with that and the chicken, made his way past the Mameluke and back up onto the deck. There he settled into a corner and proceeded to take his lunch.

When he had finished his meal, he returned to Larmenius's quarters in the aft castle solar. The guard at the door let him pass, and once inside Sinclair set about the business of finishing the first letter. He had been working for about fifteen minutes when Larmenius came in from outside.

"How much longer?"

"Nearly finished," Sinclair replied without looking up, and then as an afterthought, "sir."

"And the next copy? How long?" Larmenius sounded impatient.

"A few hours," Sinclair said. "I would hope to be finished before it gets dark."

"And how was your meal?" Larmenius asked.

"The chicken was cold," Sinclair handed Larmenius the finished copy he had been working on, "and the wine was awful."

Larmenius compared the two letters. "Yes," he said. "Greek wine, filthy stuff." He handed one of the letters back to Sinclair. "This is excellent work. You're sure you want to go back to Scotland?"

"More than anything else, sir," was Sinclair's reply.

"Well, you're certainly earning your pay." Larmenius picked up the pouch filled with gold coins and handed it to Sinclair. "I wouldn't leave this lying around."

Sinclair took the pouch and placed it in his breast pocket, where it made an obvious bulge. "Thank you, sir," he said, and inked his pen to begin work on the next copy.

Sinclair had been writing for the better part of an hour when Larmenius came to look over his shoulder.

"My, but you are getting quicker, aren't you?" he said.

"Yes, sir. It seems to be flowing a little easier," Sinclair replied.

"Good," said Larmenius. "Then you won't mind leaving me alone for the next ten minutes or so, will you?"

Sinclair closed the cap on the inkhorn. "As you wish, sir."

Outside, on the deck, Sinclair couldn't believe his good luck, and made straight for his cabin. Knowing that one of Larmenius's Mamelukes would probably be arriving within minutes, he lost no time in closing the door behind him.

Looking around, he didn't see his pistol. He went over to where Piers had retrieved it from the overhead beams, only to find it nestled in the hammock. Quickly he opened the revolver and fed the six rounds into the chambers of the cylinder. Snapping it closed, he stuck it in his pocket, changing it for the bulging bag of gold, then grabbed his life jacket—the log of the HMS *Mohle* still securely tied to it—and headed back out the door, almost colliding with the expected Mameluke.

Before the man had time to react, Sinclair was past him and up the stairs that led to the open deck. Instead of returning to the aft castle, he walked briskly forward and, as he reached the gallery deck, opened a small door on the starboard side. As luck would have it, the ship's head was empty.

Stepping inside, he closed the door and threw the bolt that locked it to the outside just as the Mameluke reached the far end of the gallery. Sweet refuge, lest the Mameluke attempt to take away his lifejacket.

In his quarters in the aft castle, Larmenius carefully spread out his prayer rug and then removed the reliquary from its olive-wood box. Setting it down on the end of the pale blue silk rug, he knelt before the golden shrine in a posture of abject submission, then straightened to carefully open the grill work that surrounded this most holy object and stare at it in near rapture.

Inside the intricate shrine, the hollow eyes of a desiccated head returned Larmenius's worshipful gaze. Slowly he closed the gates that protected the head, and once again fell prostrate before the shrine and began the recitation of the prayers of his forbidden sect of the Prophet.

Hugging the precious life vest to his chest, Sinclair waited while five minutes slowly dragged by. Finally, he closed his watch with a snap, threw back the bolt on the door, and emerged from the head.

"Your turn?" he said to the Mameluke, and walked slowly toward the stern.

When he reached Larmenius's door, he found his way blocked by the same slave who had denied access to his master's room the day before. Slowly Sinclair extended his hand and, under the baleful gaze of the guard, knocked quietly on the door.

"Enter," came the voice from within.

The red and white turbaned guard bowed slightly to Sinclair and allowed him to pass. Following immediately behind was the Mameluke who had dogged Sinclair's heels from the head in the fore castle.

"What is this?" Lamenius said, indicating the cork lifejacket that Sinclair was carrying.

"It's for my back," Sinclair said. "Sitting in this chair all day has given me a cramp."

"Let me see it," Larmenius said.

Sinclair handed it over.

Larmenius looked it over for a moment, then pointed to the words stenciled on the jacket.

"What is this?" he asked.

"It's the name of my ship." Sinclair pointed to the words, HMS *Mohle*. "And this," he said, pointing to a set of numbers, "is the ship's registration."

"And what is such a thing used for?" Larmenius asked.

"Officers wear them when they are copying charts, so their backs don't get stiff." Sinclair looked at Larmenius, and reached out his hand. "If I may, sir. It's getting late, and I still have work to do."

Larmenius started to hand back the lifejacket, then pointed at the oilskin pouch holding the HMS *Mohle*'s log book.

"And what is this?" he asked.

"A record of all of my voyages," Sinclair answered. "If you want, I'll show it to you."

"Not now," Larmenius replied, handing him the lifejacket. "When you have finished, perhaps."

Sinclair strapped on the lifejacket and settled down at the table. Dipping the pen into the inkhorn, he resumed the task of carefully copying Larmenius's letter. He had been working for nearly an hour when a great commotion broke out on deck.

Almost before he knew what was happening, Larmenius's outer guard opened the door and shouted something in what must have been Arabic. Instantly Larmenius and his personal slave sprang from the adjoining room with swords drawn. As they rushed to the door, Sinclair stood up as if to join them.

"Keep working!" shouted Larmenius, and he was out the door.

For a moment, Sinclair actually considered finishing the document, then he heard Piers shouting on deck. Without another moment's hesitation, he drew his pistol and pulled open the door.

The Mameluke guarding the door turned, and Sinclair brought the barrel of his pistol down hard on the man's forehead. The Mameluke staggered back, blood gushing from a great gash just above his eyebrows. Before he could recover, Sinclair struck him again, and this time the slave went down.

With a jump, he was over the downed Mameluke. He raced across the gallery deck and stopped at the top of the stairs that led down to the main deck. Below him, surrounded by

Larmenius's men, Piers lay on the deck. Over him a swarthy, thick-set Mameluke stood poised with a sword, ready to plunge it into Piers's throat at the first sign from his master.

There was no time to think, only react. Sinclair cocked his pistol, took careful aim, and squeezed the trigger. With a sound like a clap of thunder, the big Webley bucked in his hand, and the Mameluke was slammed back against the mast.

The silence that followed was profound. For a moment no one knew what happened, then Piers leapt to his feet, grabbing the dead Mameluke's sword.

"Jump, Sinclair, jump now!" he shouted.

"Where?" he shouted back. "Which side?"

Piers sprang up onto the gunwales, his sword pointing to starboard. "There. France is that way!" he shouted. "Jump!"

On the deck, the Mamelukes looked at Larmenius. Without hesitation, he pointed at Sinclair.

"Take him alive!"

The Mamelukes divided into two groups, one group moving to port and the other starboard. Without a command given, they rushed the two sets of stairs that led up to the gallery deck and the aft castle.

Sinclair moved moments before they did, and ran to the starboard railing. Turning, he fired two shots into the air, but the sound failed to slow the charging Mamelukes. He climbed onto the railing, and aimed at the closest Mameluke. He was squeezing the trigger when a searing white-hot light exploded behind his eyes and he felt himself topple over the railing and fall into the sea below.

Up on the fore castle, Piers leaned over the railing to look in vain for Sinclair, then dived into the sea and, with powerful strokes, made for the distant shore.

"Over there, Charley." The young man's voice was thick with the accent of the Fife coast.

"I dinna see 'im," came the reply from the stern of the small fishing boat.

"Just there, push the tiller to port." The young man heaved away on a set of heavy oars.

"Och, Geordie, I see 'im now. Can ye pull 'im in?"

"Aye, that I can," Georgie said, shipping the oars and reaching down for the boat hook.

Leaning over the side of the boat, he managed after several tries to hook the lifejacket of the man in the water, and with some great effort pulled him into the boat.

"Well, will ye look at that," Charley murmured, as the two of them cast their gaze over their catch.

By the gold stripe on his cuff, the man was a Navy officer, and young—in his early twenties by the look of him, with blond hair and the pale, translucent look of someone who had only recently drowned. Geordie had never seen a dead man before, and began to cry uncontrollably.

"Now there, laddie," Charley said. "You'll be all right once ye start rowing." The old man looked up at the sky and stroked his iron-grey beard. "It looks like weather coming up the Forth. We'd best make for Edinburgh."

Wiping his nose on his sleeve, Geordie gave a nod and heaved away at the oars while Charley steered the *Stella Maris* toward the distant shore.

INTERLUDE SEVEN

Our final story marks the return of that dynamic duo of Peter Crossman, modern-day Knight of the Temple, and his feisty partner, Sister Mary Magdalene of the Special Action Executive of the Poor Clares.

Crossman and Maggie made their literary debut in the first anthology of Templar stories—and so successful a debut it was that I encouraged their creators, Debra Doyle and James D. Macdonald, to develop a novel to showcase further adventures of these delightful characters. This they are in the process of doing. Meanwhile, they have revealed yet another of the pair's case histories. Of the present adventure, they write:

> As medievalists, we've always been fascinated by the legends of various sleeping kings—Arthur is only the most famous of them—who wait in caves and under mountains to wake when their country needs them. And as history buffs, we're interested in enigmas and catastrophes, both of which terms

certainly describe the sinking of HMS *Hampshire* in WWI. (After the war, two different men wrote books in which they claimed to have been the German master spy who had signaled a submarine to torpedo HMS *Hampshire*—in two different ways, at two different times. Needless to say, no records of such a submarine exist.) When we thought about combining the two in a story, it was obvious that only Peter Crossman could deal with the result.

Sleeping Kings

Debra Doyle and
James D. Macdonald

My name is Peter Crossman. Knight of the Temple. Only one of those statements is true, of course, but no matter. It's what you could call a white lie, a venial sin at worst. I have other, worse sins on my conscience, but I'll be going to Confession later on this afternoon.

Monday, the sixteenth, I was finishing up on some relics that someone had offered at an estate sale. The deceased had been one of those rich eccentrics who'll collect anything, from World War One British recruiting posters to pictures made out of beetle shells, and my bosses at the Temple had thought some of the items worth a closer investigation. The thread from Saint Veronica's veil turned out to be a fake, and so did the splinter from the True Cross with a drop of Our Saviour's blood on it. But the paperweight globe containing one of Emperor Vespasian's wasps was real, so I put in the winning bid, helped out by the fact that no one else at the auction knew what the globe really was.

An ordinary mission, in other words. It hadn't really re-quired the talents of one of the three-and-thirty at all, except that if the thread and the splinter had been genuine, all hell could have broken loose, and I don't mean figuratively.

Ordinary mission or no, I was still following Standard Operating Procedures. All that remained was for me to check out the bidders who had laid down some serious green for those other two "relics," and see what use, if any, the buyers had in mind for their purchases.

Like I said, routine. And routine it should have stayed.

The three-and-thirty are the Inner Temple of the Knights Templar. Not even the other Knights know about us. We take our orders direct from Prester John in Chatillon. We're all priests, all warriors, chosen for our skills in both the material and the immaterial worlds. Our mission is the same now as it's always been: to protect the Temple of Solomon and other holy things, and to guard pilgrims. It's a task that won't end until the Last Day. Even then, I expect that when the blessed enter the City of God, the rearguard in the procession will be Templar Knights.

Once the Vespasian paperweight was sent away by secure courier to Prester John at HQ in Chatillon, I requested a tail-and-report on one of the other two lucky buyers while I took the remaining guy for myself—the one with the False True Cross wrapped up in a fancy box. His path took him from southern Connecticut, where the sale had been, down through New Jersey, and back into New York. He handed off the package in midtown to a guy with a moustache, who slid it into a briefcase. I stuck with the goods.

Moustache went into a lunch spot near Twenty-third and Broadway, where he had the antipasto salad and drank ginger ale. He set the briefcase down beside his chair, next to an identical case belonging to a guy in a brown coat sitting at the next table. Brown Coat was having the Cajun shrimp and drinking tea with milk.

When Brown Coat stood up and left, he took Moustache's

briefcase along with him. He got on the subway, I got on the next car. He got off again a couple of stops later, and I picked him up and followed him from across the street.

On Canal he got buzzed into a building. I jaywalked over, let myself inside by hitting all the door buttons at once—some trusting soul buzzed the lock—and got a view of a hallway with an elevator at the end, no other doors. The elevator was ascending, no stops until the eighth floor. It paused there, then returned to the lobby empty. I'd seen Brown Coat buzz for the eighth floor. So that matched.

The lobby board—little white letters on a black-flocked background, under glass—said that the eighth floor belonged to the Kipling Society. I'd never heard of them. A front of some kind, maybe. I reconnoitered out front until way past sundown, but Brown Coat didn't come out.

Well, aside from fact that someone had spent some time and *dinero* on a bit of bloody wood, I didn't see anything to get excited about. Stuff like that happens every day. The only reason that fake relics aren't a dime a dozen on the open market is that the people who sell 'em charge a lot more than a dime.

If the Kipling Society hadn't been playing games with its couriers I would never have given the whole set-up a second thought. But that bit of unnecessary subterfuge had me intrigued. Whatever they were up to, I wanted to know more.

I went back to my hotel, reported in, and awaited results. A bit before midnight I got word that the other relic had arrived by way of a couple of detours at its final destination: the Kipling Society. Okay, two guys, blind bids, games en route. Maybe still nothing, but worth checking out.

Morning found me in the reading room over at the Public Library, looking up the Poet Laureate of Merrie Olde. Rudyard Kipling was born in Bombay on December 30, 1865, son of John Lockwood Kipling, an artist and teacher of architectural sculpture, and Alice Kipling, née Macdonald. He grew up in India, was sent to boarding school in England at age five, and returned to India when he was sixteen to become a journalist and a writer. Back to England in 1889; three years later he married an American and moved to Brattleboro, Vermont. 1896 saw him back in England. He settled in Sussex, where he lived until his death in 1936.

I came out with a sheaf of notes, amounting to zip as far as esoteric links. Kipling had probably been a Freemason, but so was every third or fourth male in England at the time, and their Famed Secrets are available for sale in second-hand bookstores all over the world.

A message was waiting for me from the Temple when I got back to my room, but it amounted to more of the same: negative on the Kipling Society, request denied for additional Temple personnel to be assigned to the case. The Masters hadn't denied me permission to pursue the matter on my own, though, so I figured that as permission granted, and started making my preparations. First step was to call Maggie.

Sister Mary Magdalene usually hangs out in a cloister up in the Bronx or in southern Westchester somewhere—she's always been vague about it, and I've never asked. Maggie's in the Poor Clares, and except for their Special Action Executive—Maggie's group—the Clares don't have a lot of contact with the World. But they do take an interest in many of the same things as the Temple, and Maggie and I have been on the same side in a couple of capers. I knew someone who knew someone who knew the SAE's contact number, and I made the call.

When at last I got Maggie on the line via a secure connection, we swapped small talk for a couple of minutes before I got down to cases.

"So, Mags," I said. "Do you like Kipling?"

"I don't know, Pete," she said. "I've never kippled."

"Ten thousand comedians out of work and you're telling jokes for free. You feel up to a little loft-and-safe work?"

"You wouldn't ask me if it weren't important, would you?"

"Never."

"What's going to be in the safe?"

"If I knew that," I said, "I wouldn't have to look. Doing anything tonight?"

"Nothing that won't wait."

"Meet you this evening, and bring your technical gear." I gave an address and a time, she okayed it, and we broke the connection.

That left me with a little time of my own, so I decided to do the obvious and reconnoiter for a bit. I'd gone into a building blind once, and when the weather is right my shoulder still aches.

A phone booth gave me information, and sure enough the Kipling Society on Canal had a listed number. I decided my cover story was going to be that I was a journalist from Brattleboro doing research on Kipling, assuming that the society was talking about the same Kipling as the rest of us. And if they weren't—well, I'd get information that way too.

The voice on the phone was pleasant and light, belonging either to a woman or to a man with a high tenor. Yes, indeed, the society was dedicated to that Mr. Kipling. Yes, indeed, I could ask some questions. Could I visit? Well . . . she—or maybe he—supposed that I could. There wasn't much to see, though. A meeting room, pretty much.

"I'm staying right uptown. See you soon." I gave my name as Roarke, for no particular reason other than that I had a Vermont driver's license with both my picture and Mr. Roarke's name on it.

"See you." The response wasn't all that enthusiastic.

After that I hung out for a while in the coffee joint across the street. The coffee shop was a good place in which to wait a decent interval before going in, and in fact I waited long enough to start wondering what kind of idiot I was, to be doing this without backup. Visions popped into my brain of meeting Brown Coat or Moustache and having one of them say, "Didn't I see you yesterday?"

Well, it still wasn't too late to back out. I already knew this place was bent. Sticking my finger into a light socket to see if the power was on didn't appeal to me.

What did appeal was going off to talk to a source. I left the Kiplings to wonder what had happened to the reporter from a Vermont rag and made my way over to the soup kitchen near Avenue A. I was looking for a guy I'd seen around there who usually had some good word for us—we were more or less on the same team.

I spotted him sitting outside, enjoying the late afternoon sun. "Ahasuerus," I said. "It's been a long time."

"Not for me it hasn't," he said. "What's the rumpus?"

"Want to go for a walk?"

"Buy me a sandwich?"

"Sure. Got a place in mind?"

"There's a kosher deli up by Houston that I haven't been in anytime this century."

It was a nice walk, and Ahasuerus was chatty as ever. "Hear anything about some guys over on Canal picking up relics?" I asked, as we settled down to some reuben sandwiches, with dill pickles on the side.

"So I should know these people?" he asked. "What, do they look like they talk to bums?"

"Just wondering," I said. "I got a feeling."

"You think you got feelings? I got feelings, because I know what a feeling feels like. You, maybe."

"So you got a feeling?"

"These guys still make good pickles."

"Want another one?" There isn't any sense in hurrying a source. He'll tell you what he wants to when he's ready.

"If it isn't any trouble. You can afford it?"

"No problem. I get paid."

"That's nice. You should have a trade if you can't be a scholar."

"I agree." The pickles were good. Traffic outside was moving well. Not too many people on the street, but not too few. I felt good. The sun was shining.

"Those guys on Canal, I think I know the ones you mean."

I didn't say anything, just let him talk. Took a sip of my water.

"They're looking for relics, but they're looking for one in particular. And here's the funny thing, they don't want it."

"What relic?"

"They're looking for the Spear of Antioch."

I wasn't really surprised. Every two-bit power-seeker for the last two thousand years has gone looking for the Spear of Longinus: the spear that pierced Christ's side, bringing forth blood and water; the spear that had killed God.

"It's in the Hofmuseum in Vienna," I said, and took another bite of my reuben. It *was* good. "Part of the Hapsburg treasures."

Ahasuerus looked at me with a smile, and his eyes twinkled. He looks old—hell, he *is* old—but he's pretty sharp. "Bubbela," he said, "that's what they tell people."

"Yeah, that's what we tell people. So. What else do these guys want besides the Spear of Longinus?"

"I hear they're asking about every schwantz who ever touched it who was a ruler."

"Big long list," I said. "What are they planning to do with it?"

"A prophet I'm not. You want prophecy, ask those three

guys up on the West side. The only guys I ever met who thought I was a Gentile."

"The Nephites moved to Utah over a century ago."

He shrugged. "No wonder I haven't seen them around lately. Well, more than that I can't help you. But this I can tell you, these guys aren't kidding around. And this one other thing: I don't like them."

"Thanks," I said. "Keep your eyes open, okay? And if you see or hear anything that you think I might be interested in, give me the word."

"Yeah, okay."

We stood and headed out to the sidewalk. I slid the old guy a five spot, and walked back to where I was going to meet Mags. Whatever the Kipling Society was up to, it probably wasn't going to work, because their relics were fake—or at least some of them were. No telling how long they'd been collecting stuff, though, and one of the items on their shopping list was the Spear. I sent a high-pri message back to HQ requesting all information on the Kips and on the Spear, with a *chi-rho* statistical distribution on any correlations, and settled down to take a nap. I didn't know when I'd get another chance.

I was awakened by a knock on the door. The light was gone outside. I looked at my watch. Maggie was a little early. When I opened the door, though, it wasn't Maggie who was waiting for me.

"You the guy calls himself Roarke?" the man outside said. He pushed past me into the hotel room, walked over to the mini-cube refrigerator, opened it, looked inside. "Hey, where do you keep the beer?"

"Pub around the corner," I said. "Drinking alone's the road to hell."

"Lots of roads go there, buddy. Want to talk about the one you're on?"

"How about you give me a name? I don't like to talk to guys named Yo."

"Call me Aurelian McGoggin."

"Right, Aurelian." I walked to the corner and sat in the more comfortable of the two chairs in the room; one where I could watch the door. "So tell me a story."

McGoggin took the other chair, turning it around so the back was to me, his arms crossed on the top of it. He'd put it so he had a good view of the door too.

"Just yesterday," he said, "there was an auction."

"I imagine there's one somewhere every day."

He held up a finger for silence. "Let me tell you a story, like you asked. Anyway, there was an auction, and some men were there, and some of them bid on certain things. And these men, they were clever men, and they knew that what they were bidding on wasn't worth much. Not anything at all, truth to tell. But there was a value. They bid against each other, these men. Just to drive up the price. And they watched, and they looked all around, these men. Are you following me so far?"

"So far," I said. I was thinking about that pub around the corner, and about that beer we'd been talking about earlier. A shot would be nice with it.

"Well, these men, they also saw a fellow bidding on a thing that they knew had some value. They didn't say a word. But they marked that man. And do you know what? That same man, he followed one of the bidders! Hard to believe, but he did. Right up to a lobby security camera, he followed. Would you like to see a picture of that man?"

"Not particularly."

"As you please. Well, the very next day, that man called from a phone booth, and before he hung up, he was seen, and followed. Now you know the rest."

"Not all of the rest," I said. "Like why anyone cares."

"The thing of value I mentioned," McGoggin said. "At the

auction. *You're* that thing of value. A man who knows the value of things, is what I'd call you. The auction was to find you, and here you are."

"And what's your interest?"

"The guys who hired me," he said. "They threw a lot of money around. Like it didn't mean anything to them. So maybe it doesn't. But I'd sure like to have some more of it."

"My advice: Take honest pay for a job well done," I said. "What did they hire you to do?"

"Bring you in."

"And you're hoping that I'll match their offer."

"Or maybe better it," he said. "I see that we understand each other."

"Altogether too well," I told him. "If I don't pay up, you'll haul me in—and if I do pay you, then you'll take my money and haul me in anyway. No dice."

"Make it worth my while and I'll forget I found you."

"I can make it worth your while," I promised. "But first, how about you give me a little bit of information?"

"Shoot."

"Who hired you?"

He looked around the room. "The Kipling Society."

"Give me this. 'The Kipling Society' doesn't do diddly. Give me a man's name. A description. So I'll know him if I see him."

"Ah. The man himself. He's named Tomlinson. A tall man, taller than you. Thin. He has brown hair, thinning on the top, but he combs it over."

"Okay." That meant it wasn't Brown Coat or Moustache. Those two were just foot soldiers.

"Now you give a little," he said. "Why do you think those guys want you?"

"They're just naturally curious."

The door opened then, and McGoggin tried to haul iron.

Not sitting like he was with his arms crossed on a chair-back, he couldn't—not before I was out of my chair and pushing down hard on his wrist. A moment later Maggie came in, tall and leggy, flame-colored hair, black sweater and jeans, black backpack, black automatic in her hand.

"About time you showed," I said. "I was afraid I'd have to keep this joker talking all night."

"No, don't stand up," Maggie said to McGoggin, kicking the door shut with her heel. She shucked off her backpack, shifting her weapon from hand to hand while she was doing it, her eyes never moving from the man. Then she came over and sat cross-legged on the hotel-room bed. The pose was spectacular.

"Don't you think you should introduce your friend?" McGoggin said to me after the silence had stretched on for a bit.

"You've got a point," I said. I turned to Maggie. "Who exactly are you today?"

"Mary."

"Okay. Aurelian, this is Mary."

"Enchanted," she said.

"The pleasure is mine," he replied. Not a lad to be fazed by staring down a gun barrel, then.

"What's the plan?" Maggie asked me.

"Well, Laughing Boy here has screwed the pooch for part one. You have any ideas on where we can stash him?"

"The East River?" she suggested.

"My conscience is clear for the moment, and I'd like to keep it that way."

While I talked I was patting down my new friend. He had a snub-nosed .38 Smith & Wesson in his left armpit and a .22 Deringer strapped to his right ankle. Either he was the extra-careful type or he just plain liked firearms. His wallet had a hundred and twelve bucks in cash, and ID in the name of William Sprague, as well as a private investigator's license and a concealed carry permit in the same name. He had a key ring with four keys and a handful of change in his right-hand pants pocket.

"So, Billy," I said after I'd tossed most of his possessions up on the bed next to Maggie but out of his reach—I didn't need either of the weapons, and taking the money would have been stealing, but the key ring went into my coat pocket for more investigation later. "What do you want to talk about?"

"My time is yours," he said. "But I do have a usual hourly rate, plus expenses."

"I assume the guy who hired you is already paying for this hour, and the expenses will cover that stuff." I nodded toward the pile of his gear over on the bed. "But I *will* pay for some straight answers. Who really hired you?"

"I told you."

"I'm getting tired of this," Maggie said. "Let's shoot him and get it over with. I have better things to do."

"Not right now, Mary," I said. "Let's see if he can be reasonable."

I wasn't even fooling myself. I doubted this guy would go for the good cop/bad cop routine. No one said anything for a minute.

"Look. Here's the deal," I said. "I'm going to let you go."

"Say what?" That was Maggie.

"I'm welling up with Christian charity." I nodded toward McGoggin—or Sprague, if his ID was telling the truth. "Get out of here."

"What about my stuff?"

"You're not in a position to worry about it. Go."

As soon as the door closed behind her, Maggie turned to me and said, "Pete, I don't know what kind of party you invited me to, but it's been fun so far. What do you have?"

"Nothing," I said, leaning my head back and closing my eyes. "A feeling."

The phone rang—it was a secure line from Chatillon. Repeat negative on the Kipling Society. All secure on the Spear, location known, nothing unusual. And a query from higher up as to what I was working on.

"I'll give you a report in the morning," I said. "A confidential source tells me that the Spear's in play."

"Your next assignment will be coming in at ten hundred New York time," the duty officer told me. "Something's going down in the Orkney Islands, and Headquarters wants you to check it out—so whatever you've got cooking in the Big Apple, you've got until tomorrow to turn it into something solid, and that's it."

"Roger that," I said. "I'll be switching lodging now. I'll report in when I'm at the next location." I broke the connection.

"Now, Mags," I said. "Let's try the streets of lower Manhattan for entertainment, shall we?"

The street out front was as deserted as it gets in those parts, which isn't very. A beggar was standing next to the hotel door. I dropped the hundred and twelve that Sprague/McGoggin had given me into the guy's basket.

"When did the Temple start paying you guys that good?" the beggar asked, and looked up from under his hat. It was Ahasuerus again.

"Call it a gift from a friend," I said.

"The friend who left a couple of minutes ago, checked suit, looked like he just ate a lemon?"

"That's the one."

"I've been asking around," he said. "You know that he was with the Kipling Society for a couple of years, and he's headed back that way."

"I didn't know that. Thanks."

"Not a problem. Who's the lady?"

"Friend of mine. Maggie, I'd like you to meet Ahasuerus."

She looked puzzled for a minute. "Have we—?"

"No," he said. "I never forget a face. One of my other curses."

"The Wandering Jew," I explained to Maggie. He'd been one of the people standing around as Christ went off to be crucified. Sort of like Joseph of Arimathea, only this guy had wound up remaining on earth until Christ comes again.

"At your service," Ahasuerus said.

"So, what brings you over here tonight?" I asked.

"Lunch was so good, I thought maybe we could have supper." He looked down at the big wad of money in his bowl. "I'm buying."

It was hot dogs with kraut and mustard, with pretzels and soda—from a pushcart vendor, this time. It was good.

Maggie looked from her dog to Ahasuerus. "I know what you're thinking," he said. "I could have saved up something by now. I tried that. You know something? The same man lives in the same mansion for a hundred years, people notice. The same man sleeps on the same steam grate for a hundred years, who cares? Less *tsuris* this way."

After we'd finished up, Ahasuerus said, "You know the Spear?"

"It's okay."

"Bet me. I know where it is."

"Canal Street."

"For a young man," Ahasuerus said, "you're pretty smart."

I decided to ignore the compliment—in part because I wasn't sure it was one. "One other thing," he said. "Whatever's happening, it'll be soon. They're making their move. The Spear and one other thing are coming into the building tonight, and none of them made any plans for tomorrow."

I looked over at Maggie and said, "So, what do you think? Frontal assault or a sneak and peek?"

"Hey diddle-diddle, right up the middle," she said.

I nodded agreement. "One of those keys I lifted from our

pal back there undoubtedly opens the right lock—and I get tired of sneaking around."

"So do I," said Maggie. "Let's go."

Minutes later, we were down by the street grating in front of the building where the Kipling Society had its headquarters. The grating was diamond-tread steel, and brown with rust. The lock on it, by contrast, was big and silver; and there was a big silver key on Sprague/McGoggin's key ring.

One thing led to another, and in short order the delivery opening in the sidewalk was open. Maggie and I walked down the iron stairway that led beneath the building.

"You coming?" I called back to Ahasuerus, but he'd vanished again, becoming one with the shadows. I couldn't tell if he was following or not.

"Interesting fellow," Maggie said. "Does he sleep out on the streets year 'round?"

"I don't know," I said, pulling out a red-lensed flashlight and shining it into the darkened space before me. "I've never seen him sleeping."

The red beam from the flashlight showed us a door, bolted on our side—keeping something in, not something out. I tried the bolt. It slid back quietly: It had been oiled. I pulled the street trap shut, laying the padlock on the top step against future need, and pushed the inner door open.

The basement in front of us was open, and dimly lit by overhead glows. I killed the flashlight, stepped in, took a step to the right, and flattened against the wall. Maggie came through the door behind me, moving like a shadow, up against the wall to the left. Her pistol was in her fist. I pulled out my own rod and cocked back the hammer.

The room ahead of us had a set of tables in it. Seven of them. Six of the tables were draped with sheets, and I could make out human forms under the sheets. That just couldn't be good.

A doorway loomed, black and empty, on the far side of the room. I looked over at Maggie. I pointed at her, at myself, and then at the door. She nodded, and started inching around the perimeter of the room, going left, her back up against the wall. I went right, brushing the plaster with my shoulder blades. To the corner, a right angle turn. I was getting close to one of the sheet-draped bodies. The basement wasn't that cold, but there wasn't any smell of rot or corruption, or any chemical smell of preservation.

Maybe, I thought, the shrouded forms weren't really bodies. I tugged on a corner of a sheet, just to see.

They were.

I pulled the sheet a little further away from the face of the man on the table, and I saw then that he wasn't dead, just sleeping. He was a big man with a grizzled beard, and he wore a rough tunic, with a silk overmantle, red embroidered with a crown in gold. He stirred, raised an arm—I saw gold rings on his fingers, and the glint of rubies—and rolled toward me. He yawned.

Then his eyes opened, and he whispered in a reedy voice, "*C'est le temps?*"

I recognized the language: Old French, close to Latin but with a German overbite to it: *Is it time?*

"*Non,*" I whispered back. "*Allez dormir.*"

No. Go to sleep.

He yawned again, stretched, and his eyes closed. He lay back again. I was getting a bad feeling. The Spear of Longinus. And a sleeping king.

The world is full of legends of kings and heroes who never died—who sleep instead, and remain sleeping until their country or their people need them. Kings like Holger Dansk in Denmark, Arthur in England, Frederick Barbarossa in Germany, or Charlemagne in France. The last I'd heard,

Charlemagne had been sleeping under Nuremberg Castle. It looked like someone had winkled him out.

Now that I knew what to listen for, the room was full of faint breathing sounds. Seven is the number of completion, they tell us, and here were six sleeping kings. Collect the whole set and . . . and what?

Another corner, another turn, and the door was coming closer. Maggie was coming up along her side of the wall, keeping pace with me. She looked bad in this light, and I suppose I wasn't looking all that chipper myself.

By now I could tell that something big was going on, down here in the basement of the Kipling Society. When we arrived at the far door, I stood against the wall to its left, and Maggie did the same on the other side. I pointed to her, to myself, and then to the door. Held up three fingers, then two, then one, then rolled around the edge, to place myself against the wall on the other side of the opening.

The lights came up in the room, and I found myself blinking at their sudden brightness. A hard object, much like the muzzle of a pistol—probably because it *was* the muzzle of a pistol—was pressed against my right temple.

Over against the far wall, I could see a man holding an automatic, and another man holding a spear. Probably *the* Spear, I thought, with my spirits lowering. This op was turning into a real screwup. Over to my left, out of the corner of my eye, I could see a man holding Maggie at gunpoint. He was plucking her weapon from her hand, even as I felt myself being relieved of McGoggin's—of Sprague's—revolver.

I turned my head slightly in that direction and saw that it was, indeed, Sprague standing beside me. Now that he had two weapons, one in each hand, he backed off well out of kicking range. The gent beside Maggie—I recognized him even without his brown coat—did the same.

The man with the Spear said, "Well, good to see you at last.

I'm only sorry that you didn't accept my earlier offer to come visit." He had the tenor voice I'd spoken with on the phone earlier.

"Now would you like to come with me? All your questions will be answered." He turned to Sprague. "Brother McGoggin," he said. "All in due form?"

"That it is. I've shut tight the door. Brother Tomlinson, allow me to present Mr. Roarke."

"My pleasure." Tomlinson leaned the Spear against the wall and walked over to me. He gave me a handshake with a peculiar grip. I returned the grip. Like I said, second-hand bookstores.

"Ah, Brother Roarke. Very good. Introductions, I suppose?" He gestured toward Brown Coat. "May I present Brother Jukes? And my associate, Brother Ortheris." He nodded toward the far wall where the man with the automatic kept watch. I noticed that no one crossed the line of fire between him and me.

The man I'd called Moustache arrived through a side door. "Almost here," he said.

We all went back into the room with the six sleepers and the one empty table. Jukes led, Maggie and I followed, and McGoggin brought up the rear. No-name went around and folded back the sheets from the sleepers' faces. Old men, most of them; some with beards, some grizzled, some bare-headed or with cloth caps, some wearing kingly crowns, some with the crowns of empire.

"Brother Roarke," Tomlinson said, "let me say again what a great pleasure it is to have you here."

"The pleasure is mine," I said. "But I'm a bit confused. What do you have in mind for me to help you with?"

"This is a case of urgency," Tomlinson said. "We are a philanthropic group; our goal is to raise and reform mankind. To that end—we shall restore the British Empire."

I have to admit that I just looked at him; I can't swear that I didn't go goggle-eyed. "The British Empire?"

"Yeah," Tomlinson said, smiling. He had a New Jersey accent, even if he did have the Union Jack engraved on his blazer buttons.

"And you'll do this . . . how?"

"With your help. I presume that I'm speaking with a representative of the Temple?"

"I'm told they're in the phonebook."

"Not the part of the Temple I need to talk with. The Temple of Jerusalem, built by the Masons—you see how it works?"

"No."

He sat down on the empty table, and leaned forward. "You want to recover the Templar Treasure, don't you?"

The Templar Treasure. Lost since the fourteenth century. The Temple in Paris had been the world's first, and at that time only, bank, filled with gold and jewels, the collateral of a thousand estates. King Philip of France had wanted that treasure—he destroyed the Temple with fire and sword to get it—but the loot was already gone: Loaded on wagons, taken to the port of La Rochelle, loaded onto ships. Then it vanished.

The thing is, what Tomlinson was offering was something I didn't care about. The real Templars already know where the treasure is, and they always have. The rent on all those safe houses over the centuries has to have come from somewhere. If Tomlinson wasn't stupid, he had to know that. He'd caught me once. I didn't want to have him catch me again. But if I played along . . .

"Sure," I said. "Finding the Treasure would be a good thing."

"I know where it is. Cast back your mind to 1916—"

"I don't know how old you think I am," I said, "but that's a little before my time."

Tomlinson laughed. "I read about it. I'll bet you have, too. Kipling knew that the war would be a disaster. He warned people."

"I read a lot of books, yes."

"Well then. Lord Kitchener—the British Secretary of State for War—was traveling to Russia aboard HMS *Hampshire* in order to convince them to stay in the war. I've figured out from books why the trip was so urgent that even a Force Ten gale couldn't delay the sailing: Kitchener was carrying the Templar Treasure to Russia to pay for their loyalty and munitions."

That wasn't the truth, of course, but it came a whole lot closer than I wanted anyone outside of the Inner Temple to be. What I especially hoped that Tomlinson didn't know was that Lord Kitchener had become a Templar during his years in Palestine, before going to Egypt to recapture Khartoum. He'd been born in County Kerry, and his secret was that he was Catholic. He took orders in the Priory at Solomon's Temple and had no social contact with women afterward. He let nosy people assume that he was a poofter rather than betray that he was a priest. And not just any priest—one of the three-and-thirty.

Tomlinson, meanwhile, was nattering on. "But alas, it was not to be, because Kitchener had saved the Empire by raising an army of three million men: 'Your country needs you; For King and Country.' Therefore he was destined to die. HMS *Hampshire* went down within sight of land on a nasty North Sea night. She shouldn't have gone out at all—her escorting destroyers had all turned back because they couldn't make headway.

"But there was one other thing about Lord Kitchener that no one knew. He had also come into possession of the Spear of Destiny, and those who possess it do not die. Friedrich von Hohenstaufen, Frederic Barbarossa, Heinrich Fowler, Gerold

Sech . . . they had all possessed the spear, and when their times came, instead of dying they went to sleep.

"Kitchener was the last of them, and he slept in a cave in the Orkneys from the day HMS *Hampshire* went down until . . . well, until today. My reading has taught me many things. I need seven sleeping heroes to restore the Empire, and tonight they're all gathered."

"Wonderful," I said. "Now how do I fit into all this?" Privately I was figuring that whatever my next assignment was supposed to be, it had just gotten easier.

"You are the expert," he said. "I need you to tell me if this is the genuine Spear."

I decided to risk revealing some classified information. "It isn't."

Tomlinson looked skeptical. "There is always that element of doubt, yes. So many fakes on the market. But there's a test. If this is the real Spear, then once the heroes are awake I will control them. If it isn't the Spear, I won't. So you see how important it is that I know?"

"Didn't all that reading of yours tell you how to recognize the true Spear?" I asked.

"It did. If I were to stab someone with the Spear, and it's the real Spear, then that person won't die. Be wounded, yes. But not die. And the Spear will heal that person. Isn't that right?"

"That's what the books all say," I said.

"But who should the person be?" Tomlinson asked. "Not one of my loyal friends, surely—suppose that I turned out to be wrong? Nor would I cause pain to any of them unnecessarily. It isn't in their contract. So . . . you will be the one."

"No," McGoggin said suddenly. "Not him. *Her.* She's the one with the East River fixation." He smiled and waved at Maggie. "What goes around comes around," he said.

"Oh, very well," Tomlinson said. "That way my knowledgeable friend will be better able to show me how to cure someone with the Spear as well as wound someone with it." With his next breath Tomlinson stood and whirled, holding the Spear, so that the point of it slashed across Maggie's thigh. Blood welled out, and she fell to the floor clutching her leg.

Tomlinson looked at me, smiling. "Now tell me how to heal her."

"You take the butt end of the Spear," I said, trying to keep my voice even. Maggie hadn't cried out, but I knew she had to be hurting. "Touch the wound."

"Like this?" Tomlinson reversed the Spear in his hands and touched the gash in Maggie's leg. A few seconds later, the blood remained, the slash in her trouser leg remained, but the flesh was whole. She rolled to her knees, then stood. From her expression, she might well have been thinking uncharitable thoughts. I know that I was. I'd have to have a word with the guys in Archives and Relics about reclassifying the spear we had.

"Ah, wonderful!" Tomlinson was enjoying himself now. He looked at Maggie. She had a poker face. "Whatever you're planning," he cautioned her, "don't even think about it. As your erudite friend will tell you, while I'm holding the Spear I can't be harmed, nor, since I've possessed it, shall I die."

While he was talking, the other Kipling Society members—Sprague, Jukes, Ortheris, and the unknown fellow with the automatic—had left the room. Now they came back, carrying a mahogany casket between them. They placed it on the empty table. Tomlinson gestured with the spear.

"That casket," he said, "contains the sleeping form of Lord Kitchener himself. Now gather 'round, my friends," he said to the other men. They formed a half-circle before him. "There's one final step in the project, the way in which all four corners of the earth will become subject to the British Empire, and the

Empire will be subject to me. Each of you represents one of the four directions, and so, therefore—"

With a great sweep, Tomlinson swung the Spear so that the edge of its blade slashed each man across the throat. They fell, red blood tinged with froth bubbling between their fingers as they clutched their throats, but they did not die.

The sudden attack left Maggie and me both free to act. I took a step, twisted, and brought my fist down on the top of Lord Kitchener's casket.

"Wake up!" I shouted.

The casket opened, and a tall man in a greatcoat sat up, slowly, blinking and rubbing the sleep from his eyes. "Is it time?" he asked, an Irish accent tingeing his vowels.

"It's time," I said.

He pulled himself upright, picked up his cap with the braid on its bill and squared it on his head. He took in the room, the Spear, Tomlinson, the bleeding bodies, all in a glance.

"Bad show," he said, "getting your own lads killed." Then he walked over to where another of the kings slept—a man dressed in chain mail, with a full red beard.

"It's time," Kitchener said, shaking the man's shoulder. "Work to do."

The second man sat up. He wasn't nearly as tall as the Field Marshall, but he wore an emperor's crown, which made up for it. He adjusted his sword belt where it rode low on his hips, and nodded. "*Fertig, brüder.*"

Kitchener looked at Tomlinson. "I fought to end war, not for any bloody Empire," he said. "But if that's what you want . . . let's take you to your mountain, eh?"

Side by side, the general and the emperor walked over to where Tomlinson stood with his mouth gaping open. Each of them took him by an elbow and all but picked him up as they marched him away. The Spear fell from his hands and clattered to the floor.

The three of them—Kitchener, Tomlinson, and Barbarossa—kept going, off into the distance, growing smaller and smaller, far beyond where the walls of the room should have been. All around us, the other kings grew misty, dim, and faded, and the sheets that covered them fell empty.

"The god that you took from a printed book go with you," I whispered to Tomlinson as he vanished.

The Spear was lying on the floor where Tomlinson had dropped it. Maggie pointed at it. "You want to pick it up?"

"Not on your life," I said. "I don't want to wind up sleeping under a mountain somewhere."

Ahasuerus stepped forward out of the shadows. I hadn't heard him follow us in, but I wasn't surprised to see him. A man in his circumstances gets a lot of practice in keeping quiet. He stooped down and picked up the Spear himself.

"Not like I care," he said. "I'm not going to die, and if I do, so what? I sleep until my people need me? The Jews of Palestine—the way the world is, I make it about two minutes before I wake up and get back to work."

He touched the fallen men one by one with the butt of the spear, then turned to face us. "I'll see this gets back to the guy who owned it already." He stepped back into the shadows again and vanished.

Maggie and I looked at one another. "I suppose that's it," I said finally.

"I guess so," Maggie said. "What are you going to say about all this in your report?"

I'd already figured out the answer to that one. "There isn't going to be any report."

"Just as well," Maggie said. "It's best to let sleeping kings lie."

A Partial Templar
Bibliography

Addison, Charles G. *The History of the Knights Templar.*
Kempton, IL: Adventures Unlimited Press, 1997.
(Reprint of 1842 London edition.)

Baigent, Michael, and Richard Leigh. *The Temple and the
Lodge.* London: Jonathan Cape, 1989.

Barber, Malcolm. *The Trial of the Templars.* Cambridge, England: Cambridge University Press, 1978.

———. *The New Knighthood.* Cambridge, England: Cambridge University Press, 1994.

Burman, Edward. *Supremely Abominable Crimes: The Trial
of the Knights Templar.* London: Allison & Busby Ltd.,
1994.

———. *The Templars: Knights of God.* Wellingborough:
Aquarian Press, 1986.

Burnes, James. *A Sketch of the History of the Knights Templar.* Edinburgh: William Blackstone and Sons, 1857.

Gardner, Laurence. *Bloodline of the Holy Grail.* Shaftesbury,
Dorset: Element Books Ltd., 1996.

Knight, Christopher and Robert Lomas. *The Second Messiah:*

Templars, the Turin Shroud, and the Great Secret of Freemasonry. London: Century Books, 1997.

Kurtz, Katherine, ed. *On Crusade: More Tales of the Knights Templar.* New York: Warner, 1998.

———. *Tales of the Knights Templar.* New York: Warner, 1995.

Laidler, Keith. *The Head of God: The Lost Treasure of the Templars.* London: Weidenfeld & Nicholson, 1998.

Partner, Peter. *The Murdered Magicians.* [Also published as *The Knights Templar and Their Myth.*] Oxford, England: Oxford University Press, 1981.

Picknett, Lynn and Clive Prince. *The Templar Revelation.* London: Bantam Press, 1997.

Robinson, John J. *Born in Blood.* New York: M. Evans, 1989.

———. *Dungeon, Fire, and Sword.* New York: M. Evans, 1991.

Runciman, Sir Steven. *History of the Crusades,* Vol. III, *The Kingdom of Acre and the Later Crusades.* Cambridge University Press, 1954.

Simon, Edith. *The Piebald Standard: A Biography of the Knights Templar.* Boston: Little, Brown, 1959.

Upton-Ward, J.M. *The Rule of the Templars.* New York: Boydell Press, 1992. (Translated from the French of Henri de Curzon's 1886 edition of the French Rule, derived from the three extant medieval manuscripts.)

About the Authors

Debra Doyle was born in Florida and educated in Florida, Texas, Arkansas, and Pennsylvania—the last at the University of Pennsylvania, where she earned her doctorate in English literature, concentrating on Old English poetry. While living and studying in Philadelphia, she met and married her collaborator, James D. Macdonald, and subsequently traveled with him to Virginia, California, and the Republic of Panamá. Various children, cats, and computers joined the household along the way.

James Douglas Macdonald was born in White Plains, New York, the second of three children of W. Douglas Macdonald, a Chemical Engineer, and Margaret E. Macdonald, a professional artist. After leaving the University of Rochester, where he majored in Medieval Studies, he served in the U. S. Navy. From 1991 through 1993, as Yog Sysop, he ran the Science Fiction and Fantasy RoundTable on the GEnie computer network. These days—once again as Yog Sysop—he manages SFF-Net (http://www.sff.net) on the internet.

Doyle and Macdonald left the Navy and Panamá in 1988 in

order to pursue writing full-time. They now live—still with various children, cats, and computers—in a big nineteenth-century house in northern New Hampshire, where they write science fiction and fantasy for children, teenagers, and adults. They are the authors of the popular Mageworlds space opera series, from Tor Books; and they are currently working on the manuscript of a full-length novel about Peter Crossman, Knight of the Temple, also for Tor.

Deborah Turner Harris grew up in Daytona Beach, Florida. After taking a B.A. in English at Stetson University, she decided that studying was (on the whole) preferable to working as a file clerk, and spent the next five years doing a Ph.D. in Medieval English Literature at Florida State University. In her final year, she was awarded a Rotary International Scholarship, and in a further bid to evade the job market, went off to the University of St. Andrews in Scotland for a year. Here (when technically she should have been writing a thesis on George MacDonald) she hammered out the first draft of *The Mages of Garillon* whilst launching a successful campaign of seduction against her now-husband, Bob Harris (who was likewise neglecting his studies whilst designing the fantasy board game, "Talisman").

The *Garillon* trilogy subsequently found its way into print under the editorial auspices of Betty Ballantine, who (continuing her role as angel of destiny) subsequently introduced DTH to Katherine Kurtz. The acquaintance thus happily begun has since given rise to the Adept Series and two historical novels set during the Scottish Wars of Independence: *The Temple and the Stone* and *The Temple and the Crown.*

DTH and her husband Bob now live in St. Andrews with their three sons, Matthew, Robert, and Jamie, of whom she says: "It's sometimes a bit like trying to co-exist with a band of Comanches on the war-path. On the other hand, you have three iron-clad excuses for indulging in every known form of adventure gaming."

Katherine Kurtz was born in Florida during a hurricane, earned degrees from the University of Miami and UCLA, and published her first novel, *Deryni Rising,* in 1970: the first venture by Ballantine Books into what became the modern fantasy genre, following on the heels of J.R.R. Tolkien's *Lord of the Rings* Trilogy. Since then, her work has run to four trilogies and a singleton thirteenth novel in the Deryni series, several companion volumes and anthologies, plus nearly as many novels in the realm of historical fantasy, such as *Lammas Night, Two Crowns for America, Saint Patrick's Gargoyle,* and the seven novels of the Adept and Temple series—these last with co-author Deborah Turner Harris. With a B.S. in Chemistry and a Master of Arts degree in English History, she is an avid researcher of Scottish and Templar lore, a student of comparative religion, a trained hypnotist, and also attended medical school for a year before deciding she would rather write about medicine than practice it. For the past fifteen years, she has made her home in a gothic revival house in Ireland with husband Scott MacMillan, two silly-looking dogs, three cats, and at least two resident ghosts.

Scott MacMillan has honed his story-telling abilities in a variety of writing fields, ranging from screenplays and daytime television, over two hundred published articles while writing for *Guns & Ammo* magazine, and editorial efforts with sufficient panache to win the prestigious Golden Spur Award in four consecutive years (roughly equivalent to the Nebula or Hugo for Western fiction). More recently, he has contributed short stories to a number of SF anthologies. The third (and final!) novel in his *Knights of the Blood* series (sometimes referred to under its working title of "Nazi

Vampires from Hell") is finally in progress, along with several other book and screen projects.

In the mold of the Victorian Renaissance man, this onetime Irish Officer of Arms (that's a real, live herald!) has raised Lipizzan horses, raced Can-Am cars, worked as a mounted police officer, served as a reserve army officer (without pay), and has little sympathy for those who say they don't have time to do the things they want to do. His interests also run to vintage motor cars, crumbling castles, heraldry, military history, arms and armor, chivalry (past, present, and future), the motion picture industry (he studied film at the University of Southern California and the American Film Institute), and the advantages of being selectively intolerant. With wife Katherine Kurtz, one of his ongoing projects is the restoration of their home, a gothic revival house in County Wicklow, Ireland.

Patricia Anne Elizabeth Genevieve Honora **Kennealy-Morrison** is a retired rock critic, a onetime go-go dancer, a two-time Clio nominee, and the author of The Keltiad fantasy series. Educated at St. Bonaventure University, Harpur College, and NYU, on June 24, 1970 she married James Douglas Morrison, leader of the rock group the Doors. Morrison died in Paris thirteen months later. Her memoir of their life together, *Strange Days,* was published in 1992, and she was a consultant to Oliver Stone's 1991 film "The Doors", in which she was portrayed by actress Kathleen Quinlan, and had a cameo in the film. A native-born New Yorker and a member of Mensa, Patricia appears on a 2001 New York Mets baseball card (third baseman Robin Ventura's), and intends, one day very soon now, to buy herself the title she has always strongly felt she should have had from birth. "The Last Voyage" is her first short story.

Robert Reginald was born in the Year of the Rat in the Orient (so it counts!)."Occam's Treasure" is his seventeenth published story, but he has published over ten thousand non-fiction pieces, as well as ninety-two books. He is also the co-author (with Katherine Kurtz) of *Codex Derynianus.*

Susan Shwartz's most recent books are *Second Chances, Shards of Empire* (Tor), and *Cross and Crescent* (Tor), set in Byzantium and Jerusalem, along with two Star Trek novels written with Josepha Sherman: *Vulcan's Forge* and *Vulcan's Heart.* Others of her works include *The Grail of Hearts* and over seventy pieces of short fiction. Her next books will be a collection of her short fiction and *Hostile Takeovers,* which combines aliens, investing, and the asteroid belt. Though she has a Ph.D. in English from Harvard University and calls herself a "lapsed medievalist," she has worked on Wall Street for the past eighteen years. She has been nominated for the Nebula five times, the Hugo twice, and the World Fantasy Award and the Edgar once each. And yes, you saw her on TV selling Borg dolls for IBM. She lives in Forest Hills, New York.

Richard Woods was born and reared in New Mexico, teaches at Dominican University near Chicago, lectures and tutors on occasion at Blackfriars Hall, Oxford University, and really lives in Ireland, in a stone cottage near Avoca, not far from the sea: paradise. A Dominican friar with a particular interest in Meister Eckhart and the medieval mystics, he has published ten original non-fiction books, co-authored one novel, published another, edited four anthologies, and authored a number of articles in spirituality, sexuality, and Celtic studies. He dabbles in watercolors, makes Celtic harps, sometimes fiddles, and sings in chapel and the shower.

Masterful Knights Templar Novels from
Katherine Kurtz and Deborah Turner Harris

The Temple and the Stone (0-446-60723-1)

Scotland, the end of the thirteenth century—and a world at war. Led by mystic visions, a band of Templars set out to save Scotland's sacred Stone of Destiny, that its spirit and power may be reborn in the soul of the Uncrowned King, warrior William Wallace. For pagan gods of blood have woken in Albion—and the fate of the entire Christian world will soon depend on the courage of the Highlander known as Braveheart.

The Temple and the Crown (0-446-60854-8)

England's tyrannical Edward I decimates the Scottish freedom fighters led by Robert Bruce, while France's Philip IV usurps control of the papacy. But far more is at stake in Europe's wars, for the French and English kings are unwitting puppets of Luciferian alchemists called the Order of the Black Swan. Now from the Highlands to the Holy Land, the Templars must save humanity itself from eternal damnation.

~More Templar Anthologies edited by Katherine Kurtz~

Tales of the Knights Templar
(0-446-60138-1)

On Crusade: More Tales of the Knights Templar
(0-446-67339-0)

AT BOOKSTORES EVERYWHERE FROM WARNER ASPECT

1215

VISIT WARNER ASPECT ONLINE!

THE WARNER ASPECT HOMEPAGE

You'll find us at: www.twbookmark.com then by clicking on Science Fiction and Fantasy.

NEW AND UPCOMING TITLES

Each month we feature our new titles and reader favorites.

AUTHOR INFO

Author bios, bibliographies and links to personal websites.

CONTESTS AND OTHER FUN STUFF

Advance galley giveaways, autographed copies, and more.

THE ASPECT BUZZ

What's new, hot and upcoming from Warner Aspect: awards news, bestsellers, movie tie-in information . . .